I0647989

CARVE

WAYS *of*

LOOK

ING

VOL. I

Edited by
Matthew Limpede
Anna Zumbahlen

WAYS OF LOOKING, VOLUME I
Copyright © 2019 by Carve Magazine, LLC.
All rights reserved. Authors hold the rights to their stories.

PO Box 701510
Dallas, TX 75370
(+1) 214-425-7860
info@carvezine.com
www.carvezine.com

First print edition, July 2019.
Printed in the United States of America.
ISBN: 978-0-578-51882-4

Cover design by Birdhouse Branding.

Carve has been publishing online since 2000 and in print/digital since 2012.
Subscriptions to *Carve* available. https://www.carvezine.com/subscribe.
Submissions accepted year-round. https://www.carvezine.com/submit.

Carve Masthead
Publisher Matthew Limpede
Editor-in-chief Anna Zumbahlen
Fiction Editor Rita Juster
Poetry Editor Ana Cottle
Nonfiction Editor Cameron Maynard
Associate Editors Zack Rybak, Bridget Apfeld
Production Editor Janelle Drumwright
Blog Editor Ariel Courage
Classroom Ambassador Amanda Conner
Resident Artist Justin Burks
Business Advisor Susan Kenny
Founding Editor Melvin Sterne

Carve is named in honor of Raymond Carver.

CONTENTS

Introduction

In "On Writing," Raymond Carver makes the claim that what distinguishes great writers is not talent. "There's plenty of that around," he writes. For Carver, the writer whose work will last is "a writer who has some special way of looking at things and who gives artistic expression to that way of looking." *Carve* is named in honor of Raymond Carver, and though we publish a variety of styles and realisms and don't necessarily hold his work as a model, something of his thinking hovers over the magazine. His presence lives in the way we preserve his energy for specificity, for celebrating the way each writer approaches a narrative in a unique and particular way. He writes, "But if writers haven't taken leave of their senses, they also want to stay in touch with us, they want to carry news from their world to ours."

Carve is focused on the personal—the story is important, of course, but also the individual, the writer and the set of contexts, influences, and obsessions they're working with on and off the page. We're interested in the news the story carries and the way the writer sees and talks about it. At *Carve*, we consider the story and then the story in the context of the writer, and in conversation we discover new ways to articulate and think about what fiction is and does. This is to say in every issue we celebrate new ways of looking, and it matters to celebrate diverse modes of being in the world, bringing the experience of one perception to another and building the empathic spaces in between. Reading is a learning tool, a tool for considering the worlds and lives out of which stories arise. In paying attention to the thinking behind them, we can consider how the craft itself might be fallible, writers and editors imperfect—but the story is a gift from a thinking, breathing person, a missive from another experience of the world.

It may be a platitude, but it is such a true thing: Reading and writing create space for empathy, for understanding experience beyond what's immediate to the reader. I believe this in the way I believe things before I can necessarily articulate them, before I have adequate language for the feeling. As I read and listen to more voices, the more I learn that the necessity and power of storytelling is held so dearly and so widely that it's a cliché, a noble truism. But even right now, when the exhaustion and precariousness of our situation as a country and as a world can make focusing on the page feel hard, I think it's fair to believe in fiction as refuge—one that grows and changes and is legitimate.

In the fall, I had the opportunity to meet the editor of a book press I really admire. We talked about writers, about supporting writers, and eventually the conversation turned to the difference between publishing a quarterly magazine and publishing books. In particular, there was the suggestion that magazines become irrelevant once they're not the current issue anymore, whereas books don't necessarily become dated in the same way. This upset me in an abstract way—the thought that interest in or readership for our stories could expire when the newest issue goes to print.

At *Carve*, we're always thinking about ways to widen the reach of our stories. Encouraging readership is one of the things that motivates the Carve Classroom, positioning our archive as a learning tool for new writers. Uplifting the stories in the archive is important because it's valuable to consider fiction outside of trends in publishing but with special attention to the empathic spaces fiction creates—thoughtful imaginings into the experiences or perceptions of others, imaginings that do not expire. Part of the project of this collection is exploring how fiction published a decade ago shifts and returns, gathers around experience, and reading from this vantage point in the future (relative to the story) might break something open, make another or a new empathy possible. The story is representative of the time it was written, but it's also representative of a particular, ongoing experience—the writer's way of looking.

. . .

I joined *Carve* as a member of the volunteer reading commit-tee years ago, but I loved the magazine before that. I discov-ered it in college and did a deep dive into the archive—it's not a stretch to say *Carve*'s archive provided me foundational training in the art of the short story as I was discovering my voice as a writer and beginning to develop my perception as a reader. In reviewing stories from these years, it became clear that selecting only eight for this volume would be pain-ful. The stories included in this anthology were published during Matthew Limpede's first few years as editor, and all of these writers expressed excitement about this project—many expressing fond memories of Matthew's editorial guidance in the beginning of their careers as writers. Most of these stories appeared in *Carve* before the conception of *Carve*'s print mag-azine (and the What We Talk About feature, the interviews of our short fiction contributors), with the exception of Jia Tolentino, who was published in *Carve*'s first-ever print issue in the fall of 2012, and Adrienne Celt, who appeared in *Carve* for the second time in Matthew's last issue as editor-in-chief in the winter of 2015.

These are a few of the stories that built and defined *Carve*'s "Honest Fiction," our tagline that helps us articulate what we're looking for in stories, poems, and essays: moments of catharsis and change, details that feel true, people interact-ing with people and their environments in messy and honest ways. Writers dealing with characters with compassion and grace, holding the characters accountable to their own authenticity. Stories that leave the reader with a gut ache. These are a few of the stories that taught me how to read for this particular kind of honesty.

Yuvi Zalkow's "When My Body Smashed Into the Sidewalk" appeared in *Carve* in 2007. It's a devastating piece that reaches outside itself, and in his interview Yuvi dives into his own relationship with reality and how he writes to connect: "Words have such a power. Stories have such a power." *Carve* published Kami Westhoff's "The Ways You Are Gone" in 2007 also, an epistolary story that follows a man grieving his missing fiancée. "I was having this thought about how if we could just grieve a little more honestly perhaps it would be less painful," she says in her interview.

"The Candy House of Roscoe, New York" by Meagan Cass appeared in *Carve* the following year, a haunting (and haunted) story about adulthood, responsibility, reality. Her interview considers influence as "reading against what you're into, or reading work that's different from what you might think of as your style." David Cameron's "And They Pillaged the Dead" was published in 2011, a story about family, music, history, and heirlooms. In his interview, he discusses writing and music and the way both of those ventures still bounce back and forth, defining his life.

Carve also published Leesa Cross-Smith's "Whiskey & Ribbons" in 2011, a story about loss and love that has since been written out and published as a novel. "It took the time it needed to take," she says in her interview. Kem Joy Ukwu's "Demetrius" also appeared in *Carve* that year, a story that became a cornerstone of her collection *Locked Gray/Linked Blue*. Her interview lays out the particular way her characters withhold from each other but not from the reader: "Fiction allows for instances where there are things unsaid—fiction allows for the writer to write out the unsaid things, because it might be unsaid to another character, but it's not unsaid to the reader."

Adrienne Celt's "The Eternal Youth of Everyone Else" and Jia Tolentino's "The Odyssey" appeared in *Carve* in 2012. "The Eternal Youth of Everyone Else" is a devastating exploration of time and intimacy, and the novels she has published since then, *The Daughters* and *Invitation to a Bonfire*, reiterate something of that tension. "The Odyssey" almost became a novel, too—in her interview, Jia Tolentino discusses how her relationship with fiction has changed as her career and interests tend more toward nonfiction. All eight of the interviews in this collection were conducted by phone as 2018 turned over into 2019 and offer different paths toward "being a writer," emphasizing that there's no one or right way to live a life of writing.

. . .

Raymond Carver had three-by-five cards taped to a wall beside his desk. These cards held mantras—for example: "Isak Dinesen said that she wrote a little every day, without hope and without despair." These mantras were notes toward how to build a life as a writer, a life around writing, a life including writing. If I were to borrow a fragment of "On Writing" and put it on a three-by-five card by my desk, it would be the fragment about fiction as "the glimpse given life." Carver writes, "The short story writer's task is to invest the glimpse with all that is in his power," to show the reader "how things out there really are." I read this glimpse as an articulation of the familiar gut ache of a *Carve* story.

When I sat down to copyedit the transcription of Kami Westhoff's interview, I found that her question, "Where are you calling from?" was the first fragment captured by the recording. I smiled at this coincidence, an echo of Carver's syntax. As I dove into the rest of the interviews, I celebrated the generosity of these writers and the different and true ways their work persists in the world. This anthology represents a sample of *Carve*'s archive, but also a cross-section of conversation that belongs to right now, reflecting these writers' lives in the present. What a gift to get to talk about these stories. The thinking is ongoing.

Anna Zumbahlen
Editor-in-chief

When My Body Smashed Into the Sidewalk

YUVI ZALKOW

September 2007

My last thought was this: I should have bought my mother a birthday present. Her birthday was the day before my jump and I didn't even call her. I had seen the blackest blue necklace at the jewelry store storefront on the way to work but I didn't have a chance to get it for her. I should have thought ahead.

My fall was 311 feet. 30 stories. 4.5 seconds. Terminal velocity is 120 miles per hour—the speed at which I was falling at the time of impact. When my body smashed into the ground, I was going so fast that a cloud of red smoke rose from my body—my blood turning into a gas, going through the blood vessel walls, through my smashed flesh, and hovering above my body as if a child had smacked two chalkboard erasers together. Poof.

A woman who had just escaped the burning building from which I jumped saw my crash from 25 feet away. It was a thunderous bang my carcass made, and she covered her head with her hands, thinking a piece of the building had just fallen. But she did not look away. She stared at that thing beside her, because in her gut she knew it was important to see.

I knew to jump the instant the fire got to my floor. The others went for the stairwell (and why not?), but I sensed something bad down there, I didn't want to die in a smoky stairwell, I wanted to die speeding through the fresh air.

Not knowing about the phenomenon I just described, she thought the cloud of blood above my crushed carcass was a soul, or it was a demon, she thought demons were escaping the scene, the horror of it, and this woman did what any sane person would do in that situation. She collapsed right on the sidewalk.

Fortunately, the man beside her was kind enough to pick her up—he was two inches shorter and twenty pounds smaller, but he picked her up and dragged her two blocks away from the scene, to a distance that was safe even when the 33-story building collapsed. The man was gone before she was conscious enough to notice him, and so he became another person lost in her dreams, a man whispering to her: It's going to be all right, my god, it's horrible, but it'll be all right.

When you have approximately two seconds to live and you know it, the wind against your ears is the most astonishing sensation.

She never spoke about the cloud above my crushed body to anyone, even during all her therapy, she refused to tell that part of the story, thinking to herself that she was cursed, and that was the only explanation for why she saw this ghost that no one else had seen. A therapist couldn't save her from ghosts—not real ones.

The building wasn't supposed to collapse, it was structurally sound. It wasn't supposed to burn the way that it did. At first, they attributed it to terrorists (and who could blame them?). There was a lot of terror in the air, especially after what happened in New York. After all, "terrorism" has more punch to it than "faulty inductor in the wiring of an old Panasonic microwave oven."

The woman who saw me crushed was named Noku. She was twenty-nine. She was no small woman, though she had the skinny fingers of her mother. Even though she was raised by her American father, it was her Japanese mother who named her before she disappeared six months after Noku was born. Noku has a memory of a woman, smelling of mint leaves, kissing her on the forehead and whispering to her, "*Aishiteru*." She'd like to think that this was her mother saying to her, "I love you," but a big part of her thinks it was just a dream.

Jumping out of a building isn't as difficult as you'd guess. When I was a kid, I hated jumping off the high dive, the jump terrified me. It was the worst feeling in the world, all those seconds standing on that horrible, wobbly plank, feeling like that jump would kill me every time. All that shame while I stood there in front of everyone. Jumping out of a burning building was far easier—because it was not a bit harder.

Noku had an abortion six months before the building collapsed. Her boyfriend drove her to and from the procedure, though he did not enter the clinic. He helped her into bed afterwards, but he didn't stay at her apartment. Noku wanted the abortion just as much as he did, they were not ready, it was only six weeks along, and when her boyfriend broke up with her the next week, Noku was not disappointed, there was nothing left between them anyhow.

My mother and I didn't get along the way I got along with my father. I worried about the possibility of my mother outliving my father and when it happened that way, I was disgusted with myself for thinking such thoughts. It's not that I didn't love her as much, it's just that we always messed up the way we expressed ourselves. When she bought me a watch, I told her she should pay attention to the fact that I never wore watches. When I called her to say I missed her, she asked why I didn't visit more often. We regretted but we didn't mend.

It wasn't until she saw the ghost above my body that Noku felt regret for what she did at that clinic. As she was carried two blocks by the man she never met, she dreamed that she had a daughter, that the daughter was trapped inside the building, that it was her daughter who was supposed to survive, not Noku. What terrified her, was that in her dream, her daughter had a name.

My mother's name is Tziona. It's an Israeli name. When I was a child, she wasn't happy living in this country. This was my father's country, not hers. She was the seventh generation born in the Middle East and however foreign you might find the Middle East, my mother found Atlanta, Georgia, at least that foreign—a camel isn't nearly as bizarre as a highway with nine lanes in each direction. But she made do. She even grew to like this country. When my mother searched my apartment after I was crushed against the sidewalk, she found two pictures that I had framed without telling her. One was from 1972, with her carrying me in her arms, her big black hair and that beautiful smile. The other was in 1967, before I was born, of my mother carrying an Uzi and (once again) smiling for the camera, with the Negev desert behind her.

Noku's mother had nightmares every night since what she saw in 1945. In her dreams, all the people she knew were dark green shadows, and she was never able to touch them. She was terrified that Noku would also turn into a shadow. And so Noku's mother disappeared, turning herself into a shadow.

My mother believes in God. She believes that the soul lives on forever. She even believes that the Bible is the real word of God. To my mother's disappointment, I didn't believe in God or the Bible. I didn't believe in devils or demons or ghosts or saints. I didn't believe that there was anything magical or mystical about that cloud of blood above my crushed body. I died, it was that simple, and the cloud was a scientifically-explainable phenomenon. There is life and there is death. But when Noku opened her journal two days later, she wrote, "I dreamed that I had a daughter named Tziona."

I might not believe in God, but I do believe in the power

of words on a page. I even believe that a story can bring the dead to life. I have to believe that. I believe it just as much as I believe in the power of the wind against your ears at 120 miles per hour.

Noku began writing more and more in her journal. After two years, the journal entries became more like stories than journal entries. After all, a journal is meant to be about real-world personal events, and most of her writing was about her non-existent daughter, who now had my mother's name. On some days, she even wrote about me.

She wrote many stories. It became an obsession. Her writing was not what they call therapeutic—it sent her further into her already-too-far-inside-herself self. She rarely let another person see anything that she wrote. This obsession disturbed the few friends she had left. (How many hours could she possibly spend on that park bench with that worn-out journal?) She squeezed the pencil so tightly that the ridges would disappear where her skinny index finger and skinny thumb touched the pencil.

At the instant I smashed into the sidewalk, I smelled like mint, like I had crumbled a leaf with my fingers and pressed it against my nose. This sensation was impossible to share and impossible to process—without an intact olfactory or nervous system.

The color that flashed in my head was the blackest blue. For a split second, I could see the world through the lens of that gem I should have gotten for my mother.

If my lips would've been able to utter a word, it would have been the word, "Tziona," with that first syllable coming out like the chirp of a small bird. My mother made up the spelling of her name when she came to this country. "Your language doesn't have the proper letters," she told my father in 1971, with me still in her belly.

Noku wrote obsessively until the time of her death. Her

death came early but not painfully—it was just a dream that lasted too long. The day before she died, she mailed one of her stories to my old address—which came to her in a dream—and the letter ultimately landed in my mother's lap, 181 days later. My mother didn't open the letter for a long time, knowing that it would be more beautiful than any necklace. And when she did open it, she too believed that words could bring back the dead.

YUVI ZALKOW's stories have been published in *Carve*, *Glimmer Train*, *The LA Review*, *Narrative Magazine*, *Rosebud*, and others. His debut novel, *A Brilliant Novel in the Works*, is about a writer unable to write a novel. Yuvi also makes videos on YouTube about writing, insecurity, and chronic pain. By day, he is a tech writer at a software company.

INTERVIEW WITH YUVI ZALKOW

January 2019

CARVE

I have a pretty vivid memory of reading "When My Body Smashed Into the Sidewalk" for the first time. I was sitting in a window seat of a coffee shop in Boulder at the time, and I'd been working my way through *Carve*'s archives. What was your process writing this story? It's been over ten years.

YUVI

It was quite a few years after 9/11, but I could never let go of the images and the stories about people who had lost their lives, and especially those who jumped out of the buildings. And at the same time I was working through my relationship with my mom. Some of my stories take a ton of work to get to a place where they're comprehensible to somebody else, and some of my stories just shoot out of me. This is one that largely shot out of me.

I was in a writing group, and we were studying story structure. I brought in this story that broke all the rules that we had studied, and no one really knew what to say about it except that it affected them. I remember we didn't even know how to analyze it, and I didn't really know how to shape it. It was a result of all of the emotional feelings that I had at the time. I don't know if that answers your question, but it was one of those odd stories that emerged almost in a complete form. Just a little shaping was required.

CARVE

What you said about the rules of fiction—I think that's interesting in the context of your work. This story is conscious of itself as a short story, and your novel is absolutely conscious of itself as a novel. In the story there's a big slowdown of time, and it jumps into Noku's life even though it's a first-person story. There's also that it's a story about the moment of death told from the past tense. Do you see yourself as bending fiction's "rules," or disregarding them?

YUVI

I've been writing seriously, whatever that means, since around 1999. When I wrote this story, I was still in a phase where I felt guilty for not following all the rules. If you study enough fiction rules, you can't write anything without being paralyzed. I eventually came to the point of studying the rules and understanding how they serve, but also how they can get in the way of the story. I mean, I love to think about the rules and they obviously have a purpose. And they often help. But sometimes they can hinder what the story is trying to do.

This was a moment where I remember coming in to the workshop fearing that the story sucks because it doesn't follow the rules. I don't remember exactly what we were studying, but some traditional storytelling structure. I always have the problem of being self-conscious in my writing, and I could never let go of that. Even when I try to write something that's not so self-conscious, it will sneak in. Over time, I realized that any rule can be broken as long as you (mostly) understand why you're breaking it. There might be some rule you're serving at the expense of another rule. I mean, you can get paralyzed thinking too hard about it. I still think it's important to study structure—I think it was really useful to learn those things and then put them on the backburner as I write a story.

CARVE

When I was revisiting your story on *Carve*'s website—we have tags that suggest something about the story, some thematic content or craft elements of the story—I noticed your story is tagged as magical realism. I thought that was interesting. I mean, it is a story told in the past tense about the character's own death. That suggests that it's bending something about reality, but I wondered what your relationship with magical realism is.

YUVI

I think I stumble into it by mistake. Every now and then, a story or a book I'm writing gets magical. But often when I'm writing I'm not thinking about magical realism. In fact, it all feels real, and I'm always blurring truth and fiction. For sure in my novel—it was such a mishmash of truth and fiction that I sometimes even forget what was what. My wife sometimes recounts stories about my childhood, and I have to say no—that was just in the novel, that didn't really happen.

Even when things get magical, I'm really not that aware. I feel like I'm always writing a memoir. At least, the first draft of everything feels so close to the heart that I don't even think about what genre or realm it fits into. But I do like magical realism. I haven't read a ton of magical realism, but Gabriel García Márquez was one of the first fiction writers that I fell in love with. Still when I revisit his stories, I love them all over again.

CARVE

It sounds like your stories begin with seeds from your own life, and then through the process of writing you'll start to take magical turns.

YUVI

Yeah. It will take magical turns, and it will also get fictionalized as I go along. I mean, this story that I published at *Carve* is a little wilder in the sense that it starts off with the person being dead. That is maybe a little bit more of a stretch for my personal life, the way it opens. But his relationship to family is something that I was working through at the time that I wrote it.

CARVE

Having revisited the story again after reading your novel, it does seem like there's consistency across the narrative voice that, like you said, manifests in the characters' relationships with parents, but also having a hard time expressing feelings, having a hard time communicating with loved ones. I wondered how you would talk about your experience of writing people who are real in your life, even though it is fictionalized and even though the story takes on magic. There are still seeds of people who are real, emotional content that is honest.

YUVI

Yeah. My wife has been supportive and awfully tolerant given how many different quirky relationships I've written about. We met in a writing group, and she really understands the way truth and fiction intertwine. In the first novel I wrote (*A Brilliant Novel in the Works*), and in the novel that I'm working on now, there is a wife character, and my real wife, with amusement, sees how it's totally not our marriage. Even if there are many other bits of nonfiction in there.

I try not to put other people in a bad light. I usually feel like the character who you'd figure is me is the one who comes off the worst. My parents are supportive, but I also think they don't understand why I write stuff that's so close to the struggles of my own life. I was a little naïve about it at first, especially when I published my novel that had so much about the narrator's relationship to his family. I think I was so consumed with trying to get the story right that I didn't think to process it as much with my family, other than my wife. I regret that I didn't—not necessarily that I would have changed it, but I should have talked to them and said, look, here are some intimate things in our history that I have put in the book, and here are some things that are fictionalized. Just to talk it through a little more. But the relationships that are closest to me are the things that are on my mind when I'm writing. I inevitably put a lot of those things into my storytelling.

CARVE

The paragraph in "When My Body Smashed Into the Sidewalk" that begins "My mother believes in God," and later the character says, "I might not believe in God, but I do believe in the power of words on a page"—I was thinking about that in the context of the catharsis, or not, of writing. I think we also see that question in this story in the way Noku turns to the inwardness of writing to deal with having witnessed this death—and her writing ends up back with his mother at the end, and in that way it does bring back the dead.

YUVI

My mother in real life does believe in God—she's Jewish, and my in-laws are Lutheran and they are very faithful. I can't remember having a belief in something concrete like that, but I still believe there's something. I think I'm a little more obsessed with how we connect as humans and what that means. When I write stories, I feel like I'm writing about people trying or failing to connect, and I'm writing because I'm trying to connect with other people too.

I don't know if it's great that I write to connect or if it's a mental instability. I actually think more toward the instability than anything fabulous, but I am writing to connect. Words have such a power. Stories have such a power. And when I look at people's religious beliefs, there's a story. I find them beautiful, and I find fictional stories just as beautiful.

CARVE

In the novel, the main character meets another character in a hospital waiting room. The novel is itself about writing, and the main character wants to use this person as a plot point, as some kind of foil. It's so interesting, in part because it's loaded with cultural context, and it also seems connected to your earlier thoughts about the expectations of storytelling and form.

YUVI

That character—I really tried to make him into a plot point in earlier drafts of the novel. It wasn't working, and the fun thing about that novel was every time something didn't work, I would write about its failure in the book. It happened to be good therapy for me. But I never feel like I'm truly part of any tribe, I don't feel like I'm of a particular group. So I am interested in what groups people feel like they belong to, and what groups they don't. In the novel, I was thinking about being Jewish—what that means, and what if you don't believe in it? You're still Jewish. But are you part of this group, or not? I don't know. I remember turning that over in the story. I'm always trying to write through, or trying to think through, what all of this means.

CARVE

It seems like in both the novel and in the short story, you as the writer—and a little bit as the character, but mostly as the writer—are examining the way strangers are connected, the way people come into each other's lives and shape something. At the same time there's this disconnect in language—it's hard to express yourself fully, even with the people that you're closest to. So to be able to shift your focus outside of your life and relationships and look at the impact of your life on the life of a stranger—is that something that you see recurring in your writing and thinking?

YUVI

I do return to this, this theme of bumping into someone who has some kind of impact—but not in some over-dramatic TV show kind of way, where this stranger suddenly becomes pivotal in your life. It's more that they bump you in a certain direction, and you may never speak to them again.

It also happens in this historical novel that I've been trying to write on and off for many years but just happened to be working on this morning. I've been thinking about how this character survives in rural Georgia in the 1930s as an immigrant. What I've been focusing on today is his relationship to strangers, these people that he doesn't know as he's trying to understand how to survive in this town. These people are reluctant to welcome him in, but they build relationships.

CARVE

What can you tell me about your recent focuses?

YUVI

I've been working on chronic headaches. It's been a big project of mine. But I'm in a better state right now. And I had a kid in 2009. It's had an impact on my world. It's been a fabulous ride. I've dabbled in a few different things. I did some podcasting and some video-making.

I haven't done as much short story writing, but I've got two novels I'm working on right now, one that my agent is shopping around. It's about how we communicate in all these crazy ways with technology today. It's about a guy trying to be a dad while working at a high-tech company, with the texts and iPads and Facebook and everything else distracting people, but also sometimes helping to connect people. I'm also working on a historical fiction project, about an immigrant family who moves to rural Georgia in the thirties. That book is not finished yet, so those two books are on my mind at the moment. But I haven't been as effective, because I have had to navigate how to live a life with chronic pain for some time. It's been interesting working through that and adjusting my expectations. That's been going on for maybe three or four years. It's been a better year as I find a few remedies that actually work.

CARVE

I've seen some of your videos—"In My Head" and "Writing Through Pain"—about giving visibility to chronic pain. I was thinking about the way you describe your projects as "self-conscious." The tone of your tips for dealing with chronic pain video resembles the tone of your novel. This tone also felt familiar to me in some way that I couldn't quite place—until, in that video, you mention *BoJack Horseman* very briefly. I was skeptical of that show at first, but then I watched one episode and BoJack says something like, "You're funny, you should do a Shouts & Murmurs." And I thought, that's it! It's the tone of Shouts & Murmurs! So, how do you think about tone?

YUVI

I think about it a lot. Whether it's a video or a story or a novel, I always try to think of the sound of the storytelling. I have a certain voice, the one that I more commonly use, which is very similar to my own consciousness—worrying about being an idiot while trying to connect with people while stumbling over my words and mistakenly saying the wrong thing while trying to say the right thing. But I also change it up sometimes.

The historical fiction project has a few different perspectives, and I have to be careful not to have the same sound in all the different storytelling voices. I need to establish boundaries, because it can get out of control.

I've noticed that my voice evolves slightly. Sometimes it matures a little bit. Not a lot—I don't want to ever get too mature in how I write—but I can tell how the voice grows with different stories or regresses into what I'm going through at the time. But I do really think about the sound of the story. To me, the voice has to be compelling. I'm not good at writing stories with a very pulled-back voice and a beautiful structure and theme and plot. I can't do that at all. For me, the voice is a giant element of the story, and the story might coincidentally have a serviceable plot.

CARVE

What is your writing community like, and who have been your influences?

YUVI

In 2002 I stumbled into two fabulous writers who have an ongoing community, a writing workshop where you come to the table and bring writing and read it, and everyone gives you feedback. These two teachers really opened the door to writing for me, Joanna Rose and Stevan Allred. They were the biggest force for me to learn how to write and to tap into a voice that was my own.

Before that, everything I wrote was me trying to write the way I thought a writer should write. They were the first people to destroy that notion and help me find a sound for myself. Now I have a writing group that meets every week. They are enormously helpful and inspiring, and we help each other along. Also, I did go to Antioch University, and I got an MFA there and studied with some fabulous people. Cheryl Strayed really helped me as I was finishing the book that I published.

Is there a particular piece of writing advice you've been given that has persisted?

One thing that I always want to start with is finding the sound of the story—how the story gets told is the thing I'm always trying to nail down when I first write something. I don't care about the shape of it quite yet. I just want to see what the story feels like, and then I figure out the shape after that. I don't know if that's advice.

How does your technical writing interact with your creative projects?

It feels like such a different, unconnected world, even though I know these two worlds must affect each other. My day job is to write to an audience of software developers—programming samples and code is part of the documentation I write. It's extremely technical, and it does sometimes have a particular voice, but it's a lot more formal and focused (and with fewer curse words).

Some of my writing, like the novel that I'm shopping around now, does have a technical bent to it because of my experience in this technical world. But I think the big thing about technical writing that helps me with my creative writing is to figure out the goal of a piece of writing. But the analysis of the goal happens in different phases. With technical writing, I'm thinking of the goal right from the beginning. With the creative writing, I want to ignore the goal for a moment to get the emotional power of the storytelling. And then I can worry about the goal after I fall in love with the sound of the story.

CARVE

What shape does creative writing occupy in your life? Is it something that you try to keep to a schedule, or does it come in fits and starts?

YUVI

I don't write fiction every day. That used to make me feel guilty. Not anymore. But I write every week. I have slots in my week, several times a week where I have some hours to focus on the writing. It gets a little fuzzy from there, depending on how busy I am. Sometimes my creative projects aren't writing, or I'll stumble into something like writing a mobile app. But when I'm hot on creative projects or trying to finish a novel, I'll be jamming in time to work on it every day, whenever I can, or I'll get away for three days—just go find a cheap hotel and write for a few days straight. So, fits and starts depending on the energy of a project, but I'm always at the table writing several times a week.

CARVE

What's something that you've read recently that has been on your mind or that you would recommend?

YUVI

Especially with the chronic headaches, I have turned to audiobooks in a new way. I'm appreciating audiobooks more than ever. *Sugar Land* is one book I loved. I once was in a writing group with the author, Tammy Lynne Stoner, and she just wrote this amazing novel. It starts out in the twenties in Texas. It's a beautiful book. She writes about being gay, being in the South, working in a prison for men, getting married, raising kids—she covers so much ground in a wonderful way. I love the voice of the storyteller in this book.

CARVE

What mantra is guiding your recent work?

YUVI

I'm going to say this and then see if it feels true to my heart—but what motivates me is having authentic connections with people. Real connections, whether it's the people close to us or the people you bump into on the sidewalk. There's something about kindness and connecting with people that I'm thinking about a lot when I write. It's easy to get overwhelmed by all of the problems and the dark things that are happening. I sometimes freeze up thinking about it, but when I think in terms of how people connect, at least I can comprehend that. Whether it's activism or writing or talking to the cashier, how humans connect is the organizing principle behind what matters to me. I think that's true.

The Ways You Are Gone

KAMI WESTHOFF

December 2007

I wait for you, because I said I would. I spend the hours I used to spend with you thinking about the ways you are gone. The length varies, as does the content. Mostly you are dead and slowly becoming food for insects. This comforts me because when this is not you, you are frozen in pieces—arm, ear, breast, leg. Sometimes you are alive but kept, and the things I imagine are things I've seen in movies—so horrific they are funny. Chainsaws, machetes, meat hooks, underground dens of torture. I think of these things when I am missing you least.

The worst thought of all is that you are you. Alive. Lungs and legs strong from years of running, beautiful from years of believing so. I don't tell anyone this, but it's what I most fear—that you are safe. Happy. Beginning things.

On the ninth of every month, I travel to where you were last known. It isn't far, nothing to be impressed by. I walk the trail they say you walked and listen to the trees and the wind and the twigs cracking under my feet. I take it in. There must be clues. When the creek is high, I imagine you shivering beside the thrashing current. When the air is water before it touches skin, you rearrange the rocks and create a pool of coolness. When the trees are fat with leaves and shocking with color, you climb them and wait. You wait.

. . .

Before I leave this place each month, I look again at the ground and the tree trunks and try to find signs of struggle or a message carved into bark. I kneel and run my fingers over any divot or ripping away of moss as I've seen people do on crime television. I lay temple to ground, close my eyes, and try to hear sounds of you—the thin snore of allergy season, the hiccups you get when I tickle you. I think hard about the relationship between you and the dirt and the trees and the condition of this place in the solid cold February when your feet last left their print. But it is just a wooded patch of land that does each season because it knows how to. There is nothing to interpret or understand. No broken nail, no earring, not even a hair, nothing but things that belong to the forest.

. . .

On the eighth month I decided it was time to forget you, not as the person you were, but as the one you were going to be, and let you just be a person gone. I kept the memory of the road you drove away from our life on, the bottle of vodka on the driver's seat, and the bag packed with two weeks worth of underwear. I kept the dents in the snow that led us nowhere. I kept the trees but not you in them, watching for me, waiting for me to figure it out, because there is nothing to figure. You were you. We were us. But now you are just something that happened.

By the next month you were again the woman I was waiting to marry. Because I couldn't think of a reason not to, I put your wedding dress in the backseat of my car before I drove to the place. I knew it was dramatic—there was no reason for me to think the dress would make you come back, or that the dress should mean it was harder for me to lose you than anyone else, but it was dramatic that you were gone: television interviews, rewards, desperate pleas to the world, psychics in frumpy pantsuits.

When I got to the place there was a family rooting for mushrooms. The children walked in slow stabs behind their father. When he knelt at the base of a tree, the children peeked over his shoulders while he carefully uncovered mushrooms from where I had knelt and crawled and slithered in search of even the tiniest piece of you. One child held a mushroom in his palms like a hairless kitten and giggled. I spread the picnic blanket over your dress and drove.

As I pulled into my driveway I decided to live our lives for us. I'd age you, sicken you, get you over with. I gave our life one week.

Monday: You are pregnant at twenty-three—younger than we'd planned. There is enough of a hint of twins in your family that I give us a boy and a girl. Everyone speaks of your "glow," but by the sixth month you are almost too massive to move. I watch your stomach during the night, pillow between your knees, but the babies don't move when you're sleeping. You are swollen and transparent, but still pretty. You give birth, a C-section, and I am relieved about the parts of you that are spared.

Tuesday: We are in our thirties. You are trim but worn, like some weight would fill out the places that are wrinkling in. You sleep naked now, in your thirties it's time to be comfortable with your own damn body, you say. I pull back the sheet and stare while you sleep. There is hair in new places. Violet veins tangle under your skin. You shiver and I cover you.

Wednesday: You are fifty-five. I'm fifty-seven. You are even thinner than at thirty-five, wrinkles too deep to see their beginning. Margaret and Jack live in other states so you travel to see them often while I keep the books for small businesses. We know we sleep with other people. It's what we both expect the other to do. When I can get away, we travel to places like Greece, Italy, and Argentina. We always return in love, mostly.

Thursday: You are seventy-five. Margaret is dead, breast cancer. Jack is fine, but fat and unpleasant. We have grandchildren who seem to tolerate you and fear me. Your C-section scar halves you now that you've finally put on weight. I said you'd always be beautiful to me, but I just find you old and finished. Though we haven't talked about it in years, on your birthday I make you tell me again about when you went missing. Your story is always the same—you needed time away to figure things out. You were only gone a little while. Don't I remember?

Friday: At eighty, I wake and the sheets are wet and I know you are dead. It had been a cold night, and I snuggled you lightly because you ached everywhere. Before you slept we both said, night, I love you. It should've meant something, but it was just what we always said before sleep. Your body finally looks soft. Not scary or sad or gross, just soft. It feels okay. Our life was fine.

. . .

Your parents invited me to dinner on your birthday. And though I wanted to stay home and celebrate—somewhere you are twenty-one and I promised we'd drink until dawn. I put on a shirt your mother gave me for Christmas and was ten minutes early. The food was nice enough, turkey, slaw, dinner rolls with real butter, but I couldn't stop thinking about how you would have never wanted this meal on your birthday and how the things of you were now things in a box. There were pictures, of course, what kind of parents wouldn't have those, but nothing else. I know I shouldn't judge or assume a damn thing about their grief, but people say no parent should ever have to lose a child and they were slowly packing you into boxes to stack in the garage.

You'd be mad to know it, you'd say it was cruel, but I asked them if they thought you were dead after your mother clanked a plate of pumpkin pie, which you hate, in front of me. She held the whipped cream over my slice, set it down, and said, "Don't you?" They looked at me, both with the last bit of hope smeared over their faces as if my answer would decide your fate. Your family was one of surfaces. Never any problems because nobody ever shared a damned thing, yet this was the deepest I'd ever been with them, maybe the deepest they'd ever been at all and I felt a little like God. I thought of sharing the elaborate ways I'd imagined you dead, the things you hated about your father, and the things your father hated about your mother.

"No," I said. "I don't."

And it was the truth. But so was the fact that I wished you were, or would hurry up and be something other than gone.

. . .

I finished my pumpkin pie, said goodbye as though I planned to see them again, real soon, and they turned off the porch light before I got to my car. At first I thought it was rude, but decided they were just done and that felt good. I was tired of sharing despair with them.

On the walk to my car I wondered if telling the truth was ever the right thing to do. The psychic, Twila Omens, held item after item, books, sweaters, hats, gloves, shoes, even your toothbrush when your mother held it out to her and said "Please?" With some items she felt you. The feeling was electric, she said, and for a few seconds we all relaxed into our bodies thinking of the vital heat and color of electricity. But the feeling, she said, was retreating like a bright light dissolves behind the back of an eyelid.

Twila had apologized as she gathered her overcoat and mittens.

"I can't imagine how hard it is for you," she said, looking at me rather than your parents. "But I couldn't just let you hope."

. . .

When I got home I opened the wine we'd been saving for a time worth saving for. It was white, which I usually hate, but had tasted fine and sweet the day we'd slunk into the winery where we'd decided our ceremony would be, the dry Napa merlot and weather wringing out our energy. I baked chocolate chip cookies from a tube that popped when I twisted it. When the cookies were done I opened your gift I'd bought a couple of months earlier. I thought you would like it, but it was hard to say, because if you were alive you must be so different and if you were dead it would be so ridiculous. A miniature tea set, the saucers no bigger than a quarter, birds painted perched in tiny trees. I hated the clank of cup to saucer, though the size and detail was impressive. In the card I'd written, Happy 21st Birthday, Madeleine, because since you'd been gone I found it hard to think of you as a Maddy.

The expensive wine reminded me you went missing with a zero balance in our savings account. My money had gone to rent and the bills and fun, as arranged, as yours was to go into savings. That's something I wouldn't have known if you weren't gone. There was money, you said, let's get married, fly somewhere and stay. I'd imagined this sometimes before I slept. I figured we'd be happy wherever we went. We'd find work or live off the land, and though I had no idea how to survive like that, I pictured us being successful, being parents. And I guess I'd fall asleep and dream of these lives but something terrible would happen and I'd wake knowing I couldn't just forget school, a career, family, friends. But there was no money. It was gone before you were. I never thought about it then, but now I wondered how I got tied up in so many things that weren't you.

. . .

Terra called me the day after your birthday. She sounded surprised when I answered.

"We should get a drink or something, sometime," she said after minutes of small and nothing talk.

Though she'd said it the way people do when they assume both parties understand neither really means it, I said, "How about tonight?"

I know she was just being kind to me because she was your best friend, but I showered, even though I already had, shaved, plucked between my eyebrows how you showed me, trimmed the hair on my chest and groin. We met at an Italian restaurant she suggested where you would've ordered a salad to avoid the carbohydrates. At dinner I laughed at her jokes because she wanted to think I was okay. She patted my hand. My nails were filed and smooth. I imagined sex with her as she decided on her meal. I imagined her lips in places yours hadn't touched since our engagement. She decided on pasta, and though I am not violent, I imagined smashing my fists into her thighs, ass, ribs, just to feel the flesh of her.

On the drive home she talked about the last time she'd seen you as though it was new information. I wanted to say it was rude for her to talk about you on our date, but there was something on the road and I hit it.

Terra looked out the back window and exhaled.

"It's okay. Just an opossum. Yuck. Such awful eyes."

I pulled over to make sure and she was right. It wasn't dead. It quivered a bit, hissed, stilled. Its eyes were black holes against the snow.

Terra stuck her head out the window and said she was freezing and needed to get home. I dropped her off and she hugged me hard.

"Maddy'll come back. I know it."

. . .

After the date I snuggled with Margaret. Though your parents took everything in from your dorm room, they asked me to keep her. We're dog people, they said. With you gone, Margaret loves me more than anything. I call her Mags, though you'd be crazy to hear it. When I first met her I asked you what kind of name Margaret was for a cat, but you needed to think it was a beautiful name, as it was to be your daughter's, after your grandmother, so you gave it to something beautiful.

. . .

I saw you alive a week after your birthday. You were in between a walk and a run as people are when they are in a hurry but don't want to draw attention to themselves. Your hair was red and straight and long and you were wearing a flowing hippy skirt and a tank top, both were shades of your hair. When you finally looked at me I understood she wasn't anything like you. She was older and heavier and more like a woman who had lived a lot more life than you. How long would I keep seeing bits of you in everyone else, in people I don't know or that I hate, people you would hate that I saw you in? How long would it be before people would say, You really should move on, and stop looking at me like I've buried or burned or chopped you into bits, though they all loved me before, loved us together, offered their services for our wedding, asked us how many kids we would have and when they could babysit.

Because people asked about it, I often think of our last

night together. There must have been something, people say, and they are right. There was something—normalcy. It was a weekend, so you were staying the night at my apartment. There was television, frozen pizza, a salad with blue cheese and walnuts, a shared bar of expensive chocolate after dinner. You went to bed first and were asleep when I joined you. You flopped away, moaned a little, and went back to sleep. I snuggled against you until there was sweat between us. You kissed me in the morning and said, I love you, Drive safely, It's snowing, and you were gone.

Maybe you told me you were leaving in a hundred ways that night. The way you flipped through the stations and the one you decided on. The red peppers you chopped and arranged next to the shriveled pepperoni. The way you slapped at the snooze button only once.

. . .

I was surprised when Terra invited me to a BBQ for the loved ones of missing loved ones. I agreed to go because I figured it would look bad if I didn't, but the more I thought about it the more I wanted to see what these people looked like. I wanted to know if they had lived their loved ones' lives before killing them off then begging them back into life. Those sorts of thoughts must leave a smear like I see all over my face.

Though Terra offered to pick me up I drove alone because I lied about having places to be later. It was a BBQ, so I brought plain potato chips because people would eat them even though nobody ever bought them. Multi-colored ribbons were tied around the fat trunk of an oak tree. Maybe you would've said it was pretty. There was a white banner stretched between two trees. It read: NOT UNTIL THEY'RE HOME, each letter a color of the rainbow. Many people wore t-shirts with iron-on pictures of their missing.

"Who's your missing?" I turned to the hand on my shoulder and saw Marc.

He'd written his name in all caps on his nametag. The woman on his shirt was pretty even with the feathered hair and ruffled collar.

"My fiancée, Madeleine. I don't have a shirt."

"This is my fifth. Sarina's been missing since '85. The faces wear out fast."

"Girlfriend?" I asked.

Marc laughed. "Little sister. Good luck with your Madeleine." He laughed again.

People chatted as though familiar, but stood away from each other. I felt sorry for them and I felt better than them. I helped myself to a hamburger and chips.

"Hello, Jack. I read about your Madeleine last winter. How are you?"

I nodded, bit into the burger, and waited for lowercase Denise to ask me if there were any new leads as people did when I saw them at the store or school.

"Getting by," I said.

Denise wasn't wearing her loved one. I guessed a missing daughter because her voice fluttered like your mother's.

"Get used to it. It doesn't get any easier."

I wanted to say, Thanks, Denise, for your comforting words, but my "loved one" will come back, so fuck off. But what did I know?

Denise joined a cluster of women. Though some of them were laughing, they all held themselves as if they were waiting for a gunshot.

Marc found me again.

"Found a burger, huh? Don't mind Denise. She thinks she can say anything because hers was the worst. Alex was tortured. Her killer sent a letter with the details and photos but nothing about where the body is."

"So she's not really missing anymore, I guess, huh?"

Marc looked at me and shook his head. "They never come home."

Marc walked away like someone who really wants their words to resonate and though I hated his dramatic nature I felt a little better. During the first few months you were gone, everyone had words of comfort and advice—"You're in my prayers," "She's a strong girl. Try not to worry," "Don't give up hope." Words as thin as the air they were spoken into.

I finished my burger and realized it was likely some of these people knew where their missing was. Maybe they were the ones that looked the most destroyed. I knew people suspected I had something to do with you. Why would a girl with everything pack a bag, cash her paycheck, drive into the middle of nowhere, and disappear? Some nights I woke up sure they were right and that I'd simply blocked it out to protect myself. I saw you in my trunk, ashy arm pinned beneath the spare tire. I watched black and blue explode over your throat. Dreams are never literal, I told myself, though each time it took hours to convince myself it wasn't me that made you gone.

I used the bathroom and got into my car. I'd tell Terra later it was just too hard to be there, but I almost had to laugh at the scene. Ribbons and t-shirts to bring back the dead, or even more ridiculous, the missing who didn't want to be found. How could I tell which one you were? I promised to wait for you, but how do you keep a promise to someone who isn't anywhere?

I stopped at the store for some beer. It was lit softly, nothing like the usual blaring glare. It was my first time in a real grocery store since you'd been gone. Of all the places we'd known together this was the one I imagined I would miss you most. You were everywhere. Life cereal. Red delicious. Double roll toilet paper you insisted on though it cost more. Pink razors, black beans, the red and yellow peppers I said we couldn't afford. I'd avoided it because I feared the scene I might make by gathering all the things of you into a basket, dumping it over myself, holding the boxes and bags like they were the bits of you I loved most. Crying, of course, because people commented I hadn't done much of it, yelling, blaming anyone who tried to console me because how could they ever have a fucking clue what I felt like?

But I didn't make a scene. I bought beer and three cans of Fancy Feast for Mags, food you never would've let her eat, and made a joke about the combination to the checker.

At home, I slopped it onto a plate and set it on a foot stool so she wouldn't have to strain her neck to eat. I'd read to do that somewhere. She looked at me, then at her all-natural-anti-hairball-weight-managing usual. I moved her close to the treat and pet her from head to tail.

"Go ahead. It's okay."

She looked at me again and sniffed the food and I heard the flutter of a purr. She bit into the food with quick deep breaths, waiting to be shooed away. She ate until she heard the deep gut sobbing and looked at the mess of me. It was the most gone you'd ever been.

"Sorry, Mags. Go ahead. Finish."

I slid my hand over her fur. She lifted her back into the pet, turned toward the food, sniffed, and took another bite.

———————————

KAMI WESTHOFF is the author of two poetry chapbooks: *Sleepwalker*, winner of Minerva Rising's Dare-to-Be Contest, and *Your Body a Bullet*, co-written with Elizabeth Vignali. She teaches writing at Western Washington University in Bellingham, WA.

INTERVIEW WITH KAMI WESTHOFF

January 2019

CARVE

"The Ways You Are Gone" was one of the first stories I read in *Carve*'s archive, years before I became involved with *Carve*'s staff. It is truly one of my top most revisited stories, one that made me fall in love with the magazine. Last night I reread it in anticipation of this conversation, and I found I almost couldn't because I knew what was going to happen, how I was going to be devastated, but it still gave me shivers multiple times. What do you recall about writing this story, and what has your experience of revisiting it been like?

KAMI

It was inspired by a student that I had when I was teaching as part of my MFA at U-Mass in Amherst. I had her as a student during the fall semester, and then she went missing in February of that year and hasn't been found. There have been *Dateline* features, all kinds of shows and reporting about her disappearance. She was a nursing student there and I didn't know her all that well, I just had her as a student for a brief period of time, but I just thought this waiting—this idea of waiting for someone that you love to come back, who now hasn't come back even eleven, twelve years later—it just really struck me. In the story I use a few of the real details, like the vague geographic location of where she went missing, and she did have a fiancé at the time, but I tried not to go into it any more than that. I tried to really fictionalize it.

I wrote this story a long time ago, when she'd only been missing for probably less than a year. A lot of other details have been revealed since then, and it's all stuff that I didn't know going into the story. So it's really very loosely based on her, but it's more about the concept of having someone that you love go missing, and never knowing where they are, and trying to approach grief in a way that isn't idealized. The bitterness and the anger that the character felt, even though he felt guilty about feeling it. That's where it came from.

CARVE

I had no idea this story was based on a real missing person. That's so fascinating, so devastating.

KAMI

I know. I feel a little weird about it now that her story has become so prominent. I just finished also a collection of poems that are about women in my community who have been murdered, and I'm nervous about appropriating these tragedies. I'm trying to pay homage to those women, but it's something I'm thinking about a lot. But this story, it was one of those stories that just came. You know, you get one or two of those in your life—that you just have to sit down and write.

CARVE

I'm so interested in what you said about the way this story portrays grief, the way the character is considering his grief. The flashes of uncertainty and bitterness are so important, but there's also so much intimacy in the way he thinks about his missing fiancée. I read it as an epistolary piece, the way the character composes his thoughts addressed to her, and that feels so intimate. Did this story ever take other narrative forms, take other points of view?

KAMI

You know, it pretty much stayed this way. I wrote it after I finished my MFA program so it wasn't even a workshopped piece—which was new for me at the time, to not have my fiction workshopped. I had the first line, "I wait for you, because I said I would." It was the kind of line that comes to you when you're on the bus, or whatever, and the story follows. From that line I knew it was going to be a first-person narrative, but a really close, intimate address to another character. Sometimes I forget that it's in the first-person and I think about it as a second-person piece. It seems so directed, even though it's not technically that. One thing that I did add a little bit later was the imagining of the life lived, where he goes through Monday, Tuesday, Wednesday, Thursday, Friday. I wasn't sure how I felt about that section, and it's funny because I've had so many people point it out as their favorite section of the story.

CARVE

I think about that section all the time.

KAMI

I'm glad I added it. I must have known it needed it.

CARVE

What was the uncertainty?

KAMI

I think I was worried it was a little too heavy-handed, that I was pushing in their life. At the time I had also just become aware of the Andrea Yates story, the woman who drowned her five children in the bath. The idea of protecting somebody from an imagined life rather than letting them live that life stuck. I was really interested in the idea of imagining a life that was worse than reality, that provided some sort of reason to be less upset about the character's current state. But I wondered if it was a little too writerly.

CARVE

I love the imagined life because, like you said, it's not an idealized life. He's mourning the chance to have had that life, but the life isn't perfect—there's infidelity, the daughter's death, the son is unpleasant. In fact, a lot of this character is not ideal—I'm thinking about his date with Terra and the way he imagines feeling the flesh of her. That part is uncomfortable, the terms in which he's thinking about her. But that moment combined with the way he imagines the marriage through a series of selves and the way he's conscious of the drama of a missing persons case, the drama of bringing the dress to the place where she went missing, and the drama of the news—I'm fascinated to know this story is inspired by a real case, but I'm curious about your character in particular. As you created this love and this relationship, what were your other influences?

KAMI

That's such a good question. I remember thinking that I wanted to try to write a convincing male perspective. When I was rereading it this morning, that line that you brought up, when he's imagining crushing into the friend's body—I'm certain I wouldn't write that today. But at the same time, I don't think it's too far. It's a moment of anger and honesty. But it's disturbing too.

I'm sure I was being influenced by certain styles of writing, but I think it's my personality to be really cynical about grief and prescriptions for grief. My epiphany—which, of course, many other people have had—is that the entire way we grieve is based on the capitalist inclination to make money around the funeral industry. I was having this thought about how if we could just grieve a little more honestly perhaps it would be less painful.

CARVE

Who were your major influences at the time?

KAMI

I had gotten into J. M. Coetzee because he had come to U-Mass and he won the Nobel Prize that year. I read *Disgrace* and a couple of his other books. I was really affected by his visceral language and his refusal to make things prettier than they were. I was reading some José Saramago at the time too, and Lydia Davis, but I don't see her in there really. Flannery O'Connor and Grace Paley were people I was really into.

I also write a ton of poetry. I'm really into concision of language, I try not to have any extra words. I think it takes me a long time to write a short story because I write it like a poem. Rereading this story after so long, I thought I would cringe. I saw one extra word, an "in," and I thought, that's not too bad.

Which reminds me, when I was revisiting this story I came across *The Literary Roadhouse* podcast talking about it. Did you see that?

CARVE

Yeah, I did. Did you listen to it?

KAMI

I did and I was so flattered, first of all, because it was really nice that they took time to discuss it. But it made me see the narrator in a different light. Yes, he can be ugly, but that's how grief is too. I think I like him a little more than they seemed to, but when I reread the story I was like, "Yeah, he really is a jerk." If I were to edit the story now I think I'd lose a little of that ugly honesty because of my concerns about the way it represents violence against women.

CARVE

Considering gendered violence—you mentioned your poetry and composing fiction like a poem. I think I can see that in your work, in the way you use sensory details and how you place your plot points and your images in the narrative. Your book of poems, *Sleepwalker*, seems like it has a consistent character with a particular narrative, a narrative that deals with violence and intimacy. I wondered about your process writing that book, what the relationship between form and narrative is for you.

KAMI

I wrote *Sleepwalker* one April, during 30/30. Its narrative is based on my mom's first husband. I had a lot of material to work with, unfortunately. He was a pedophile, and my mom wasn't aware of that until she became aware of it when he was arrested. I wrote it as a sort of homage to her. People would say, "How did you not know?" I tried to focus on her, and it was really a way for me to connect with her too, to realize that instead of focusing on how I wanted her to be stronger, actually, she survived this.

I got her permission, of course, and she gave me a lot of the details. I added some other details and used my poetic license on some things. But the real violence of the story, the pedophilia—a lot of that stuff was true.

I don't know how to get away from writing about this kind of stuff. It's just where I am. And I started this new project about women who have been murdered.

CARVE

Right, which you said is based on true stories also. What was your process? What kind of research did you do, and where do you draw lines between, as you said, your poetic license and the real events?

KAMI

As you might imagine, it was very difficult to do the research. I did it this past April, also during poem-a-day, and I really wanted something with a theme. Last November a friend of mine and her five-year-old son were murdered by her husband one night. I'd actually done my master's degree at Western with her, and we'd shared poems about sexual assault. It was very traumatic and upsetting and horrific.

I wrote a poem for her about her funeral and some other things, and then I realized that was my theme. So I started to do research. I had connections with a few of the women that I wrote about. I went to community college in Bellingham, and a woman was killed there on campus. We had to be on lockdown because of her ex-husband. And then there were women I didn't know personally. I did notice that I referenced one of them in "The Ways You Are Gone," and I had forgotten that—a woman named Mandy Stavik, who lived in our county and had been killed. Recently, just in the last year or so, her killer was found and put on trial.

It was all part of my community, it was sort of all over me. I thought, "I've got to write about this." I started researching the ones I knew, the stories I knew. There's also the Hillside Strangler who murdered two women, students at Western, in the seventies. I don't know if this is just a northwestern thing, but people claim there are lot of serial killers and murderers here. The Green River Killer was also in Northwest Washington. The process of doing all this research was horrific, as you can imagine. And it's so hard because these aren't my stories to tell.

CARVE

In these poems, is there a poetic voice that belongs to your perspective? Or is it from the perspective of the women? Or a third-person narrative?

KAMI

The majority of them are in the second-person toward the victim, but there are a few first-person poems, like from my friend's perspective, about other people that I had a little bit more of a personal connection with. I knew my friend, of course, but the other ones I didn't know firsthand. I pulled a few details that I found on Google, in our local newspaper, in some Seattle news sources. I began with details that were public knowledge and then I tried to create. They ended up being nature poems too, which was interesting. I guess I'm finally realizing I'm a nature poet. I use a lot of mountain and water imagery, and trees. Which is what I have around here to look at.

I've published a few of these poems and had a number of readings. People have responded really well to them. Sometimes I'll apologize before I read them. I had an older lady come up to me after a presentation I did this last fall, and she said, "Please stop apologizing for these. They are beautiful and they're important, and you're brave. Thank you for writing them." She started crying, and then I started crying. Right now I just can't stop writing about violence against women and girls.

CARVE

In the poems of yours that I've read, I can recognize the things your poetry shares with "The Ways You Are Gone"—considering, like I said, sensory detail, but also the relationship between the physical movement of the body and the emotional movement of the voice. I also came across *Your Body A Bullet*, which is a collaboration. I wondered what you could share about your experience creating and publishing a collaborative manuscript.

KAMI

I mean, what a gift to have a poet to work with. She's one of my best friends, Elizabeth Vignali. When we started 30/30 back in April 2014, she was my partner in that. She's read pretty much everything I've written in the last five years. I'm so afraid of being heavy-handed and overly dramatic, to which she said, "Your images are great, but sometimes you can just say a line that has emotion in it, a direct emotion." And I thought, okay, I'll try.

So we had this idea for a collaborative project and the subject matter would consider collaboration too: a parasite/host theme. We thought, what's more collaborative than that? I think the first one we wrote was actually the Cuckoo Bird, or maybe it was the Angler Fish. Those are some of the early ones. And then a lot of them ended up being essentially mother poems.

We both have two girls that are between ages eight and twelve now. We were thinking a lot about bodies and perceptions of bodies, how to keep bodies healthy. Essentially all the parasites are trying to do is keep their young healthy. I think whatever's driving me emotionally works its way into the poem, so the poems became about facing motherhood. I write a ton about unconventional experiences of motherhood, experiences that are messier than what I had seen, what I was surrounded with before I had kids.

Liz has a line in one of her poems: "I didn't know you'd be so hard to love." It's a bird looking at its baby. I thought there was so much honesty in that, and I think we were able to approach that emotion about motherhood more honestly through these parasites than we could have if we were writing about our actual children.

As for the process, one of us would do a little research and begin to write. Most of the poems are call and response, but not all of them. Some of them we just wrote separately and saw how they worked together. It was interesting because I tend to go inward. I'm all gut. When we were doing our final revisions, she said, "You have so many guts and throats." I mean, parasites—sometimes they just look like long throats. But Liz is less about the body, her work isn't as visceral in the blood and guts way. So it was really cool to see how her poems were working and think about how I could be a little bit less internal or less gory and still get my point across. I don't want to seem gratuitous, and that's something I'm really concerned about when I'm writing poems about actual people that have been killed.

I hope most people think like this when they collaborate, but it's so nice to not feel alone in the world. We live in the same town and we're doing our book release on January 12. It's just a warm environment, and to have someone to stand up next to you while you're reading is really nice too.

CARVE

What is your community in Bellingham like?

KAMI

Our community here is great. I teach creative writing at Western, and I have all of these students that I'm so in awe of. They're creative and kind and so empathetic toward each other and toward me. I love my job, and I love them. They're constantly keeping me connected to the younger community of writers.

Liz and our friend Deedee run the Kitchen Sessions. It's a monthly event in which a person—Liz—gives her home over to people that want to come together and eat healthy, warm food. Well, it doesn't have to be healthy—I should say comfort food. And be warm together. Right now we're in the dark of winter, as you are in Missoula. It's good to share work in a safe space. So every month, we're surrounded by amazing writers of all different skill levels and all different experiences, and we support each other. And we're so happy for each others' successes, too.

A lot of my community here comes from teaching and from the poetry community. There are a lot of cool events. A woman heard me perform at the Kitchen Sessions and invited me to be part of a reading on Sunday, art and poetry, that arose out of the women's march that we had in Bellingham in 2017. And I said, "Are you sure? My work is pretty bleak," and she said, "I know what you do." In Bellingham I feel very supported as a writer, as a poet.

CARVE

Do you think it's in part because you have this poetic space that is lovely, collaborative, and cozy that you are able to take these emotional, thematic risks in your writing and explore these things that are difficult to look at?

KAMI

That's so much of it, I'm sure. I'll actually extend that credit further back—when I started writing about some of the trauma from my own family, I was fortunate in that I met a person, my husband, who was a very grounded, safe space for me. I think once I felt settled in that support at home, I could really get into the unpleasant, painful stuff. And that just continued. But I didn't write for a long time after I had children, because it was so much emotionally harder than I expected. Now that I have this poetry group for each April, they go through it with me and they give me so much love and support.

Also, I've been buoyed by people from the community telling me what I'm doing is important, that it's important for the victims that I'm writing this. Because I do feel worried—I don't want to take anyone's story. I mean, I try to do it with so much grace and give all of these victims and their families privacy—I don't put any names in anything. I try to write with grace and honor and try to breathe a tiny bit of hope, if there is any, into it. I don't think I could do any of that work without the close group of friends that I have lifting me.

CARVE

You mentioned how your process for poetry and your process for fiction are different. What do you mean by that?

KAMI

I'm not sure if this is just my community or not, but I do feel like there is a stronger support system for poets. There are more opportunities. And, I don't know, poetry just takes up less space on the page when you submit it. Fiction feels far away right now. I'm also doing a little bit of creative nonfiction here and there.

CARVE

It seems like nonfiction often comes along with poetry.

KAMI

Yeah. It's newer for me. But my mom has dementia, she's in the mid-stages so she still knows me, but it's constant heartbreak. I've been writing about that. I think it's that some topics belong, for me, in nonfiction or in poetry, and some don't. I also feel like writing fiction is a little bit lonelier, and I'm not sure why that is.

In my fiction usually I have an idea or a question like, what would happen if a person did this? And then I write the story. I was very interested in the idea, like I said, of unconventional mothering, inspired by Andrea Yates, and I kept thinking about what drives a woman to kill her children. Or to abandon her children. So as in the poetic project or in the nonfiction, it's still about motherhood, but framed differently.

I'm also aware that I'm representing a very heterocentric identity approach to motherhood, which I'm not proud of. It's not
something I'm intentionally trying to do, but it's the only voice
I have right now, so I am trying to be really aware of that. And
I would say the majority of my fiction has characters that are
trying to figure out how to navigate a world that is painful to
exist in, but that still see a little bit of light and a little bit of
hope and grace in it.

CARVE

You've spoken about your mother's influence and presence
in your first poetry collection, and how writing became more
emotionally difficult after having children. And now your
mother has dementia, which is prompting you to experiment
with a new genre. So much of this seems connected. How
has the evolution of these thoughts and concerns influenced
your writing? Do you think there have been other effects of
it, beyond moving away from fiction and into poetry and
collaboration?

KAMI

One thing that I am looking at now—whenever I write it's personal, of course—but now it needs to mean something else.
It needs to matter beyond my experience. I'm trying to give
my students writing that I think really matters socially, that
says something, that has a voice. I appreciate humor-writing
and that sort of thing, and obviously humor-writing does matter and can be very socially charged. I often find myself reading and thinking, okay, everybody should write anything they
want. I fully believe that. But, with my students, when I read
their work I always push them to consider how their writing
can connect to the world, to the larger struggles of humanity.

I'm teaching a lit class this winter and I'm pulling in
texts that deal with contemporary examples of captivity in

American culture. One of the texts I'm teaching is called *There Should Be Flowers* by Joshua Jennifer Espinoza. It matters so much, engages so much beyond the individual poet. I think we need that.

So I think, as far as my writing—and I get that this is tiresome for people reading my work sometimes—but if my writing doesn't have a social issue that it's addressing, then I can't even bother with it. But I also know that I'm probably shutting myself off to some important writing that could be therapeutic in a different way.

CARVE

Do you think this attitude is a result of the politics of right now?

KAMI

I'm sure it's partly that. My writing has become a little bit more focused on exploring, more based in nonfiction. The collection of stories that I completed most recently was about mothering and characters trying to mother when they themselves were victims of trauma. How to move forward when we have these small children that we're trying to protect and the world is so scary. I think some of it is that poetry allows me to get at that kind of grossness about the world, but then also it's spring and right outside my window there's a cherry blossom. It's easier to move between thoughts and images.

Once in a while I'll write something and ask Liz if it's too sentimental. She says, "No, please, give us a moment of sentiment." Poetry is that way, isn't it? It lets you do both, I think. I feel like it connects me to the world more than fiction does. You know, I've always said fiction is my genre, but I don't know if it is anymore.

CARVE

You've spoken about what you're teaching and how it's connected to your personal work. How does the act of teaching
interact with your writing? What's the relationship between
your teaching life and your writing life?

KAMI

I don't write as much when I'm teaching, of course. I know
some people do. I don't get as much material done, but I feel
like everything I'm reading is building the material for when I
sit down to write. I have colleagues and know writers who are
writers first, and then teachers. I have never felt that way. I've
felt equally a teacher and a writer, if not more so a teacher. I
think it helps that I don't resent my time with my students. I
look at working with them as though they're giving me a gift
and I'm hopefully giving them a gift too. I think that helps me
not feel stuck in a way that I know some people struggle with
when they're teaching more and unable to write as much.

But I think it's more that I have the same philosophy as a
writer and as a teacher: that fiction—I mostly teach fiction—
but fiction and stories really matter. It's important that we say
them as well as we can and as clearly as we can. I want to hold
myself to the same standards that I try to hold my students
to, about engaging with important emotions, and the more we
read the more empathetic we become.

I am also very open with them about my struggles when I
write, and that's always fun. I bring them my rejections. I tell
them to build a supportive community, to find a couple of people that understand what you're doing in this class and hold
onto them. Then April comes around. I usually have a lighter
spring quarter, which is great because then I can write a poem
a day. I'll go into class and say, "This is terrible, look what
I've written, what am I doing?" I think they enjoy seeing the
writing struggle too. Liz and I, our children all go to the same

elementary school. We've done an after-school enrichment writing club with eight- to ten-year-olds. They're so brilliant.

What's your experience of teaching creative writing at the college level versus working with elementary school students?

KAMI

The first thing I would say is that ninety percent of the elementary kids want to share everything they do, which is so cool. Especially the third-graders. We work with third, fourth, fifth—by the time they're in fifth grade, some of them start to feel more self-conscious. But elementary kids do the best similes.

I would say teaching college and teaching children is pretty similar in a lot of ways. We all just need to be supported by kindness when we're writing. Not that we don't need to be critical of each other's work, and all of my students are empathetic with each other. One big thing is that third graders are not caught up in ego yet. And when I say ego in a college-level creative writing classroom, it's not a critique at all—it's just that there's so much pressure being in an MFA program. We're all very vulnerable and sharing really important work. I'm the same way when I share with my friends, too. But if we're supported, then it's okay.

CARVE

What mantra is guiding your recent work?

KAMI

Something I think a lot about when I'm writing poetry—I tell my students this, and my family members—is that poetry hurts, but it heals too. I have that in my head a lot: "This hurts, but it heals."

I try to look at writing as a way to find grace, especially with some of the stuff going on with my mom. How do I find grace in my mother slowly forgetting who I am? That's the one connection that I thought I always had. So in addition to poetry hurting and healing, I'm trying to find some grace in the tragedy that surrounds us all the time. I don't know that I'm necessarily always doing that, but sometimes when I write poems, I feel at the end that I've found a little bit of grace. And that's something to hold on to, for sure.

The Candy House of Roscoe, New York

MEAGAN CASS

December 2008

They woke in the night, in their childhood homes, with a strange, mawkish hunger, a sprain in the chest, a clench of the gut, a small, dull-toothed animal stirring. The girl lived upstate, the boy lived downstate, and they did not know each other, had just taken degrees at different universities. Yet at one, two, three in the morning they each crept into their parents' kitchens to find that nothing edible satisfied them. They took to sampling fistfuls of dirt from potted plants like pregnant women, to biting at their own cheeks, to sucking the briny copper of pennies but still, they could not sleep.

In the murky dark of a Monday morning in August, they packed up their cars, each headed for the other's region. They were hopeful. They had each been making things out of words for some time. Living in a new place *fires the imagination*, they told their parents, who stopped throwing things at each other just long enough to hug them too tightly, to press crumpled dollar bills into their hands, to offer the standard words for separation, unremarkable and yet vaguely haunting, like a pile of chicken bones: Goodbye, we'll miss you, take care, best of luck, be careful.

They drove fast with the windows down, the pastoral

scenery blurred, green ribbons out their windows, the herds of grazing deer not looking up as they raced past, mosquitoes hitting their windshields and dying in spindly stars. As the sun rose and the clouds burned off, the boy and girl were metallic and in control, cutting across the sleepy, ragged belly of New York State. Merging onto Scenic Highway 17, they imagined all the word things they would make in their new lives, perfect houses of narrative built to the right proportions, wildly original and yet so hospitable. Gabled and all that.

Imagine flying above them in an airplane, seeing their toy cars creeping closer toward one another through the inky spills of cloud shadows. They believe in their own independence. They have woven no tenuous threads home. They have thrown up their isolation quickly and clumsily, like so much cheap housing. You know it will not hold.

At noon, just as they were about to pass each other, they were starving again and saw the billboards. Since they were traveling on opposites sides of the highway the billboards were facing opposite directions, but they said the same things. "America's Only Candy House! So clean you can eat off the floor...OR THE ROOF!" the first proclaimed, the bubble letters striped red to look like candy canes. "A Fine Family Adventure! DESSERT IS ON THE HOUSE!" insisted another. A third pictured a woman dressed like Nougat Nancy from the Sugartown board game the boy and girl each played as children. Only this Nougat Nancy's skirt was hiked up above the knees, she was curvaceous, and her turquoise eyes took up her whole face like two disco balls. She held a bright yellow lollipop, her other hand held coyly behind her back, the words "America's Only Candy House...STOP IN FOR A LICK!" beneath her.

"Christ," thought the girl. "It's either got really good chocolate or really weird porn."

"It's ridiculous enough to be worth a stop," thought the boy.

He pulled off at the appropriate exit, onto a service road and fell in line behind the girl, the two of them following the pointing hand of an anthropomorphic gummy bear that served as a road sign. "You're Almost at America's Candy House" was written across the bear's wide, glistening stomach.

Flung deep in the woods several miles from the interstate, the place had more of the air of a shoddy vacation cabin than of the roadside extravaganza they had expected. The gravel driveway was lined with plastic swizzle sticks that had seen better days, tilting in either direction, and the mailbox, a giant Pez dispenser with a rabbit head, was covered in bird shit, one of its vacant black eyes weathered away. The full, August trees shook with wind, cropping the noonday sun into shifting rectangles of light. Famished, they stood blinking at the structure before them, a squat, brown cottage with a trippy candy cane pattern painted around the windows. The white roof was black with a few plastic-looking nonpareils affixed to it like a ruined game of Othello. The air smelled like sulfur from the refinery one town over. Someone had graffitied "Fuck You Suzanne" across the front walk.

They were the only ones in the lot, despite the billboards, and they took a moment to check each other out, the way any two humans of the same age group will. She did not think him particularly attractive, though there was something about his muscular shoulders, his long torso, the thinness of his black t-shirt that made her uneasy. He did not think her particularly attractive, with her skinny legs and her cloud of frizzy blond hair and her fussy cardigan. She had an air of fidgety aggression in her, in the way she tapped her foot and squinted her face while looking up at the Candy House, which made him want to elbow her in the stomach.

A wiry man in jeans, purple cowboy boots, and a t-shirt that said "No Fear" burst from the house.

"I would shoot myself in the foot for a cigarette right

now," he said, crossing his arms over chest, sticking out his hips. "But I've quit. And the gum is not the same, don't believe anyone who tells you that."

His hair was greasy, his sunken face pitted with acne scars, and he had one of those mustaches that curls up on either end in a perpetual grin. There was a dark red carnation pinned to his shirt, as if, as an afterthought, he'd decided to go and crash someone's high school prom. He smelled like hot tar.

"You own this place?" the boy asked.

"Is this the Candy House?" the girl asked.

"I don't know what you were expecting," said the man. "A chocolate river? You're not in paradise, folks, you're in central New York. But we do what we can. Decent selection of high quality chocolates. Hot chocolate in the winter months."

He spoke with the boisterous, theatrical air of a ringmaster, waving an arm to display each sentence.

"College kids? All of life before you and all that shit?"

The girl smiled, slid her hands in her pockets. The boy looked down at his feet. They each muttered something about being on the way to somewhere.

"Well, well, that's great for you," said the man. He cut his small, dark eyes back and forth between them.

"This way, please. We'll fix you with something good."

· · ·

Inside the house was unremarkable, boring even. On the living room floor yellowed copies of Penthouse were stacked in messy piles like precarious monuments. There was a hokey display in the vestibule featuring a miniature boy and girl with rosy cheeks and curly hair standing on a circle of synthetic grass, giant lollipops clenched in their fleshy fists. The place smelled like what they thought of as an old person's house, a combination of cough syrup and mothballs.

Yet there was something subtly unstable about the living room walls, which were the color of chapped lips, and the marshmallow-white leather couches, cartoonishly big for the space. The lollipop wall art, metal garbage pail lids painted with clumsy swirls, the decadent crown moldings around the doors and windows in reds and pinks, the giant plastic rock candy sticks leaning in the corner like cavemen's clubs, and the jelly-bean patterned throw rug, created the lurid, dirty feel of a funhouse at a Fourth of July carnival in a small town. The wood floor, they noticed, was sticky, from God knows what.

Still, they were hungry. They looked at each other, decided that the other was unlikely to cause any serious harm. They looked at the yellowed postcards on the rack in the corner showing the Candy House in its glory days, the yard a flourishing garden of blown glass lollipop ornaments, the old man standing in front of it, younger looking, his teeth white and straight, his body muscular, a woman with gallons of messy hair in his arms smiling widely, the title "America's Sweethearts" printed beneath them. The boy and girl peered into the small kitchen off the living room, where the old man was puttering in the cabinets. It was a standard kitchen, blue-tiled with yellow walls.

"Ah ha," said the man. From deep in one of the cabinets he pulled a chocolate gift box, the kind of thing given to an elementary school teacher at the end of the year or to someone half-loved, and led them back into the living room. "We don't get much business at all," he said. "People have lost their sense of nostalgia, their sense of wonder. They only like to stop for fast food."

A breeze blew through the open window, filling the room with the spicy musk of cinnamon.

"Is it really?" said the girl.

"Is it stable?" asked the boy

"Now I have one question for you," the man said, putting

a hand on each of their knees. "Have you ever been in love?"

The boy and girl laughed, looked at each other. Who was this guy? What a nut job.

"Of course," they said, though neither had been on more than a few disappointing dates.

"Was it terrible?" asked the man.

"Of course not," the boy and girl said.

"Then you've never been in love," the man said, rubbing his hands together, putting more chocolates into their hands.

The boy and girl leaned back on the couch. They were suddenly very tired from driving. This quaint cottage, carved into the mountains, its living room windows filled with the merciless green of the Catskill Mountains, seemed a wonderful place to rest. They each took more candy. It tasted like chocolate should, the thin milky casings falling apart easily to give up tangy cherry centers. They watched each other's thin, supple wrists, watched the other's hands grab, extend up to mouths. The man stood up so he towered over them, said it'd be rent-free in exchange for some light maintenance, keep the candy racks full, the peppermint sticks polished, the giant gum drop bouncy balls inflated; pick the fruit and vegetables from the garden out back or wild animals with sharp teeth will be at your door, grown arrogant and vicious with plenty. Do not dare eat any more of the candy.

He showed them the two small upstairs bedrooms, each furnished with a twin bed, dresser, and a child's-size desk, all done in faux wood. They watched him peel out of the drive, a cigarette in his mouth, and then the house was quiet as a cube of glass.

. . .

For weeks it was a workable life. They spent their days in their separate rooms kneading paragraphs, mixing index cards scrawled with ideas. The furniture was small, but they were able to cram themselves into the desks, bend themselves into the beds. Sometimes they would pass each other on the way to and from the bathroom and joke that they were peeing in America's Only Candy House.

There were few visitors. In late August pairs of university students on their way to upstate or downstate schools came into the Candy House and laughed at all the kitsch and wrote the name of their universities in the guest book, the forceful acronyms shouting on the yellowed paper. BU. UB. NYU. SUNY. The couples fumbled shyly around the copies of Penthouse. Their bubbly, repetitive curiosity quickly grew tiresome to the boy and girl. They fell into the habit of leaving the boxes of chocolate on the coffee table for the students with a sign that said "eat me." They had never claimed to be people persons.

Then there were the lonely, restless people, the divorcees, the widows and widowers, the worried parents, their children away fighting the latest war. The boy and girl sat them down, poured them glasses of the pomegranate juice the old man had left them in the fridge, listened to their stories, offered them plates of neatly arranged chocolates. They never questioned their own prohibition. It made perfect sense. They were like bartenders, existing around vice but not engaging in it. Calm. Removed. They nodded with what they thought was sympathy. If there had been clean, white gloves they would have worn them.

Labor Day a herd of minivans converged in the parking lot. From their windows the boy and girl watched boys in yellow-and-black soccer uniforms spring from the sliding doors and run toward the Candy House, punching and tripping each other on the way, their parents and siblings trailing behind them. The boy and girl stopped making word things and presented the boxes of chocolates, a large bag of swizzle sticks, a package of sucking candies and some licorice. There had never been such a big group and they were slightly embarrassed of the shape the house was in: they had left dirty juice glasses on the coffee table; the television was tuned to a cooking channel; and there were still the piles of Penthouse.

But the boys did not seem interested in fairy tales, in witches or magic or Hansel and Gretel. They quickly ate the chocolates, sucked on the sugar sticks, chewed on the licorice, their little cleats making sucking noises on the sticky living room floor. As they ate more sugar they got more rowdy, kicking at the giant, plastic gumdrops resting in the corners, passing them back and forth like soccer balls. They ran up the stairs and looked into the bedrooms, complaining that nothing was really made of candy and why were there papers in a candy house. One of them tried to bite into the purple banister.

Then the soccer player parents were there in khakis and jeans and white sneakers, yelling that it was still soccer season and the boys had signed contracts not to eat any junk food and they were just here to *see* the Candy House and have a little snack. The soccer player boys threw their candies into the garbage in the kitchen one by one, their faces assuming the guilty seriousness of baseball players caught taking steroids. Their older siblings hung back around the postcards, signed their names in the jellybean-patterned guest book. An overweight teenage boy in a t-shirt with a giant, grinning skull on it explained that they were a select soccer team from Rochester, The Yellow Jackets, and that they had been eliminated in the early round of a prestigious tournament on Long Island. "It's been a hard trip home," he said, picking at one of his cuticles, then letting his large hands drop to his sides. "I got one of the mothers to give me a blow job in the hotel elevator, though," he whispered, glancing quickly over his shoulder at a trim woman in tight jeans, heeled boots, and a blazer, wiping chocolate from a small boy's face with a handy-wipe.

"Liar," the boy and girl laughed when the teenager and the rest of the caravan were gone.

. . .

That night they met in the kitchen, poured glasses of the pomegranate juice. They had come to love drinking it in small doses from the tall, thin glasses in the cabinet, sucking it up like nectar. They drank the juice and talked word things for hours, each unimpressed with the other's conversation but nonetheless content. They noticed that the pitcher of juice kept refilling itself in the refrigerator. This odd abundance made them uneasy, but it was good to talk, to forget about the mocking green out their windows and the small, neat boxes of their rooms. "I am happy," they told their family and friends over the phone.

In September they came together most evenings to cook dinner. The vegetable garden was bountiful—zucchini, tomatoes, pumpkins, and squashes hung heavily from the plants— and the old man had left them a well-stocked spice rack and a good black pot. They got adventurous in their cooking, bungling soups and stews, making their own stock, laughing at each other's foibles, sometimes moving out to the front stoop afterwards to sit in the cool night, their new world cupped in darkened hills, verdant and mysterious and claustrophobic. Horizon-less.

After a particularly successful dinner, they moved to the couch, paged through the guest book, read and chuckled over its fading travelers' messages. "Your candy is simplistic and your décor is overwrought," Eric and Melanie from Manhattan had written in July 2005. In 2000 Mark from Troy, New York said, "Down with the man, down with corporate candy, Vote Nader."

Then there was a spree of messages from the Reagan era

about the value of such a wholesome family rest-stop. "What sweet kids! We'll never forget the fruit punch fountain!" said Constance and Thomas of Elmira, New York, 1981.

The '60s and '70s were more ambivalent about the Candy House. "How come there weren't any Gobstoppers?" complained Bruce from Ohio, 1979. "Gone to Canada, not coming back to this Godforsaken country. You can have your candy," wrote Anonymous, 1968. The last entry: "Free candy free country. And keep putting whatever you're putting in the marshmallows!" wrote Steve from Port Washington, Long Island, June 1967.

The boy and girl took long sips of their juice, sighed with the easy melancholy of people who have suffered but have fallen, inexplicably, into a kind of bounty. They did not notice that the house was changing shape with each new thing shared. The roof was leavening. The wooden beams in the living room, the house's skeleton, took on the shiny, red gleam of hard candy. The boy and girl in the vestibule were awakening, bringing their lollipops up to their mouths over and over again, their acorn shaped heads swiveling back and forth.

"This has been a productive day," said the boy, on his fourth glass of juice. He looked at the girl's buttoned up cardigan.

"We have an amazing setup here," said the girl. She looked at the boy's t-shirt, could almost feel the thin fabric in her hands.

Afterward they thanked each other politely, dressed quickly, slipped into the small, cramped, separate beds, giddy with the easiness of it. Satisfied.

. . .

The next day, moving about their chores, working on word things, each avoiding the other, they noticed a change in the light in the house. The panes of glass in all the windows were tinted red and green and yellow. They wondered if they should call the old man, but they figured it must have something to do with the new fall cool. They sprayed the windows with a bottle marked "saccharine preserve" they'd found under the sink and went on with their work, which was taking odd turns. Ideas like strange vegetables—cucuzza, mirliton, celery root—bulged and then went bad on their pages. They looked out their stained windows. At night they crept back toward each other again.

It was this way for several weeks. During the day they would forget about the head resting in the crook of the other's shoulder, the plate of the bed, the salty, warm bread of each other. They would pretend that the teeth marks, sprinklings of paprika on each other's necks, then hands, then arms, were from some central New York insect they didn't know the name of yet.

In October the hills pulsed with fall color, and busloads of fall foliage tours arrived, moving hesitantly through the house, the men in flannel shirts jammed into worn jeans, the women in those seasonal-themed sweatsuits with pumpkins on them.

"Aren't you two darling," a middle aged woman from Pensacola said one day, smoothing down her hair. They were all in the living room, the boy and girl passing out candy.

"You two married?" the woman asked.

"No, of course not," said the girl quickly, wanting to punch the woman right in the pumpkin.

"This thing sound?" her husband asked, pressing at the walls, staring up at the ceiling.

"It's fine," said the boy, though in the nights now, when the northern winds blew down from Canada, they could hear the joints of the place creaking, could sense its imminent collapse.

Despite the early frosts the back garden continued to

thrive, grew monstrous in its thick vines and bulging offerings, but by November they had lost their appetite for vegetables, preferring mainly to suck and lick at the house's exposed beams, which were all red now, like they were living inside a flawed, tinker toy heart. At night they could hear deer and rabbits rustling amongst the tomatoes and squashes, biting down on the soft fruit with coarse teeth, scratching at the door of the house. All the beige walls smelled of vanilla and the crown moldings around the doorways and windows became almond-flavored toffees. When they were hungry and in the middle of unwieldy word things, the boy and girl liked to reach out and break some off, tonguing the stringy pieces into knots. The windows thickened to hard candy like Jolly Ranchers, making it harder to see the outside world, the trees rendered vague, underwater forms, the sun a blurry, glowing ball. They did not mind. It was so warm in here. They could almost believe they had imagined love this way. They listened to the sound of the children downstairs, crawling around, sometimes answering the door and offering food to visitors, sometimes speaking with their parents on the telephone, telling everyone how very happy they were. At night the boy and girl slept fitfully, their lips lined with sugar. One by one they lost their teeth.

In the nights, he would imagine folding himself up and slipping into the freezer amongst the cut vegetables, the slow drain of blood from the limbs, the gradual ebbing of desire. In the nights, she would imagine him in a cage, imagine closing her eyes and believing he was the twig, the denial of love he thrust out, a thing she could break over her knee and walk away from. In the days, in the slow, stock-taking hours, they still worked index cards into word things, hoping that their ideas would become plenty for the whole of them in the nights when they lay, curled like beans, wanting dreams of a candy house with walls made of words and no oven.

The night the roof came down they went to the basement, ducked into the musty dark of it, sat down on the cool concrete, and turned on the lights. It was here, in the solid gray, that they noticed the loss of mass. They were like stick figures woven of blood red licorice ropes. And then they knew that the man and the woman in the postcard had slowly claimed parts of each other, had whittled each other away. And they understood the nature of the haunting here. And they could leave then, could help each other back up the stairs, could return to their dusty cars and, in new cities, relearn how to eat Cream of Wheat, to bite the hard, tart flesh of apples. They would not sneer at other people's desperation.

But every once in a while, in the evenings, a husband and a wife sleeping beside them in good beds, in brick houses, they might lick their lips. They might sit up, go to the kitchen for a bowl of sugary kids' cereal, and think how some nights they had so enjoyed it, the sweet, tangy taste of their own disappearance.

MEAGAN CASS' *ActivAmerica* won the Katherine Anne Porter Prize in Short Fiction. She is author of the chapbook *Range of Motion* and her stories have appeared in *Hayden's Ferry Review*, *DIAGRAM*, and *Puerto del Sol*, among others. An assistant editor for Sundress Publications, she teaches at University of Illinois, Springfield, and lives in St. Louis, MO.

INTERVIEW WITH
MEAGAN CASS

December 2018

CARVE

Where were you in your journey with writing when *Carve* published "The Candy House of Roscoe, New York" in 2008?

MEAGAN

I was in the PhD at the University of Louisiana, Lafayette. I believe it was my third year in the program. I remember being in a very anxious place as a writer. I was trying to figure out what kinds of stories I wanted to write. I was very fearful that I wouldn't figure out what my obsessions were in short fiction, and I think I also just didn't have a lot of confidence in my work. I remember reading "Candy House" out loud for the first time at a conference at UL—I remember running into the bathroom before the reading and doing line edits on the story right before I was supposed to read.

It was a time of a lot of growth. I was reading a lot of really different writers. Everything from Angela Carter and Kate Bernheimer and Rikki Ducornet (who was my mentor) to Stuart Dybek and Edward P. Jones. I think I was synthesizing a lot of different influences. Yeah, it was an exhilarating but also a very anxious time.

CARVE

Your collection, *ActivAmerica*—"Candy House" isn't part of that collection, and the collection has a pretty clear throughline, thematically and in terms of place. I think "Candy House" falls into some of the thematic questions that exist in this book, and the place, upstate New York—it shares that too. But *ActivAmerica* is so defined by its own sense of Americanness: sports, divorce, and sugar, consuming, excess, and alcoholism. Sugar and trying to find your way as a young American person exist in "Candy House," but the sport and activity—that focus is not at the center of the story. You mentioned that when *Carve* published you, you were going through a process of figuring out what your obsessions were. How would you describe that process over the last few years, up until you published *ActivAmerica* in 2017?

MEAGAN

I think in part it had to do with establishing a writing practice that fit me better, that fit my imagination and my psychology better. Before "Candy House," I was writing erratically. I would write for a four-hour stint and then take two days off, or a few days off. And then there'd be a deadline, and I'd buckle back down. As somebody who has struggled with anxiety and with depression, that way of writing fed into that, because I would think, "I'd better make this count. I haven't written in five days. I have seventy-two hours to do something that people are going to read." And I think it was just not a healthy practice for me.

I know a lot of writers can write that way, more sporadically, but I realized that I needed to devote a certain amount of time every day, preferably at the same time of day, to let the work be messy and be surprising and to be able to let go of control. I think "Candy House" was one of the first stories that was part of that. Then after leaving the PhD program I was really able to let it impact my work more, so that these things that had been on the edges of my stories, like soccer and booze—they started to come more into the center of the pieces I was writing.

I also started to find that I was even more excited about the revision process. I think when my stories are messy in that good way, where I can let the writing surprise me, then the revision process becomes part of that—learning more about questions that I didn't even know that I was asking, that my subconscious had been forming through the process. I think that was another thing that showed me that I had found a different and maybe more healthy way of being a writer—to be able to enter into that ambiguity in all of the stages of creating.

CARVE
What were your scholarly concerns in the PhD?

MEAGAN
We had four exams at UL at the time that I was studying there. They were in different focus areas. Mine were in Modern American Literature, Women's Literature and Feminist Studies, Creative Writing Pedagogy, and Modern British literature. I was especially interested in fairy tales and how particularly women writers were reinhabiting the fairy tale.

I wrote an article about Angela Carter's *Nights at the Circus* and how Carter was thinking about nineteenth century concert divas and ideas of femininity. It's a very strange and bawdy story about a woman who has wings and is a trapeze artist, and there is this ambiguity surrounding whether the wings are a gimmick, a part of her circus act, or if they're really a "natural" part of her body, tapping into a lot of anxieties that folks had (and of course still have) about women making art. I was fascinated by that and in what Kate Bernheimer calls writing in "the fairy tale way," how that way of writing could interact and root itself very specifically in historical questions and conditions. It wasn't directly influencing my creative writing. I think maybe it's starting to now, ten years later.

CARVE

It's funny, I have a page of notes toward this conversation and I'd written, "Candy House—fairy tale…" But you've mentioned some of your influences. How do you negotiate influence and what persists? What do you take from your influences when you come to your own writing?

MEAGAN

I think I negotiate them in a few different ways. Sometimes an influence can give me permission to write my stories how they seem to want to be written. I remember reading Stuart Dybek's *I Sailed with Magellan*, which is a linked story collection or a novel in stories, depending on how you define it. But the way the stories in that book move is very associative and very much through memory and tangents, and it's all located in a little village in Chicago in the fifties and sixties.

I had this idea, I think particularly coming out of my MFA, that my stories needed to move in a linear way. They needed to be very firmly located in the realm of prose. Reading Dybek and seeing how he was using association and discursive leaps as a way to fuel a story—it was like, okay, that's actually how my mind works. That's actually the way that I most constructively write a story.

Right now I'm writing these stories that are in this weird seven- to eight-page length. And I have a little self-consciousness about that, like I need to read some writers who are also inhabiting a space that's not flash fiction but also not the traditional fifteen pages. Amina Cain is doing that, for example, so I'm studying how she's using compression to get a richness out of eight pages.

I also think part of influence is reading against what you're into, or reading work that's different from what you might think of as your style. I just finished Guadalupe Nettel's novel *After Winter*, and it's a more realist novel that is told in retrospect but pretty much moves linearly in switching points of view. Stylistically, the prose is really, really spare, and there's not a ton of figurative language. I was glad to read that book, I think, and have that dissonance to what I consider my moves or the signature things that I do.

Lately, I've been thinking more about visual art as influence and how walking through an exhibit and getting obsessed with a new artist can filter into fiction-writing in different ways. That's a new vein that I want to explore more.

CARVE

What shape does that take? Is it the tone of a piece of visual art, or a character, or a setting?

MEAGAN

This is going to sound opaque, but I think right now it's shapes and colors. For example, I saw this amazing Hilma af Klint exhibit at the Guggenheim. She has these abstract, surreal paintings—she calls them the temple paintings. Many of them they have these spirals and snails. In addition to being a painter she was an illustrator for biological textbooks, I think, and she illustrated a veterinary textbook and that filters into the work. Some of them are really mystical, surreal shapes. I think the story I'm writing now is drawing on that contrast a little bit.

I think it also helps me give a different context to images I'm drawn to, thinking about how they can be mysterious. She has snails in all of these paintings. I've been obsessed with snails lately. I want to cook them, but also I think they're really cute. Then I saw the Klints, with all of these pink and purple snails. So, okay, I need to write a story about snails. How can I make snails strange for my character?

CARVE

In your book, you have a couple of stories that are in some way in conversation with poetry. In particular, I noticed a story engaging with James Wright. Do you compose poetry too? Or are you primarily a reader?

MEAGAN

I'm primarily a reader. When I start to figure out the central obsessions of what I'm working on, I always turn to poetry, to poems that speak to my obsessions in some way. I like thinking about my stories as speaking back to, or speaking with, that work.

I also want to be rooted in the compressed, vivid, nuanced space that I associate with poetic language. The fiction writers that I admire are big poetry readers too, and often incorporate sonics. I have at least as many poetic influences as I have prose influences, because those elements are an important part of fiction writing for me.

CARVE

It's been at least ten years since you wrote "Candy House." Do you remember what the seed of that story was?

MEAGAN

I reread it this morning—I think part of it was a really unhealthy romantic relationship that I had been in a couple of years before I wrote it. I went to school in upstate New York, and there was this roadside place called Memories. It was some kind of antique shop and we never stopped to go in it, but we always passed the billboards for it going from the suburbs of New York City up to Binghamton. I always wondered about it though. I think that inspired the Candy House, and also being interested in that middle space between upstate and downstate and people on their way to other places having this interaction.

CARVE

That sense of people being on their way to other places—I pulled a line out of the story too, to keep in mind as we talked today: "They each muttered something about being on their way to somewhere." I think something of that sense persists into your collection. Even the characters who are rooted in their suburban lives, their domestic lives, there's a tension around the idea of movement and elsewhere that takes a lot of different shapes but persists. I was struck in particular by "Girl Hunt." I wondered who your characters are to you and whether they return to you, or have returned to you?

MEAGAN

I think it's interesting that you've asked this question in response to "Girl Hunt," because the girls in that story are some of the characters that have returned to me in current work. That was one of the earliest stories I wrote for the book, when I was still in Louisiana.

One story whose characters returned to me over the course of years were those in "Jews in Sports." I started writing it during my MFA. The scene about the temple being defaced actually happened in my hometown, in the temple that we went to growing up. In the early draft, the story didn't work at all. The narrator was a teenager getting bar mitzvahed to please his father and the story felt really dogmatic. I put it deep in a drawer and moved on.

Then, I guess it was six years later, I started writing about this bathroom book that I remembered my dad giving to my brother when we were kids, the book from the story's title, and then characters from the older draft, and the temple scene I had written all those years ago bloomed back in. It felt magical to me that characters and images I knew I needed to write about but wasn't ready to returned when I was ready for them.

CARVE

It feels like many of your stories and characters are grappling with the way women and men interact. How have these obsessions and anxieties shifted or persisted into 2018?

MEAGAN

I feel a little strange speaking about this because the project I'm working on now is still nascent. Maybe I can speak more to how I think about the stories in the book in relation to this theme. Looking back at them now, I'm even more aware of the suburban space as a privileged, highly patriarchal space, and as a problematic space in terms of race and class. A space that in many ways upholds oppressive aspects of how we define Americanness. Particularly the patriarchal, capitalist idea of individual accomplishment, of individual striving for a quantifiable definition of success.

Lately, I'm thinking about how they also translate to artistic production in the academy. I haven't written a lot about being in academia, but I've been there for I guess my whole adult life. I see connections between the way that the world of sports is wrapped up white supremacist, patriarchal capitalism, and the ways that academia is too. And how that impacts marginalized people in specific and harmful ways. How it impacted and impacts me as a queer woman. My current work is interested especially in how women artists living with mental illness grapple with these painful structures, and how that impacts romantic relationships.

Also, thinking about queerness in the book and in current work—I'm increasingly interested in making the experience of bisexuality more visible. As a bisexual person who encountered no narratives from that subject position growing up, who struggled a lot with coming out, I see representation as crucial.

There was one story I wrote, not long after "Candy

House," about a bi character that didn't make it into the book. It just wasn't ready. I remember reading it in Decatur, Illinois, and these two queer undergrad girls were there. In talking with them after, I felt that excitement of reading your experience when it's historically cut out of the "American" literary tradition. It's vital that those narratives are accessible, are in the world.

CARVE

You've anticipated what I was going to ask you next, which is: How do you think fiction is equipped to change the way people interact with each other, and think about each other, and think about themselves?

MEAGAN

I think about it primarily in terms of the form of attentiveness, a way of being aware of the nuances and complexities that are happening in the world around you. I know that when I'm writing and reading a lot of fiction, I pick up on things. Somebody's subtle reaction to a particular phrase or the tension of a room, the way that people are sitting. What those things mean about the politics of the room. I think fiction asks us to be aware of our bodies and other people's bodies and the space we inhabit. To pay attention.

Fiction also requires a certain level of—how do I phrase this? I think it helps us to be less naïve. I think clinging to naivete is one of the major things holding a lot of folks back. Or claiming innocence, you know, "I said this thing that hurt you. Well, I didn't intend it to. I didn't know it would." I think fiction asks us to interrogate that. "Well, why didn't you know? Did you really not know? What in you led you to say that thing?"

Fiction requires, asks of us, that we improve our consciousness of power, of how we move in the world.

CARVE

Being from the suburbs of New York City, a space that you've written so much about, how do you reconcile that with your present life in the Midwest? How do you negotiate place in your thinking?

MEAGAN

I don't know yet. I'm sort of struggling with it. Because yes, that book was so located in a place that I don't have a day-to-day interaction with anymore. And in a lot of ways it was about my memories of that place. I'm starting to feel even more, when I go to New York, that I'm going as a tourist, or at the very least as a visitor. I left, not just my hometown, but my home region. I've lived in five states in the last ten years. I have to think about place differently than somebody who is forever located in or close to the region that they write about. I'm trying to figure out what that means for my identity as well as for my writing. How do I exist and write about a place where I still feel like an outsider, or where I don't have long-standing memories? How is place something we bring with us? These questions feel alive for me.

CARVE

What can you share about the literary community of St. Louis?

MEAGAN

It's amazing. There are so many writers here doing, I think, some of the most important work happening in America right now. Justin Phillip Reed, a St. Louis poet, just won the National Book Award. Danielle Pafunda, Carl Phillips, Mary Jo Bang, Paul Tran, Aaron Coleman, Angela Mitchell, Ron Austin, and so many more are all based here. And we have at least five reading series. It's an active, diverse, supportive community.

At times, it can feel a little fragmented. There's different

MFA programs that have their own scenes, as happens. And it's a writing community that, like any in America, requires you to think critically about who's in the room, who's not in the room, and why. St. Louis remains a very segregated city. The effects of racist housing policies like redlining filter into everything. A reading that's held in Maplewood is often less inclusive than a reading that's held on Cherokee Street, and the politics of that are important to recognize.

But it is a full, rich writing scene, and I feel grateful to have found an incredible community to nourish (and that nourishes me). We also have Dorothy, an experimental feminist press, here—their books are gorgeous. And there's *River Styx*, one of the oldest lit mags in the country. And Bottlecap Press just opened a bookstore.

CARVE

I think *december*'s there too.

MEAGAN

Yeah, *december*, and *Boulevard*. And there's also a thriving zine and comic book scene that feeds into all of this. We have the Small Press Expo every year in October. It's free to attend and held at the public library. You get to see how many creators we have doing limited edition zines about such a wide range of topics. Indie publishing is flourishing in St. Louis and that makes it an exciting place to be as well.

CARVE

And you're an assistant editor and board member for Sundress.

MEAGAN

Yeah! I started reading for Sundress when I was an undergraduate. I was a reader for *Stirring*, one of their online magazines. Since then I've gotten the opportunity to take on a few different roles. Right now, my work is primarily screening manuscripts, which I love. When we have an open reading period I get to read and evaluate manuscripts that come in. As a board member, I get to be part of shaping the kinds of programming we're taking on. I was part of the conversation surrounding a new fiction wing. We're open for the first time for fiction. I can't wait to see what we get.

It's a not-for-profit organization entirely run by volunteers. One of my dear friends, Erin Elizabeth Smith, founded the press as well as *Stirring* and the anthology *Best of the Net*, and the residency program in Knoxville. It's remarkable how many folks are invested in amplifying writers still excluded by mainstream publishing. Everyone from interns who are helping us revamp the website and have a social media presence, to folks who are doing heavy book design work pretty much for free.

It's really—I don't know if I want to use the word inspiring. I feel like that's a squishy word, but it does make me hopeful. The press has been around, starting with *Stirring*, since 1999 and it's continuing to carve out spaces that still don't exist in the broader industry.

CARVE

You also teach at University of Illinois, Springfield. What do you teach?

MEAGAN

I teach courses in creative writing, composition, and American literature. I get to teach a little bit of everything, which I like. I also teach a class in independent publishing that's challenging and also a lot of fun. My students did a zine project this semester. Each student created their own zine meant to be for a specific community that they're a part of. It was great to see the range of what they came up with. They had to create twenty copies each and actually distribute them.

CARVE

I would have loved to take a class like that in college. How do you build your reading lists for your literature and creative writing classes?

MEAGAN

A few different ways. Partly through recommendations of friends who are teachers. I'm always talking with my friends about what new books they're liking, or what they've taught that opened up something for their students. And I just do a lot of reading about new books coming out, reviews, lists, the catalogues of presses I love, trying to keep up with what's compelling each year. It's really important to me to change my reading lists continuously and to have them reflect as many different perspectives as possible. I hope all of my students can see themselves reflected in what I bring to the table.

I also find a lot of things through literary journals, particularly for my short fiction workshop. Stories published online or in print that I can give my students access to—it's important to me to show them work by writers who are not too far ahead of where they are now, in addition to writers that have already won awards and all that kind of thing.

CARVE

You also help coordinate the reading series there, right? What does that look like?

MEAGAN

Every year I write the Dean a memo explaining why there should be a reading series, and we cross our fingers. And then, hopefully, he continues to fund us. My first year we didn't have funding, but from then on and for the last six years we've been able to get a budget to pay writers to come in. I work with my colleagues in creative writing to talk about how we create a diverse series that has as many perspective as possible. We're always thinking about what perspective has been missing from the series. We usually meet over the summer and we bring in, depending on where people are at with their own work or other things going on, two or three people a semester. This semester we have Amina Gautier and Jenny Xie coming. And then we set up a master class or a class visit, so they meet with undergraduates and talk to them about writing and some-times give them a writing exercise or a craft talk on a specific element.

It's been nourishing for me, selfishly, because when I got to the University of Illinois, Springfield, I was the only cre-ative writer on faculty. It was a way for me to research who the other writers were in my region and figure out how to meet people and how to think about my community here. But it's most important for the students, especially because we are such a small department. We have two full-time creative writ-ers on faculty. When I was a student I valued hearing different people talk about how they write and knowing that there isn't just one way to be a writer. It's a lot of work, but it's really rewarding, I can say now that the semester is over.

CARVE

You have several different pursuits in the literary world, between teaching and editorial work and coordinating the reading series. How do the other literary things you do inter-act with your writing time?

MEAGAN

It's really hard to find time to write during the semester. When I'm on my game I'm up early, and also thinking about how the writers I'm interacting with and the editorial work I'm doing connect to the questions I'm asking creatively. I'm the nerd who always has a notebook at every reading or when I'm reading submissions, recording questions that pieces bring up for me. I'm always thinking about those kinds of connections.

Particularly for women and non-binary people, queer people, and people of color in the literary community—a lot of us are doing more service work because we want to create spaces for our perspectives and for the perspectives of other marginalized writers. So that's awesome, but it can also make it hard to nourish our own practice. It took me a long time to figure out how to articulate that. And I'm still trying to know when to say I need to pull back a bit. The writing is the one thing that you get no immediate social feedback for. No one's going to be like, "Good job. You wrote for an hour or two today."

CARVE

You published *ActivAmerica* through winning a book prize. You've also sat on the other side of that process, of course, at *Sundress*, screening manuscripts. How did you go about the process of submitting, and what did you learn in the process of being published that way?

MEAGAN

As I'm sure you know, there aren't that many presses that publish short story collections. I was looking at smaller presses because I believe in the missions of many smaller presses to be inclusive, and I was looking at ones that had published things that I had liked in the past—places that had published writers I thought it would be cool to share a catalogue with. Places where I could see how their mission aligned with what my goals as a writer were. I think I sent to maybe around ten places. I also reworked the book a couple of times within that. It was a two-and-a-half year process, so it didn't happen on the first round.

Something I learned is that everyone's taste is really specific, and if you're doing your job as a writer, your work is not for everyone. I think about the person who chose my book—I'm a huge fan of her fiction. It makes sense to me that somebody whose work I was partially immersed in while I was writing these stories would find something in my work. So I'm trying to learn, as I head into the next body of work, to not take a book rejection as a referendum on the book or whether the book is good. But it's hard. Any rejection is hard, any rejection of any kind. When I put my full book out there—I just wasn't prepared for how much it would set me back in different ways to have the whole project not get picked up at first. I've hopefully learned some ways to cope with that and resist it as a measure of whether the book is good enough or whether the book matters enough.

CARVE

So publishing your book was a matter of finding your community?

MEAGAN

Absolutely. There's so many publishing houses. There's so many small presses right now. I think it can take some time to figure out what the right fit is and what conversation you want to be in. The same goes for magazine publishing.

CARVE

Yeah. Which is to say, if you're a writer trying to publish, you need to be reading too, keeping up with what presses and magazines are doing before submitting.

MEAGAN

Yeah. Absolutely. I think a lot of us that come up in the MFA system read a lot of stuff from major presses, like "the top five." And that's great work, but there's so much else going on. You have to train yourself to be attuned to that. You can go to AWP—that's a great place to walk around and see. But that's also not an accessible place for a lot of people, so finding other ways in is important.

CARVE

What mantra is guiding your recent work?

MEAGAN

Can I give two?

CARVE

Yes, absolutely.

MEAGAN

Cool. This is a quote from an Audre Lorde poem: "Don't let me die still needing to be stranger." I think when I'm stuck the most, sometimes it's because I'm not letting the fiction be weird enough. Or I'm trying to sound like another story that I think I should sound like.

And then this one, from Amina Cain: "I cannot write anything else except sentences."

And They Pillaged the Dead

DAVID CAMERON

June 2011

The strangest part was that smoking hash with grandma wasn't the strangest part. But no one else wanted to hear it. Like Brendan's sister.

"You couldn't spend a few hours with Omi without doing drugs in her *house*?"

"And my car."

"That wasn't your car. That was Mom and Dad's car. You visit Omi and then do drugs in mom's car?"

There was more to the story. Tons more. But his moral collapse was all that stuck.

. . .

Omi meant grandma. It was the German word. Her name was Eva, and she and her sister Inge, who she lived with, had grown up in Hamburg during the Second World War. As a small child, Brendan listened to gruesome stories involving shrapnel and air raid shelters and Berlin hospital wards and when he was older, the carnal atrocities of the Russian occupation in the east.

He hadn't seen Omi in years.

It had been whispered, but seldom discussed, that Omi was prone to spells of darkness, which at times had resulted in her needing to "go away" for indefinite periods. He couldn't help wondering if this part of her, this shadow, explained why whenever he thought of her, he immediately recalled a certain photo taken in the mid 1930s, outdoors at a campground, her in the front row of about a dozen stern-faced and stringently sober teenage girls, white blouses with black ties and ash-colored skirts: a group photo of the Hitler youth.

. . .

Brendan thought of that photo as he drove to visit Omi in Pennsylvania, having just left his latest residence: his parents' house in Long Island. It was a beautiful home, thousands of square feet of colonial living space, a sprawling lime-colored lawn, a built-in kidney-shaped pool. But luxury had nothing to do with it. He was there because he'd run out of couches to crash on.

There was, in fact, a long lineage of relatives and friends whose hospitality he had drained (including his sister's who had only tolerated him for one night), and he knew damn well that Mom and Dad, despite their membrane of benevolence, were covertly making the case for kicking him out of their gated-community nest and back into the urban wild. And if he were them, he'd do the same.

. . .

A year ago, as 1999 folded into 2000, his life had fallen apart.

He lost his job as an HTML coder, his garage-rock music career was going nowhere (the major-label signing frenzy of the early '90s leaving him in the dust), and worst of all, his girlfriend of almost a decade, Nadine, a half-Thai half-Dutch photographer who made her own clothes and sold them at shows, walked off with nearly everything he owned. He had discovered this late on a Tuesday after waking up on the kitchen floor.

He knew perfectly well why she chose such a vengeful exit. He had taunted her into leaving through habits like lying on the couch all day breathing bubble hash from a vaporizer and searching the wall for beauty in the patterns of cracked plaster while she, often fighting tears, described how watching him self-destruct was like swallowing glass, one shard at a time. Also, he cheated.

But he never expected she'd steal his favorite things: his Gibson SG and Fender amp, his collection of vintage Keds, his Japanese comics, his zoot suit, the vaporizer, and that LP of John Coltrane's *Blue Train*, autographed by his father's father, a crazy drunk and semi-professional musician who insisted up to his dying day—which occurred when Brendan was four— that he had played drums on three of the album's five tracks. Brendan was probably the only person on earth who still believed that story, and it was a belief he guarded.

Over the years, Brendan had cultivated an image of soulful indifference to material things, but as soon as these possessions were gone he tried frantically to get them back. Nadine had moved in with her brother, a cop, a guy who hated him so much that Brendan suspected something Freudian in their relationship.

After months of couch-crashing, moving in with Mom and Dad was humiliating. It rubbed in his face the unavoidable truth that so far, at age thirty, he had failed spectacularly at being an adult. It fueled the terror that he may never pull it off, that he simply lacked the courage to ever be anything more than an expiring adolescent.

Why not take off now before they kick him out?

But some vestige of dormant wisdom compelled him to stay, to reach back to a time that predated Nadine and his whole façade of punk-rock stardom, to grab hold of something that had existed long before these last ten years of post-college life. Childhood was a place where tomorrow could mean anything because today meant nothing. Maybe some totem still existed somewhere that could shuttle him back into the past and reveal why the present was so shattered.

. . .

As he drove his parents' Toyota Avalon straight into the October sun, the dirt speckling the windshield shimmering like glitter, spread out on the passenger seat were CDs that at any other time would have fueled the ride: Teenage Jesus and the Jerks, Television, New York Dolls, The Stooges, and last but not least, his own imploded brainchild, Mary Jane Rotten Crotch.

But what currently piped through the car's stereo system—and the windows were sealed tight in the event someone he knew blew past him on the interstate—was his mother's copy of *Rumours*.

When he was four or five, he recalled a brief period when his mom played Fleetwood Mac relentlessly, shouting along and moving to "Don't Stop" while he blocked her path, begging her to shush. And sometimes when he charged her thighs and she grabbed his wrists and he tried to pull away, their struggle dissolved into a dance.

Now, this one song, this template for all musical clichés, lured him back into his childhood living room, and he saw it as a child would see it, eyes level to the surface of the radiator, books stacked in shelves beyond reach, dust particles levitating in columns of light that fell through the high windows, and his mother's waist, her blouse tucked loosely into a woven leather belt, his mind clear, his heart accessible.

. . .

After two hours on the road he arrived. Eva greeted him at the door.

"Hi, Omi," he said.

"Hello, Brendan," she said, holding open her arms. Hands on his shoulders, she kissed each of his cheeks. She smelled of coffee and perfume.

"You look like you are a beatnik," she said, jiggling a tuft of his choppy sand-colored hair. He had tried to look as "normal" as possible, remembering to remove his eyebrow ring and to wipe off any traces of black eye makeup. His "Black Girls Have More Fun" t-shirt was hidden inside of a russet colored V-neck sweater that covered his narrow torso.

But he should have shaved. And the rip in the armpit of his Army jacket sagged like a mortal wound. Still, hearing "beatnik" spoken with a German accent made him smile. He had always loved how the accents of his mother's relatives roused their speech into new and spirited arrangements of all-too-familiar melodies. The difference between a German accent and Long Island American English was the difference between a French horn and a car horn.

"Come," she said, holding the door.

The old house was spacious, free of the family mementos grandmothers typically horde. The air had the faint, charred smell of a carpet that's just been vacuumed.

Eva looked magnificent for a woman of eighty. She wore a silky red blouse and dark slacks, and her pepper-colored hair, fresh from the salon, was styled and firm. Her face, clearly beautiful when she was young, was handsome, strong. She stood tall, her spine so far having withstood the force of age.

"Inge is sleeping now," Eva said. "Her nap, every afternoon. Sit. I will get you a cold drink. Coca-Cola?"

"Thank you, Omi," he said and took a seat on the Danish sofa, a piece of furniture he immediately recognized, the wooden legs and armrests glistening like marble, the bluish gray cotton surface so tightly upholstered he could probably bounce a silver dollar on it. It must have been fifty years old, but it looked as good as new. He reached over to the ceramic dish on the coffee table and helped himself to a Viennese chocolate.

He looked around the room: surfaces utterly dust-free, paintings that at one time must have seemed subversively experimental, light from the southern-exposed bay window gushing over the sofa and armchairs and the radiator—so familiar and yet now so alien. The room's mid-century modernism had changed little since his earliest memories of it, memories like mother prodding him to refine his posture to accommodate Omi's queries, "Who do you love most? Tell us a joke! Sing!", the smell of boiling meat wafting through the air and mingling with piano sonatas that seemed to issue from nowhere in particular, background music for Omi's stories about life in a war-torn land that to him felt as ancient as Rome. All as he sat on that very same sofa. He was a prodigal returning to a home he had abandoned, one in which he barely recognized himself. It didn't feel good, but it felt right, and it had been ages since he had chosen feeling right over feeling good.

"Here you are," Eva said, entering the living room and handing him a tall and narrow glass filled with ice cubes and fizzy, crackling cola. She set it down on the coffee table atop a white, needle-lace coaster. She drank the same.

They chatted idly for about a half-hour, a kind of conversation he almost never had, the kind that stuck to unarguable topics (the weather, how there was rain, how there was sunshine). They chuckled over the Y2K frenzy, mourned the recent 9/11 attacks, after which he guided her on a tour of the tattoos swathing his forearms. The ability to navigate intergenerational dialogue made him feel older than his years.

"Ah, here she is, little sister!" Eva suddenly announced.

And across the house, shoulders arched over a walker, Inge approached, moving slowly but firm, unfaltering, like a tortoise.

Any stranger would have considered Eva's comment "little sister" a nasty joke. But while Inge easily looked ten years older, she was actually three years Eva's junior. To highlight this contrast, Inge wore candy pink polyester pants, a red sweater, and a bright floral patterned vest that looked psychedelic. Curved across her messy white hair was a headband with a sprouting clump of red paper flowers at the top. As for the finale: white sneakers.

Brendan wasn't sure if he should rise and give her a hand. She made her way right at them, steady and determined, staring at Brendan through black-rimmed glasses that looked more like goggles. Slowly, he sank back down into his chair. When she was no more than ten feet away, she halted, looked at Eva, and spoke, each word scoured by unrelenting German phonetics.

"He works at a zoo? Look at him! He works at the zoo!"

"He works at a magazine," Eva said, shaking her head.

"Website," he corrected, and then added, "*worked*."

"*Ja*, him? Ha! He goes to the *zoo*!" Inge said, resuming her inexorable gait.

. . .

For dinner Eva served a stew prepared in white cream sauce ladled over rice. It was a dish he had only ever eaten in her home.

"You're quite the chef, Omi," he said, feeling the distance between childhood and this very moment collapse as the pungent, flowery blend moved over the back of his tongue.

"You are kind," Eva said.

More than any other place in the house, the dining room

evoked another era, a grandmother's world from generations ago. The wooden table was solid and vast, wide stretches of worn, dark surface, inlaid with rosewood patterns. With only the three of them, it felt stark. The china hutch-buffet that spanned the narrow wall behind Eva also seemed imported from another time. The glass cabinets encasing plates and serving dishes and crystal were as clean and free of dust as every other surface, yet the objects inside, from certain angles, looked skewed, shimmering with irregularity, edges slightly buckling and then straightening—if you moved while looking, a prism-effect of century old windows.

Eva and Brendan drank white wine from crystal glasses with beveled surfaces. Inge drank beer from the bottle. Like Brendan and Eva, Inge too ate heartily, but he had the feeling she would have shown the same enthusiasm for Spam.

"So, Brendan," Eva said, dabbing the corners of her mouth with the embroidered edge of a white napkin, "we are all sorry to hear about what you have been experiencing. Your fiancée. We are sad for you."

He would have corrected her, but "fiancée" felt like such a respectable term. "Oh well, you know, shi—*stuff* happens," he said. "I'm better off, she's better off. But thank you."

Inge stared at him with the tip of the bottle suctioned between her lips.

"I'm actually not all that sure *I'm* better off," he continued, shrugging. "I'd be lying if I said it's been easy. I've been really lonely." He swallowed. "Family, friends have helped out, but I can be a handful. Seriously. I'll think of something. But thanks for all this." He gestured sweepingly at the table. "I think I might be starting to see things that I've been ignoring for way too long, and that's kind of why I'm glad I'm here. Not sure if that makes any sense."

Eva nodded as she poured herself more wine. She offered up the bottle to him. "Nothing is as new as something that has been long forgotten," she said as she poured him another glass. "Brendan, you are a handsome young man."

He laughed.

"You are," she said, setting the bottle down, "even though you hide it. You have a strong face, generous eyes. And you have character—long ears and a short tongue, as my father would say. Your next wife will be good to you."

"Well, I certainly appreciate the thought, but let's be honest. It's not her fault, it's mine. The whole mess." Her misuse of the word "wife" had unexpectedly emboldened him. "She's no saint, but I was the one who... I was the one with the bad habits. I was... in all honesty, I was unfaithful—among other things."

Acknowledging his sexual appetites made it hard to swallow. Inge stared. "I'm sorry. That's just the way it is. I've spent too long trying to cover it up. I need to start telling the truth. That's my new resolution. From now on, truth." He decided to skip the drugs. Honesty had limits.

Still, he looked around the table, expecting some sort of proxy cheek-pinch from the elders, something that demonstrated their pride in his dedication to virtue. But Eva continued eating, scrutinizing her plate, one eyebrow raised as she slid rice onto her vintage fork with her vintage knife. Inge was pinching a strip of gristle, lips condensed.

Brendan looked over Inge's shoulder and into the living room, noting how the evening had been leeching the flailing light, leaving the room dim and grainy. The chandelier above their table offered the only luminescence in the house. He could see the back of Eva's silver hair reflecting in the skewed buffet glass behind her, and as she shook her head at his words, she and her likeness moved in synchronicity like two gears meshing.

"You should not be sorry," Eva said. "It does you nothing good. Besides, you are a man, and forever is a long bargain."

Inge, having successfully extracted the gristle, wiped it like a booger on the edge of her plate.

Brendan croqueted a caper around with the fork tines until Eva finally lifted her eyes and gazed at him over the rims of her half-moon bifocals. It was a while before she spoke.

"Brendan, you are a sweet boy and a good man. But here is your choice: You are the anvil, or you are the hammer. It is one or the other. You feel good being a... a penitent. Fine. But too much being humble is *narzissmus*. Do you understand that?"

He wasn't sure. Her words evoked for him one particular evening of Nadine-induced psychodrama, her on the closed toilet seat with her head between her knees while he ranted about how, if it would make her happy, he'd wallow in remorse like a baby in its own filth—a thought that was sickly appealing—and he wondered if some people fucked up on purpose just so they could slosh in their own penitence. *Narzissmus*.

She went on. "Your mother tells me that she took many things of yours, this *wife*. That she stole from you and refuses to return them. Is *that* something you feel guilty of?"

"No," he said, shaking his head. "But you know, it's like Shakespeare said, 'He who steals my purse steals trash.' You know? Stuff is just stuff. 'But he who steals my good name makes me poor indeed.' You know that one?"

Eva smiled indulgently, then swiveled the wine in her glass. "A proverb for the sentimental."

And he thought once more about his Coltrane LP. It had become a family joke, evidence of the wretched life of his father's father, the idiocy of giving an almost-three-year-old a jazz album for Christmas, just an excuse to once again carry on about how if it wasn't for his altercations with some highly influential recording engineer, *he* would have shared percussion credit on the album. Brendan alone defended this story, arguing that the old man *did* drum the post-war jazz circuits in New York and Chicago. Later in his life he even tried to eke out a musical living in LA in the 1970s, a card-carrying member of Local 47 until, when Brendan was still a preschooler, grandpa's girlfriend found him dead in Compton in the passenger seat of a Buick Skylark.

He had signed the album, "Never stop bebop. With love, grandpop."

And now he realized that under Nadine's watch the record was nothing more than an old dreg in a storage bin in a dank basement, grandpa's words abandoned with the milk crates and wine boxes stuffed with misfits, and the desire to get it back from her at all costs, and to have the act of doing so degrade her, seized him.

Omi said. "Pick up your fork."

The request confused him. So Eva demonstrated. She picked up her fork.

"Look at it closely. What do you see?"

A fork. But on closer inspection, a beautiful fork. The handle, engraved with a floral pattern encircled in a motif that looked serpentine, and at the base an ornate, cursive "R," felt smooth and textured against his thumb. But Omi's last name was Eichberger, so he asked, "What's R stand for?"

"*What?*" Eva said, the question coming from the back of her throat, German shrapnel cutting through the skin of that single English word. "Rosenbaum! Do you know Rosenbaum?"

Vaguely. Distant relatives of Mom's and Omi. But he was afraid to say anything more.

"It is time," Eva said, rising. "It is time for *cake* and *Cognac!*"

. . .

He had already drunk too much wine (all white, which typically made for a bloodthirsty hangover) but the word "Reserve" in the Cognac label caught his eye. The three of them had moved to the TV room. Eva switched on the two rod iron lamps, one on each end of the sofa, then returned to the kitchen. The lampshades glowed a dull, opaque orange, two symmetrical setting suns. As Brendan sat on the couch reading the label on the Cognac bottle, *Chateau de Fontpinot*, he noted a silver cigarette box with a hinged lid at the edge of a shelf in the bookcase lining the wall. Beside it was a series of framed, black-and-white photo portraits, and below that, LPs lining the two bottom shelves. Inge sat across from him in a rocking chair, filling her pipe, and he asked her, "Got Coltrane?"

She looked at him, her tongue working at something distasteful on her gums.

"Mozart?"

"Ach, Mozart." She held the pipe between her teeth and lit it with a silver lighter, her crooked thumb working the lighter's wheel deftly. "*Mozart*," she said again, sucking air into the pipe bowl. "Mozart is all of this da da da *da-da*." She embellished her point by plinking the air with an arthritically bent index finger. "Mozart is for the children. Not me." She drew smoke into her mouth and let it drift idly through the gaps in her large teeth. The tobacco smoldered.

"Then who do you like?"

"I like so many!" she said. "All of the *B's*. I love *Bach*. I love *Brahms*. I love *Berlioz*. Beethoven when he was old. I love Strauss. And so many others. And *I* have them *all*."

"Ach mein Gott!" Eva said, setting down the tray on the coffee table. She cut three pieces from the round, orange dessert, licking the icing off her thumb. "The smell of smoke. It is sickening."

But Inge ignored her.

"Rosenbaum," Eva began. "You must know this name, Brendan. When *schwester* Inge was a baby, our mother, your great-grandmother, died of an infection. She died in the hospital after many nights. Our father, your great-grandfather, soon married again, a Jew, Hannah Rosenbaum, a woman older than he, a woman who had lost her husband and two sons in the first war. One daughter, older than us, all she had. Hannah Rosenbaum was a well-off woman, almost rich, at least to us. And she raised us with the whip. When we would cry, she would tell us that to taste what is bitter is to know what is sweet. Do you agree with that Brendan? That is what the cruel say. As we were older, Inge and I, dressed for a night of dancing, she called me a prostitute. I can still see her as she says this, tall, black hair pulled tight, her chin, her lips, her black evening gown."

Eva sat in an armchair beside her sister, who had begun to rummage through a wicker basket beside her chair. Inge's body language, lavish with disinterest, clearly indicated that she would need to occupy herself while big sister spoke.

"So, the Jews began to go away, but not Hannah. Any Jew married to a Christian was saved. But then, as you *must* know, in 1941, our father, her protector, died. Mounting a staircase, he collapsed. It was his heart. And Hannah was alone.

"Inge and I had been sent to Omi and Grossvater in Braunlage, in the mountains, away from the cities, which soon would be rubble. On Grossvater's birthday, Hannah Rosenbaum came and showed us the letter. It was from the Hamburg police, instructing her to arrive at the police station on Monday, with a change of clothes and one toothbrush. The entire letter, that sentence. Brendan, do you know this? Has your mother told you this?"

His body was still acclimating to the atmospheric variance of white wine and Cognac. He shook his head.

"Well, you know what it meant, the letter, as did she, as did we. We *say* no one knew what happened at the camps. And we didn't. But we did. We saw no one come back. People, families. All at once, gone. And we knew the old and the sick did not live, and we knew Hannah would not live. So did she.

Hannah knew that to die at home was better than going to some barracks. That is what she came to tell us. She even showed us the bottle with the pills.

"Grossvater jumped up and said he'd take her to Switzerland, and she laughed. If he were apprehended—and he would be!—everyone, man and woman and baby, all of us, to the camps. They would rip out the whole garden. Who would risk that? No. Hannah Rosenbaum would die at her own hand. Alone. With all the possessions she loved. She said, *cry for me now, but don't cry then*.

"I didn't cry. I was young. Inge, too. Inge didn't cry. What to think? We hated Nazis, but Hannah had been cruel. The scars on our backside, our hands, they bore witness. So confusing.

"But I have a story, Brendan. Listen. Hannah Rosenbaum did not want to die alone. She wanted to be with someone. Most, she needed to be sure the pills did the job. How horrible would it be to take all the pills, but then, a miracle, she wakes! Someone, someone she could trust, must be there to make sure her eyes never open again.

"But who? The Rosenbaum family, they had vanished. Her daughter was lucky, living with a husband in Sweden. A few left for Britain early on, some for Zurich, and those who stayed behind—who knows. Omi and Grossvater, too old. They wept. They had no stomach for this. So who?

"Who could do this without temptation to make her live?"

"Me," Inge said through a cloud of smoke, knitting together two balls of pink yarn into something neither hat nor scarf. The pipe was still wedged between her teeth. She puffed relentlessly, the red paper flowers in her headband bobbing as she nodded.

Eva looked at her, an accusatory glare. She began to nod. "Yes," she said. "You."

"I'm confused," Brendan said. "She was... w*hat*?"

"The chosen one," Eva said. She held the large and bulbous Cognac glass in her hand, swirling it. "She was chosen because... Well, you can see." Eva glanced at Inge, then rolled her eyes slowly and melodramatically for Brendan's audience. "Hannah needed a flesh and blood soul whose heart was salt. And Inge, let us just say, also had no love for Hannah Rosenbaum, and no one knew that better than the old woman herself."

Inge shrugged, then let her shoulder slowly drop, and Brendan thought he heard a joint click somewhere in this gesture. The pipe had migrated to the edge of her mouth. Her eyes never strayed from the knitting project on her lap.

"So the family agreed, and Inge, barely even sixteen, took the train back to Hamburg with Hannah that Sunday. Inge had one objective: See that Hannah Rosenbaum is dead on Monday morning."

Brendan wished that Inge would say something, give some kind of voice to the tragedy. Her knitting compelled her more than the story, and that unsettled him. He wondered if she was knitting anything in particular, or if the rhythm of pins and yarn was simply automatic.

"So they arrived at Hannah's apartment in Hamburg. It was strange for Inge to be there. It was familiar, and it was strange. Pictures of Hannah's first husband, her sons. Her daughter and son-in-law. Pictures of our father. But of us, nothing.

"In the dining room, on the old, dark table, the one Inge and I sat at every night for years, never allowed to speak, she had placed flowers. In the vase that had been her mother's vase, chamomile, edelweiss, spindle. The flowers smelled like the blood of summer.

"Inge told her how lovely the flowers were, and Hannah said, 'Yes, thank you. Today there must be something beautiful. When you are done, you can have them.' She said this plainly. You see, Hannah Rosenbaum was a proud woman.

"For much of the afternoon, Hannah stayed in the kitchen, cooking. She prepared a small feast. It was early in the war, and food was still plentiful if you had money. Inge helped stuff the chicken. She thought, 'Chicken, when was the last time I had that?' Chicken was a delicacy in those days. A holiday supper. Inge chopped leeks for Hannah to steam, and potatoes. There were baskets of potatoes, and those also Hannah said to have when it was done.

"But mostly Inge was left to her own.

"What must it have felt for Inge to be back in this place? And for *this*. For me, who knows. I am sentimental. And you too. But I think Inge said to herself, 'To hell with all this.'"

"Ach!" Inge said, the sound rising from her mouth in a smoky gray cloud. "There is no *hell*. Do not make it up. It was a fine house!"

"You can tell the story if you like," Eva said. "Go ahead. It is yours. Please. Tell us."

"Nonsense," Inge said. "You are the narrator. We are the audience. Just tell it right."

"Do not test me," Eva warned her sister. And she sighed and waited and soon Inge was once again absorbed in her knitting.

"Well, now, Hannah brought the chicken out to the table on a tray, scolding Inge for the mess. Inge had found a box in the living room chest that contained photographs of Hannah's family, the family before our family. The photographs were spread on the table and Hannah said, 'Put those away, now! It is time!' The photos didn't bother Hannah. It was the clutter. And Inge remembered how Hannah used to always say, 'A place for everything, and everything in its place.' Inge was fascinated by these pictures, and longed to ask Hannah many questions, but she put the photos back into the box and put the box back into the living room chest.

"Inge wondered, what happens to these photographs when it is over? And what happens to all these beautiful things of Hannah's?

"The dinner was delicious, especially compared to Omi's stews, food with no taste, us picking bones to make shapes on our plates. Inge had not eaten such good food in years.

"Hannah Rosenbaum ate little, and that should not surprise. They drank wine from the same glasses you and I drank from here at dinner. And Inge, thinking now was time to reveal her soul, placed her hand on the table beside Hannah's, but Hannah said to her, 'It is easy at a time like this for you to be tricked into a feeling you think is love, but it is not. It is something different, and I feel it too.'"

And deep inside of Brendan, the elevator cable supporting his stomach snapped, saved in the last second by an emergency catch. He swallowed a gasp inside a fake throat-clearing.

"I'm sorry," he said abruptly. "I need to... I think I left some allergy medication in the car. Will you excuse me? I'm sorry. This is a great story, really. Do you mind if I just pop out and come right back?"

He wasn't sure if either of them grasped his question. Eva looked to her sister as if for translation.

Inge said, "All young people are allergic these days."

Brendan laughed nervously. "Yes, yes, Aunt Inge, they are." And Inge resumed her knitting.

"Go. Then return," Eva said.

. . .

Part of him wanted to hit the gas and take off, just drive, maybe route through Philly or Manhattan, take in a show, find a place to crash. Just flee the heaviness.

He thought about this as he sat behind the wheel, his hand pressed against the keys in his coat pocket.

He reached under the passenger seat and took out the brown lunch bag. Usually he liked to mix the cough syrup with Sprite or 7Up, even throw in pieces of candy. A friend called it "Texas tea." But now he simply swigged straight from the prescription bottle. He'd grown to appreciate that orange-jelly aftertaste. He took out his keys and turned on the car battery. The dashboard lights glowed, igniting Stevie Nicks's alto rasp. Little by little the codeine snaked through his skin, a warm tickling itch crawling toward his fingernails. Soon he was buoyant, his head filled with pure, perfect blood.

He leaned back onto the headrest and ejected Stevie, displacing her with Iggy. *Fun House* had always been his favorite. Something in the unalloyed animal attitude of Iggy's howling contained the power to do what little else could: make him feel normal. As the jungle beat rattled his bones, he reached for his wooden hash pipe, the one he bought in England years ago, then pinched off a corner of brick, rolling the hash between his finger and thumb for a bit then stuffed it into the pipe bowl like a dentist packing a tooth, topping it with a sprinkling of lemon kush.

He turned off the battery and, keys in pocket, pipe in hand, headed back to the house.

. . .

"Hi," he said, reentering the TV room, struggling with his breath. Inge remained absorbed in her knitting, but Eva eyed him closely. On the coffee table, beside the cake, sat a china tea set: three cups on saucers, a pot, a creamer, and a sugar cube bowl, blue roses and soft green leaves painted below the gold trim.

"Welcome back," Eva said, spooning two icy white cubes into her tea cup. She pinched the spoon between her thumb and finger and stirred slowly, then rested the utensil on the saucer. Brendan kept standing.

"Hey, look," he said. "I'm wondering, I'd hate for Inge to smoke alone, so do you mind if I smoke my pipe as well?" He held it up, a rust-colored cylinder, Sanskrit painted in ribbon script, a thumb-sized smoke stack for the bowl.

"That is no pipe," Inge barked. "It is a kazoo!"

Brendan buckled back into the couch. He balanced the pipe in his lips with two fingers and angled the lighter over the bowl. "You mind?" he asked Eva through the corner of his mouth.

She brought the teacup to her lips.

"Please continue, Omi," he said as he exhaled, the peppery sensation dabbling his tongue like needlepoint, a honey narcotic balm. Everything around him moved at the speed of dreams. He poured himself more Cognac.

"What else is there to say?" Eva said, resting the teacup on the edge of the shelf, then fanning the air beneath her nose with her hand. "They ate. They drank. Inge cleared the table, washed dishes. They sat in the living room and listened to Mozart, Hannah's favorite. Especially the sonatas. Especially this one," and with eyes closed, lifting her chin, Eva began to hum a simple minor-scale tune that jolted Brendan's memory. Her voice, with the timbre of crystal, moved along the imaginary piano keys as her right hand lifted off her thigh and began stroking the melody's surface, and a spasm of despair swirled through him. Inge coughed, and the sonata vanished. The silence was boundless.

"*Anyway*," Eva continued, "at some point, Hannah Rosenbaum announced that it was time. Just like that. She could have meant, 'It is time for the dentist. It is time to bake bread. It is time.' And so she walked into her bedroom, put on her white gown, and sat up in bed. She asked Inge to bring her a glass of white wine. And Inge did, filled to the brim with Riesling. Hannah took the glass in her hand and Inge unscrewed the top of the bottle, placing three, four pills at a time on Hannah's tongue. Hannah swallowed them down with wine. And it was done. The bottle, empty. Many dozen pills, gone.

"And Hannah Rosenbaum lay down on her back, looking up at the light, at the paint on the ceiling. She stared into her own fate. And in her cold, winter eyes there was victory. 'You will do what you need to do, if you need to do it,' Hannah Rosenbaum said. And Inge, stupid girl, she must have gasped, because suddenly Hannah grabbed Inge's wrist and made her promise to stay until morning. She made her promise on the grave of her father. 'Do not leave. You must not leave. Promise me this now!' And Inge swore, and Hannah told her that she would know from beyond if Inge lied, and as Inge knelt beside the bed, making even the sign of the cross to convince this old Jewish woman—*stupid girl*—the pills began to take effect, and Hannah Rosenbaum drifted away, still grasping Inge's wrist.

"It was after eleven o'clock. Brendan, what do you suppose it could have been like for her, a girl of sixteen, to spend the evening in the home of a woman as she slowly dies?"

"Ask her," he said, startled at how disembodied his words felt, like an echo without the antecedent voice. A tingling that began in his stomach had spread into his throat, coating the base of his neck and crawling along his scalp. He scratched the buggy tickle. Although Eva's voice dominated the room, she seemed to recede in her chair, her spine contracting, shoulders narrowing.

"Inge, what was it like?" Eva asked. "Brendan insists I ask! What was it like for you to spend that night in the house of a woman dying?"

Inge turned, and Brendan could no longer see her face, only his grandmother's as she and her sister stared at one another, and for a few moments a look of deep sadness moved over Eva's face like an eclipse—and was gone. Inge shrugged.

"There was nothing. I read. I slept. I went home."

Eva sighed loudly, theatrically, closing her eyes and lifting her chin toward the heavens. She seemed to have regained both stature and command. "Brendan," she said, placing one hand on the bookshelf and slowly pushing herself up. "I want to show you something. A photograph. Will you come with me? Inge, stay."

Brendan felt as though his muscles had become porous and brittle, freeze-dried, cracking at the slightest strain. When he finally made it to his feet, he didn't trust the relationship of his body to the floor. He moved cautiously, the nerve endings in the soles of his feet not quite synching with the pressure of his boots against the carpet.

Still, he managed to follow Eva back through the living room and into a dark hallway that led to the bedrooms. She stopped and turned to him. The darkness had turned the topography of her face into disembodied cheekbones and chin, her eyes and mouth hollow and black. He moved closer to her, and for a single and shameful moment hoped she would grab and kiss him.

"I needed to bring you away from her to tell you this," she whispered. She placed her fingers on his shoulder. "You must understand that Inge is not like us. She does not *feel* like you or I feel. She is not a bad woman, no. But she can do the things you and I cannot. Then sleep like a child." Her touch squeezed. "Do you think that is a bad thing?"

And he said, "Omi, look who you're asking. I'm a mess. I fail everyone. Something inside makes me screw the people I need. It's out of control. I wish I could be something else. That shit I take helps me forget myself. I'm here because I want to rewind my life. I'm looking for a totem to bring me back. Can you help me? I need help."

Or at least that is what he wanted to tell her.

The empty hallway startled him awake, and in one jarring

instant the passage of time soared through him and he tunneled back to the point when Eva had asked that question, most likely interpreting his silence as a kind of meditative impulse. And so she returned to her sister, leaving him alone (unknowingly) to consider her words, standing there one minute, two minutes, three minutes, hash pipe in fist, speaking, at last, to a dark corridor.

. . .

"It is late," Inge said, placing her knitting down on the floor and her pipe onto a dish at the edge of the shelf. Fists latching onto the hand-bars of her walker, Inge grappled with her body until it remained upright. "Stay the night," she said to Brendan, who sat stiffly and upright on the couch, flexing the muscles around his eye sockets. "You are dangerous on the road."

"Look who's talking," he said, and she coughed what might have been a laugh. "Good night, Inge," and she moved out of the TV room, moving with the poise of a young soul reconciled to an ancient body, her skewed frame weighing heavily on the walker as it somehow held her aloft, leading her to bed.

. . .

"I need cake," Brendan said, cutting another piece and sliding it onto his palm and feeding his gaping mouth.

"Have more. Have all the cake you like. Eat and listen. Here it is: Inge spent the night examining Hannah Rosenbaum's things. She wanted a glimpse into the meaning of this woman. Inge, I think, spent the evening as a soul outside the body. And then, six o'clock the next morning, the milk truck woke her.

"She sat up in the armchair. She forgot where she was, and

then, her mission, all came back. She stood and crept down the hallway, down to Hannah's room. She pushed the door with one finger, the hinge creaking as it opened slowly, and there lay Hannah on the bed, just as she had left her. A fly, she saw, buzzed and landed in her hair. Inge turned to leave—who wants to stay with a dead person?—when she suddenly heard the smallest sigh." Eva swirled the Cognac. "Yes, God's cruelest miracle. Hannah Rosenbaum lived."

Eva set her glass down beside the dessert plate. She flattened her palms on her thighs and stared at the veins mapping the back of her hands. "It was one pillow. And one minute. And she could leave. And she could forget."

It took Brendan a moment to grasp the meaning of "one pillow, one minute," and when he did a cold current coursed through his gums. He shivered and grasped his knees, and his mind began to race through a collage of black and white—iron bed frames, open mouths, gowns, gray hair, and most vividly of all, a trembling hand lifting toward the ceiling.

"I need to go to bed," he said.

"Ha! But that's not even the story! Here is why I chose to tell you all this. Listen! Grandmother told Inge to lock the apartment after the police had taken the body away. No one could enter. Friends of Hannah Rosenbaum insisted on access, insisting they had spoken with her daughter in Sweden, or her brother in Britain. But no one was allowed. When a family friend brought a locksmith, the things inside had vanished. Heirlooms of china, silverware, fur coats—gone. First she is dead. And they pillaged the dead.

"After the war, distant relatives came from nowhere calling on us, wanting explanation, demanding these *things*, but grandmother had nothing to say."

Eva stared hard at Brendan. "Wow," he said.

"Wow, ha! Yes. Certainly *wow*. Look, things appeared. People received them as wedding gifts, anniversary gifts.

Relatives of Hannah Rosenbaum were invited to *your* relatives' houses, only to find themselves eating a holiday meal with spoons and knives engraved with the Rosenbaum 'R.' So much anger. But who was wronged? The Nazis chose Hannah, and Hannah chose Inge. And these things, all these beautiful things, like dandelions, they are everywhere."

Eva stopped speaking. The silence filling the room felt like the inside of a large and empty glass bowl.

Eva reached for her Cognac glass and drained it. Brendan picked up his and tipped it over his mouth, but there was nothing in it.

"I can't drive," he said, the muscles around his eyelids collapsing beneath the strain. "I can barely move. Can I sleep here?"

"Of course you can. The spare bed is in Inge's bedroom. It has sheets. I'll make you breakfast. *Brendan*," she said, and something in her voice made him freeze midway up from the couch, his knees bent. Her tone had lost its music, and the loss was jarring. Her eyes, for the first time that night, were an old woman's eyes, glassy, rheumy. "Listen to a grandmother's advice," she continued, throat hushed, and he fell back onto the couch. "Do everything to get those things back. It doesn't matter what. You must retrieve them. People come, people go, they live with you, they die without you, but the *things*, once they leave your hands, they are everywhere, and people will find your secrets in them. I have gathered all things under this roof and they will stay as long as I breathe. You—your eyes betray you. Do you have secrets, Brendan?"

Beside her, on the shelf, he noticed the spoon by the teacup, its handle jutting over the saucer's golden trim, and he nodded, he nodded fiercely, his secrets too numerous to name.

. . .

Inge breathed loudly from her bed, a slight wheeze, air working through her sinuses. Without turning on any lights, he pulled off his boots and fell back onto the spare bed. He didn't even bother getting under the sheets but simply lay on top of an unplugged electric blanket. He could hear Eva rummage through the bathroom, the medicine cabinet creaking open and shut, the toilet flushing, her bedroom door sighing closed. The objects in Inge's room were faintly outlined by the blue glow of her digital clock reflecting off the metal support bar that ran the length of her bed. The air smelled medicinal, moist, and minty, like a topical ointment.

The combination of intoxicants immobilized Brendan's body, yet his mind churned manically, a deluge of images and sounds, no single thing related to another, a flipbook of erratic noise. Despite the room's hospital warmth, he began to shiver.

"You are not sleeping?" he heard Inge say, after he failed to locate the wall plug for the blanket and instead cocooned himself inside of it.

"Sorry," he said, jaw quivering. "I thought you were asleep."

"I don't sleep anymore. Sometimes I sleep. Mostly I just remember."

"I'll try to relax."

"I have sleeping pills. Right here next to me. Sometimes they work. Take one."

"From *you*?" he said, trying to chuckle as his torso shook.

But neither the frenzy in his head nor the trembling in his muscles showed any signs of abetting, so he got up and, still sealed in the blanket, lifted a prescription vial from her night table.

"Just one," she said. "They are strong. Give me one too."

From the glow of the clock, he saw her extended tongue as she said, "Ahhhhh." He worked off the child-proof cap and dropped a tiny pill into her mouth, her tongue and lower lip grazing his thumb. He popped one on his own tongue as well, wincing at the aftertaste.

"Now we sleep," she said.

Brendan returned to his bed and stared at the ceiling, watching as translucent blue orbs, retinal ghosts from the digital clock, tracked his eye movements, then faded. Soon, a warm, syrupy sensation moved from his chest and down his legs, warming the bones beneath his face. The memory of her mouth on his thumbnail felt like the trace of a cold and wet brush stroke, and as he raised his hand toward the ceiling, the ground beneath him opened.

"It wasn't you was it," he whispered. "It was her, Omi. Eva was the chosen one."

Her breathing stilled, but she said nothing.

"That's okay," he said, "I'll never tell."

"It should never have been," Inge said, her voice disarmingly calm. "She nearly lost her mind. So I took it from her." She breathed. "Now it is my story. *Für immer*."

And soon Brendan would sleep. The next morning he would leave, early and quickly, with little ceremony, arriving back at his parents' house. He would tell the story, not sure where to even start, talking animatedly on the driveway beside their emerald lawn when his mother finds the stash under the passenger seat. He grapples for new words, new ways of trying to explain why he is the way he is, but this is Mom and Dad's free ticket, and they can now throw him back onto the streets for his and their own good. He without a single earthly possession. And while he never really lands on his feet, he will never hit bottom either, always finding someone to help him make it through the week, even managing to finally reclaim Grandpa's LP and everything else his ex has taken, his sister allowing him to hide these things in her basement, and he, realizing that Omi would love to hear this news, decides to visit her again, but he should call before he visits, and write before he calls. But he never writes.

Like an old couple, Inge and Eva will die months apart, and their possessions, glassware and coats and spoons, divided and dispersed and exiled even deeper into the world—the Diaspora diluted into extinction.

Für immer.

That last German word, which even he in this state understood as "forever," echoed slightly in Inge's room, and as the darkness multiplied, rolling over him in waves, he tried to smile, tried to speak, tried to tell Inge that she was a good sister, and that while some things need to be left alone, others beg to be taken, like memories.

He wanted to say this and so much more.

DAVID CAMERON lives with his wife and children near Boston, Massachusetts, where he works in biomedical research communications. A Pushcart nominee, his fiction has appeared in *Ploughshares*, *Boulevard*, *The Literary Review*, *Carve*, and *Digital Americana*. He can be reached at djcameron@gmail.com.

INTERVIEW WITH DAVID CAMERON

January 2019

CARVE

What is your community like? What do you do in Boston?

DAVID

I've been working in academic research public relations for a long time now. I work at an independent research institute that has connections with both MIT and Harvard, mostly the medical school. It's a biomedical research institute. I've been here for a year-and-a-half and I do mostly editing at this point. My title is Director of Media Relations and Communications. We do press releases and news stories for our website that try to give an accessible, lay person's version of the research that goes on here. There's a lot of genetics. The whole institute is devoted to finding the genetic causes of all sorts of diseases, common diseases, rare diseases, and so forth. It's a deep dive into the world of genetics. The communication department is the public face of the institute.

CARVE

How did you land in that world?

DAVID

Total, total, total happenstance. I was working in social services, working with an agency that helps homeless people find employment. As you can imagine, it was hard to make too much of a living on that. My wife was pregnant with our first kid at the time. I went to the Cambridge Center for Adult Education. I started taking courses in proofreading and copy-editing, and someone who I knew worked for this medical society that published all these newsletters and stuff. They were hiring for a proofreader. I didn't have to know anything about the content. Just had to know punctuation, essentially. So I got that job and went from there, and I got a copyeditor/staff writer job for *Technology Review* magazine, which is published by MIT. Again, I knew nothing about the material. I just started doing that and I worked there for a few years. That put me in this world of technology, science, and research. I have a bachelor's in English literature and a master's degree in religious studies and theology. I had to develop familiarity with the terms and the overall concepts, and not be afraid to ask stupid questions. I think the secret of this has just been shamelessly asking stupid questions. Gradually, through osmosis, things kicked in. That's my professional life.

I've always been a writer. I have also done music, so creatively I've bounced back and forth through periods of my life when I'm focusing on writing and other times when I'm focusing on music. In terms of writing and community, a big part of that has been Grub Street here in Boston. I know a lot of people involved with that, and I've done workshops there. I'm in this program right now called the Short Story Incubator, which is a year-long program. Rather than a typical workshop with a standard workshop critique, it's really geared at taking a very deep dive into revising stories. I'm currently in the middle of that program right now.

CARVE

Carve published your story in 2011. What role has fiction played in your life since then?

DAVID

I've had a few publications since then. Right after *Carve* I had a piece published in *Digital Americana*, which was the first literary magazine that existed purely as an app. It was kind of interesting. They were around for a few years. They have a website still, but they haven't published anything since 2014, unfortunately. I also had a piece in *The Literary Review* and one in *Ploughshares*. *Boulevard* just accepted one of my stories. I was really excited. All of this, as I'm sure you're not shocked to hear, was punctuated by reams and reams and reams of rejection.

CARVE

I'm interested to know that you have a master's degree in religious studies and a background in music— both of those things feel relevant to "And They Pillaged the Dead." Are those things that persist through your other fiction work?

DAVID

I never studied music, really. It's more that I've been playing guitar all my life, not that I ever studied music officially. I was in a few bands doing local stuff. I have a Soundcloud page where I put some of the electronic things that I've been dabbling in. Nothing huge. I think the character in the *Carve* story—I mean, that's not me. I've never had a drug problem, I was never surfing couches. But obviously my psyche is in that person, to some extent. That image of a nineties grunge wannabe type—I think I've certainly related to that at certain points in my life. But it's an interesting question that I'm not sure how to answer. I get ideas and I start pursuing them. Most of them might just be a few drafts before I give up on them, but a few actually make it to the finish line.

In terms of writers who have inspired me, I know that when I wrote "And They Pillaged the Dead" I was really into

Jennifer Egan. I was deep into *A Visit from the Goon Squad*. It had either just come out or was about to come out—my sister was working in publishing at the time and she actually got me the galley of it. "Safari," one of the stories in there, had just come out in the *New Yorker* around that time too. Even the technique of doing a quick flash forward at the end of the piece is something she does in a number of the stories. I did that in the *Carve* story and that was very self-consciously inspired by her.

Since then I've discovered and delved pretty deep into George Saunders. Joy Williams is another one. They're two very different writers, they're very distinct, but they're both ideal writers in my mind. I wish I could somehow be the love child of Saunders and Joy Williams. That would be a wonderful thing.

CARVE

What is it about each of them that you identify with so strongly?

DAVID

George Saunders, he's easy. He's so unbelievably entertaining, and he's funny. I'm fascinated with humor in stories and how it works. In fact, one of the things we're doing in this Short Story Incubator, each of us is embarking on a different project, finding something about fiction that we want to explore and doing a deep dive into it. I chose humor. Specifically, how humor is used in character development. Sam Lipsyte is another. Today on my way to work I was reading a story by Lipsyte called "Dungeon Master," which is a really funny story, but it's devastating too.

Humor in fiction is fascinating. It works very differently, obviously, from humor in film or television. Saunders is probably a master of that. There's such a generosity of spirit, I think, in his stories. He's not afraid to go for a happy ending, too.

He's not afraid to run the risk of almost being sentimental. His story "Tenth of December" is a good example of that. That could have ended in so many different ways. His heart is equal to his imagination.

Joy Williams is just fucking weird. Even the latest story she just had in the *New Yorker*, "Chaunt." Everyone I know who is a reader—I'm like, "You've *got* to read this story." There's so much about it I just don't understand. I'm drawn to her in the same way that I'm drawn to David Lynch movies. I can't really explain most of them at all, but there's this atmosphere. She draws you into the moment, too. A lot of her stuff is in the present tense. I feel like, as a reader, you're being held by the hand and slowly walked into this very strange world. In "Chaunt," you're not even sure when you're in reality, when you're in this person's mind. To what extent is it even in the real world? Who is this person experiencing this near-death event? Is she in purgatory, in some sense? It really is that sense of being taken by the hand and very deliberately, very carefully led into a very strange place, and then just left there. I think Saunders is a huge fan of hers as well.

CARVE

So your influences are interacting too.

DAVID

They're all talking to each other.

CARVE

I think there's something about the voice of "And They Pillaged the Dead" that's relevant. I think I'm partial to unlikeable characters, but I also think it has to be an unlikeable character with heart and humor and honesty. That's this character—he's made mistakes but he's also endearing. I wondered what you could tell me about where this character came from.

DAVID

It's interesting what you say about unlikeable characters, because I have never been one to think that I have to like characters. They just have to be interesting. If you can just get into their head, if they come alive to you. I've written a lot of stuff where the characters are not likable—maybe it's something I should explore at some point. I've gotten feedback saying, "Yeah, I really didn't like this person." But when I get that feedback, I pay no attention to it. Characters don't have to be likable.

Where this story came from connects to how the character came out. My mother is from Germany and grew up there during World War II, before she immigrated when she was in her twenties. There is a family story about a great-aunt, or something, who was in this situation—a woman who was Jewish who was married to a gentile. Her husband died, and then she got a notice to appear at the police station. They knew what that meant. She did take her own life, and she did have a member of the family, a teenage woman, my mother's aunt, stay with her while this happened because she didn't want to be alone. Then there were all of these rumors afterward. It's a story that I heard in a very solemn, hush-hush way.

For years, I would think about that. At some point it occurred to me that I had to put it into some kind of story. At one point, I tried to do the historical fiction thing, put all the action in 1940 in Germany. The story itself was too intense, at least for me at the time. It was too direct. Some writers can do that really well. They can take something very harrowing and just go deep. There's all sorts of decisions you have to make to do it that way. It almost would be easier if it was 300 years ago, or something, because it's a world that's another world, but it's still very close to our world.

At some point it occurred to me that the only way I could do this would be to come up with the context in which it is a story that is recounted—a story within a story. I felt like I could access it this way. I could get my head around it and start exploring it. I tried different kinds of characters, just tooling around. At some point I settled on using this person. I drew a lot from myself. The character is thirty years old and having a life crisis. When I was thirty years old, I was having a life crisis. I wrote the story later, but looking back, it was a crazy year in my life as well. For different reasons. But I had similar fantasies about being a musician. At one point I came to terms with the fact that that's just not going to happen. I also grew up in Long Island, New York, visiting German relatives.

This notion of older German women—I could hear their voices in my head. Intergenerational stuff is always interesting—the fact that he could be sitting there getting stoned and smoking from his hash pipe. Maybe I was listening to Weezer—"Hash Pipe" has always been one of my favorites— and that put the idea in my head. Give him a hash pipe and just sit there with these two old ladies.

CARVE

That's what I love about this story—the way it balances with levity. That opening line is funny. But it's also a hard story. I'm thinking in particular of the photograph that's discussed in the beginning, and also the conversation about what family is and having a complicated heritage. Physical things, too—and why they're important, why it's devastating that his ex-girlfriend has stolen all of his things, and also the family heirlooms being lost. Did any real physical objects help inspire this story?

DAVID

I reread the story last night in anticipation of this conversation. I don't think I've read this story since it was published, so it's been a while, but it's the only story of mine that exists online. Whenever someone asks me what I've written, that's what I send them. But this is a very heavy story, and I wanted to do everything I can to remove any sentimentality from it. The idea of the materialism of it appealed to me because I knew that there was going to be this notion of objects being missed, you know, from the original story. And then his girlfriend walking off with that stuff—at some point the connection was made, but I wanted there to be a materialist element to it.

It struck me again when I was rereading the story—the power of things, the power of stuff. On the one hand, it's very superficial. Stuff is stuff. But there's power to objects. I was wondering, can I work this very self-consciously and overtly materialist element into this emotionally fraught piece? Stuff is stuff, but stuff is more than stuff too. Stuff possesses parts of ourselves in all sorts of ways. I wanted that element to be there.

CARVE

And part of the story is what a luxury it is to have your stuff around you, to be able to hand your stuff down to other generations. And not take that for granted. I think that's significant.

DAVID

I think about that a lot now. My parents are very elderly at this point. They just sold their house and moved into a smaller apartment. What to do with the stuff? There's so much stuff that goes back generations. My wife's mother is also getting up there in age and is downsizing. My wife's been visiting her in Pennsylvania and going through all the stuff from her late father. What do you do with that stuff? Things that have profound meaning to you that would have no meaning to someone else. The way stuff migrates is interesting. It means something. I wanted to at least put it there and let it be.

CARVE

You mentioned this is your only story that's available online. I think it was your first published piece of fiction as well. And you reread it last night for the first time in years—how do think about this story now in terms of content but also maybe style, the form the story takes?

DAVID

That's a good question. From a purely technical standpoint, if God smiles on me and I ever get a collection out and the story were to be in there, I probably would pare it down a little bit. There's a lot of details in there. I think I could probably shave off upwards of a thousand words, maybe. But that's a very technical thing. I read it and I felt good about it. Obviously it's not perfect. I think for this particular story, certainly at the time, it's the best I could have done. The story lived through many drafts and revisions. I feel good about it still and would proudly show it to anyone. There are other things that I have written and every once in a while I'll go back and find things and get that feeling—yes, this part's good, but this is kind of embarrassing right here, and what was I thinking?

CARVE

In the years since you wrote this story, has your way of working and writing and revising changed?

DAVID

I don't think in any substantial way, other than the natural evolution. I've gotten better at being a self-editor. Once we can really edit ourselves, that's a good thing. Nothing else has really changed.

I remember when I was younger and there were fewer constraints in my life, I could just carve out a huge chunk of time and spend three hours on a Saturday writing. Sometimes

I could do that now, but it's different. The older you get the more life just becomes life. I was joking with someone the other day, saying you almost have to treat writing as if it's an illicit thing, like a gambling addiction. You do it whenever you can, because unless you're a professional writer who gets up in the morning and writes for seven hours—if you have jobs and other things going on and kids, that's a lot. It's like, screw this mentality of needing my office and everything set perfectly, the temperature to be set, a certain time of day, to write. Man, I'm sitting on the bus and typing with thumbs into Evernote. I've done a lot of writing when I'm commuting, sometimes a little bit on my lunch hour. When you can do it, you have to do it. Gone are the days of long stretches of luxurious free time to just indulge.

CARVE

You're involved with *Talking Writing* also. How would you describe that project?

DAVID

Martha Nichols is the founder and editor-in-chief of *Talking Writing*. Her background is mostly in journalism and expository writing. She teaches a feature-writing class at the Harvard Extension School, which is their evening program. I got connected with her through a mutual friend. The publication itself started literally as the title, as its name says, a place where writers can get together and talk about writing.

The fiction part of it—I've been the fiction editor—we don't publish too much fiction because, and this is largely her call, of how she sees the nature of the publication. It's more expository writing, interviews, and poetry. She and I go back and forth about the nature of publishing fiction online versus print and how that works. Every few months out of the year we'll open it up. We only publish a few short stories a year.

There's nothing specific or thematic. We'll have writing contests that are thematic, but those wouldn't be the fiction ones. Those are more essays. The bulk of the energy of the website is essays and poetry. I just published an interview with a poet on there. As the editor, I'll have things recommended to me and I'll go through it and do a more final round of editing and line-editing when we get ready to publish, which is something I really enjoy doing.

What is your relationship with poetry, as a reader or as a writer?

Poetry—how would I describe my relationship to poetry? I feel like I'll go a few years and barely look at it, and then suddenly I'll take a deep dive and read all the poetry that I can, and then come back out of the deep dive and two years later go back in. Ben Purkert is the poet I just interviewed. He was published in the issue of *Ploughshares* right before the one I was in, and he read my story and contacted me. He just said that he liked it. He teaches creative writing at Rutgers, and at another point they were using the story in their class and he had asked me to Skype him. Unfortunately I couldn't do it at the time, the timing just didn't work. But we kept a correspondence going, and then it turned out he was doing a reading right here in Boston. He had just published his book. I went to that, and I think his poetry is fantastic. He's fairly young, I think he just turned thirty. He's definitely a name that we're going to see in the future.

I never get writer's block. I actually think that I have more ideas than I will ever put forth in a lifetime—for short stories, that is. But sometimes I find myself burning out on fiction, and I am suddenly almost amazed that I could complete any story and have it be something that I feel like I want to show to the world. Going from inception to that moment, when you actually feel secure enough to put it out there, I feel like you're climbing a mountain. Even if it's just a twenty-page short story, the engineering that you have to do—it starts with inspiration and with a mood, and with a moment, and the inspiration is what pushes you forward, gives you the impetus. Then after a few drafts you almost feel as if it's all engineering, at that point. Like, how do I bring these things together?

At times it's overwhelming and I get burned out. I like to lapse either into poetry or trying to explore music, and do my own compositions just for myself. Not with any grand ambitions, certainly with music. It just releases another part of my brain. I mean, poetry is profoundly difficult as well, but it's another part of your brain working. It's more forgiving in terms of intuitive moments. When I was talking with Ben about that, the revising that he puts into very short pieces— it's endless. I've written my own poetry and I feel like I'm constantly revising it. But it has allowed a different part of my brain, the very intuitive part—I'm not talking about meter and rhythm and things like that, or even structure. It's the dream-like quality of it. What makes a piece of music appealing to someone? It's on another level. It's not subject to analysis in the same way. At times I think I just need to put myself through that other kind of creative process.

CARVE

A few years ago you published an essay about reading the slush for *Tin House* and the concept of being a literary doorman. That's something I think about a lot, and I'm really interested in looking at the ways that it's complicated to be a literary gatekeeper—the subjectivity of editorial decisions and the fallibility of the editor, as a human. That essay is great because it was written long enough ago that Submittable was still Submishmash. It's been a few years. I wondered, what is your take on submitting now?

DAVID

A very good friend of mine who is a writer said that he is pretty much burned out on that. He has the means to go to AWP every year and just spends the whole time getting to know every editor of every journal that he can. I think that's great. I would love to be able to go to AWP every year and do that. But it's weird. Anyone who chooses to do anything creative and then try to get it beyond their own kitchen table, put it out in the world—it can't ever have been easy. People are always mentioning prior golden eras. There was a time when there were tons of short story journals out there. Kurt Vonnegut used to make a living just cranking out a story a week at one point, in the 1940s or something. The volume, however, that is out there—do you use Duotrope?

CARVE

I get overwhelmed by it.

DAVID

Well, there you go. I mean, you beat me to the punchline. When you look at their statistics, which I think are only a quarter or a fifth of what's out there, and you see that currently *Missouri Review* has two thousand stories pending—you realize the volume of that. When I was a reader for *Tin House*, the majority of pieces that were submitted probably were not ready to be submitted. They struck me as stories that were a first or second draft. I've experienced that with *Talking Writing* too. It's maybe just a smaller fraction that feel like their stories have really been carefully thought through and revised and worked over. But there are not enough journals out there to give homes to all of the stories that warrant a home. I think every journal is under-resourced. Even the top ones—I'm sure the *Paris Review* would love to have more readers and more editors and be able to publish more than they do.

Certainly as a writer, you have to understand that you are rolling dice so much of the time. But you just have to. I don't know what the answer is for submitting. Do you submit to every journal out there or are you selective? According to Duotrope statistics, submissions at many journals are going up every year.

CARVE

That's the thing. I've been involved with *Carve* for longer than I've been actively submitting, and I think it's made me very careful about submissions and also realistic about how much it depends on being in the right place at the right time with the right reader. And it depends on knowing the magazine. If writers don't read magazines but they do send out all over to try to play the numbers game, it's tricky. I think you have to play the numbers and you also have to be thoughtful.

DAVID

Yes. The story that I have coming out in *Boulevard*—they rejected that same story two years ago. It wasn't a personal. It was just a standard form rejection. This time, I happened to get the right reader. This is so profoundly subjective. I do think readers at bigger journals are looking for a reason to reject the story. If they've got a word count of five thousand words in their submission guidelines and someone sends five thousand five hundred words, nope. That was easy. That submitter just made your life as a reader easier by violating some letter of the law.

But it is a problem and I have no idea what the solution to it is. I remember once hanging out with some friends— one guy who is a painter and one guy who is a musician and actually rents his own recording studio. Another guy, who is, interestingly, an interior designer—we were just having dinner. I probably started complaining about the submission thing. The guy who is an artist, a fantastic painter, began to weigh in. Then the musician guy, too. You just swap out poetry for painting or short stories for demo tape—we're all seeing the same thing. I think probably with any kind of creative pursuit, you end up having a conversation about the choke point of volume versus outlets to give a home to the art. Can you imagine if you're a painter trying to make it in the New York City gallery scene?

As gatekeeper and as an aspirational writer, I think you just have to completely reconcile yourself to the rules of the road, that this is how that world works. We haven't even mentioned anything about money. You're a poet—you have it easy, because no one ever told you that you poets make money. That's a given. There's no movie about the rich poet who is rich because of their poetry. Whereas prose writers, especially novelists and some really duped short story writers, might actually think that this will be something that could lead to some sort of financial reward.

I know *Carve* pays their contributors. Many journals don't. Even many that charge for submissions don't. The value of getting paid for your work—it's less a profit thing than that you can now deduct all the money that you've expended on this from your taxes. Submission expenses and things like that, or workshops that you took. Even if someone gave you thirty dollars in one calendar year, you are now able to do that. You are a paid writer.

CARVE

All of that being said, it feels significant to reflect on *Tin House*'s announcement that they're closing their print magazine. What magazines are you reading and excited about right now?

DAVID

I subscribed to *POETRY* recently. I think that's such an amazing publication. I was so happy that *Boulevard* accepted my story that I immediately subscribed to them. I just got my first issue, their one hundredth issue. I read the opening short story and I thought it was hysterical. A really well-done story by an author who is, I think, not yet established. I haven't delved too much into the smaller ones. I've subscribed to *Tin House* on and off over the years, but they've got their books and their conference. *Glimmer Train* is closing too.

This has happened before. There's the magazine that Joyce Carol Oates' husband was the editor-in-chief of—*Ontario Review*, a really established publication. He died and I think they shut down that magazine. The *Partisan Review* used to be really huge. The *Mississippi Review*, which has morphed into an online thing and is very different from what it was. So these things do come and go. There's a new one called *Lit Mag*. Have you seen that?

CARVE

I haven't.

DAVID

It's a brand new one, but they must have a lot of funding behind it because they're paying their contributors a lot of money and they've only had two issues out. They've got very big names. Of course I read the *New Yorker*. That goes without saying. People like to, over the years, take pot shots at *New Yorker* fiction and say it's sterile, or whatever.

CARVE

But I love the weirdness of what they sometimes publish. I think the *New Yorker* is operating on some other trendsetting plane, in terms of fiction.

DAVID

I think that they publish great stuff. There have been so many stories that I've read there that made me think, damn, that was killer. I like their poetry podcast too. The format is really simple. They take a poet who has been published in the *New Yorker* and they pick out of the *New Yorker* archive another poem and read it, discuss it, and then read one of their own poems that's been published in the *New Yorker*. Then they discuss that as well. Kevin Young is really good. Just his energy.

CARVE

What mantra is guiding your recent work?

DAVID

What have other people said?

CARVE

That's cheating.

DAVID

It is cheating. What mantra? You know, when we do the Short Story Incubator, each session begins with a quote. The guy who leads it writes a quote on writing on the whiteboard and we spend five, ten minutes meditating on it. There was really good quote from Pamela Painter, who is probably better known as a fiction teacher than as a writer. She has this beautiful quote: "A story is a journey that begins somewhere and ends in illumination somewhere else."

But the one thing I have to keep reminding myself so I don't lose my mind: Writing is revising is writing.

Whiskey & Ribbons

LEESA CROSS-SMITH

September 2011

I cut my hair when my husband, Eamon, died. Dalton did, too. Everyone says you're not supposed to cut your hair when you're pregnant, but I don't think that applies if you're a pregnant widow. I don't think that applies if the father of the child was a cop and was gunned down by some motherfucking sixteen-year-old kid who skipped school. I don't think it applies. I think an exception can be made. I cut my dreads and I shaved my head and I felt like a little chicken somehow. And Dalton hadn't shaved his face in years, but he did. The bottom of his face looked tender and raw and red sometimes. I was afraid to touch it.

That was six months ago. Our son, Noah, is five months old. I asked Dalton to move in with us because he was Eamon's best friend and they were practically brothers. Eamon's parents took him in after his mom died because Dalton didn't have any other family and never knew his dad. He lived with them until he and Eamon went away to college.

I like Dalton being here because I don't want to be alone. And being with him feels like being with Eamon. And when it was just me, I hated taking out the garbage by myself and I hated being scared at night. And I needed someone. I needed lots of things then and I need a lot of things now, but having Dalton here fixes a lot of things that are broken in my heart.

His lease was up last month so he officially lives here now. He sleeps down the hallway in the blue bedroom.

I don't have to worry about money. Eamon took care of all of that stuff, and I have enough. I stopped teaching ballet when I got too pregnant. Dalton owns a little bike shop, and if I even look like I'm thinking about bills or money, he tells me not to worry about it. I know he has plenty of money. His mom left him a chunk that he got when he turned twenty-five. I've been letting him take care of the money because I don't have extra brain power for anything like that right now and I trust him. I don't take that for granted in him or anyone. I fucking hate being around people I know I can't trust.

I read once that Bill Monroe said that bluegrass music "has a high lonesome sound." Dalton and Noah and I left in this world without Eamon, that's what we have. We sound like one banjo playing slowly. We sound like one fiddle playing into the wind of the Blue Ridge Mountains. We sound like a sad country song that hasn't been written yet. We go to bed at night in deep darkness and wake to these thin-as-a-communion-wafer mornings with their dirty white winter sunlight and hush.

. . .

I swim up out of the thick sleep that hitches itself to the trains of whiskey and winter. After the bathroom, I walk into the kitchen wearing a tank top and pajama pants and I pull my grey wool sweater down over my head. Dalton touches me underneath one of my arms.

"I like your armpit hair," he says softly.

It tickles so I smile a little. His fingers aren't as warm as I want them to be if he's going to touch me there.

"I hate to shave," I say back.

"Me, too," he says reaching up to touch his beard.

He tells me that Noah is still sleeping, but that he was up for almost an hour during the night.

"I didn't hear him," I say, holding both of my hands up to my mouth. The sleeves are too long. It was Eamon's. I'm convinced it still smells like him, but I know that it can't be true.

"No worries. I heard him. We hung out for a little bit and then he fell back to sleep," he says, smiling, as he goes over to the coffeemaker and fills it with tap water.

"I feel awful for not hearing him."

"Don't," he says, putting his hand on my shoulder for a moment.

. . .

I take Noah to my parents' later. They really want to see him, and I could use some time to myself. I let myself in like I always do, and my mom walks into the foyer with a plaid dishrag draped over her shoulder and holds her arms out for my baby. He grins and grins.

"Come here to Nana, you big, big boy," she says, grinning back.

"I'll come back and pick him up later. I think I may run some errands. Maybe go see a movie," I say, lying. I want to go back home to sleep but I don't want her to worry about me.

"Why don't you leave him here tonight? Get some rest," she says, grinning at Noah and then looking up at me with that sweet look that moms get—worry mixed with love mixed with suspicion.

"Well, I didn't bring his pajamas," I say, looking into the diaper bag to see if I put more than one clean outfit in there. Noah leans forward and reaches out for me, and I take his hand and let him grab my fingers, while I root through with my other hand.

"Evi, I went out last night and bought him two new sets of

pajamas. Aren't they so cute?" She squeals and points towards the ottoman, where she has them laid out. One is brown and blue stripes and has a little hood with bear ears and one is a pair of red footie pajamas. I turn back to her, but she and Noah are already headed to the kitchen. He's looking at me over her shoulder with the same dark eyes that Eamon had. He's got the fabric of my mom's shirt balled up in one of his little brown fists. I reach my hand straight out to wave to him and say "Hey, Baby," and he makes the happiest squealing baby sound that echoes off of everything in the kitchen. That echoes off of everything inside of me and then shoots straight up to Heaven to Eamon's waiting ears. I have to believe it does.

. . .

Eamon was over the moon when I found out I was pregnant. We'd only been married for a year, and I thought maybe we should wait until we'd been married for longer, but life happens and it only took me half a second to feel over the moon, too. If I think about the fact that Eamon never got to see Noah's face in this life. If I think about the fact that Eamon never even got to touch his baby or hold his baby or smell his baby's head. If I sink down and let my bones steep in those feelings for too long, I have to put my hand to my heart. I have to make sure that I'm still breathing because it's hard to understand how I could be. It doesn't make sense.

I put my hand to my heart as I am driving back home. I'm still eating the oatmeal cookie my mom shoved in my hand when I left. And I'm looking forward to not having to worry about Noah waking up in the middle of the night tonight. I won't have to feel guilty that Dalton hears him better than I do sometimes. I hear a *thumpadumpdump* and know something is wrong with my tire.

I pull over and get out and see that it's flat. I could call

AAA. I could call my dad. I could change it myself. I could call Dalton. I'm only about a mile from home. I decide to walk home and wait for Dalton, and we'll come back down here. We'll change the tire and get it fixed, and it's fine and I know it's fine, but I start crying as I get my purse out of the car. I keep crying as I walk onto the sidewalk and head towards home. The sky is starting to do some sort of sleet-snow mix, and I keep crying and walking, and I cross my arms. I hear a honk behind me and think Oh God, Please Don't Let It Be a Weirdo. I don't want to turn around, but I do and I see Dalton's big black truck, thank God. And he's not alone. There's a girl in the truck with him. He pulls over and gets out.

"Evangeline? What's up? Noah's with your mom?" he says quickly, looking around. I know he worries about me. Everyone does. I'm sure he's worried I've left Noah somewhere or that I've lost my mind. And sometimes I think that would be easier.

"He's with my mom," I say back to him, wiping my eyes.

"What's wrong?"

"I'm just tired," I say.

"The tire's flat?" Dalton asks, sizing up the situation. He looks down the road where I left my car. I haven't walked very far. The sleet makes a hard and constant sound as it falls on my puffy vest. I should've worn my bigger coat.

"I was walking home to get you. Who's that?" I nod towards the truck. The girl in there wipes the fog off of the window and holds her hand up and smiles. I mirror her and smile back quickly.

"Her name is Cassidy. She comes into the bike shop sometimes. She needed a ride," Dalton says, looking back at her and then again to me.

"Oh," I say. I'm jealous. He tells me to get in the truck and we'll take Cassidy home and then come back and fix the car.

I step way up into the truck, and Cassidy scoots really close to Dalton, and I hate it. I can't stand it. I say, "Hi," and then look out of the window, and then I look down and watch Dalton's keychain swing back and forth and back and forth and back and forth in the ignition. There's a little flashlight on it and a green bottle opener. I bought it for him. I bought Eamon one, too.

Cassidy's place isn't too far up the road, and when we get there I get out so she can slide across the bench seat. She does a hair flip-fluttery-eyelashes-smiley goodbye to Dalton, and I say goodbye to her, too, before I get back inside and close the door.

"She likes you," I say as soon as he drives away.

"Well... it's not like that, really," he says.

"I don't feel like I'm in a place to say anything," I say, starting to cry again. I'm tender. He knows that. Everyone knows that. I can't hide it and I don't try.

"Don't cry. Hey. You're not crying about this, are you? About me giving a girl a ride home?"

He keeps turning to look at me even though he's driving and it's sleeting harder now.

"I'm crying because of everything, Dalton. Because of my life," I say, crying harder. I put my face in my hands.

"I love being a part of your life," he says, "everything about it. You and Noah."

I shrug and don't say anything.

"And Cassidy's not my type anyway," Dalton says, putting his hand on my leg for a second to get my attention.

I look over at him as he stops at a red light.

"It's not my right to say anything even if she is. I don't know how to handle stuff like this... I mean, eventually a girl *will* be your type. Then what?"

He starts shaking his head.

"What?" I ask.

"It's not going to happen like that," he says as he pulls his truck behind my stalled car on the side of the road.

. . .

I stand with him while he puts on the spare tire. He keeps telling me to get back in the truck. He keeps telling me it's too cold. He keeps telling me that he'll be done in a second. He flips up the collar of his coat. His hair is wet and dripping, and I take off my red toboggan and put it on his head and pull it down over his ears. And when he's finished I get back into my car and follow behind him slowly as he drives up the road and turns right, headed back to the house. Then I drive around and pull in first so I can go into the garage. He says he'll pick up a new tire for me tomorrow. We go inside, and then I go upstairs to my bedroom so I can put on warm, dry clothes. Pajamas and my warmest slippers. When I come back down, Dalton has on his pajama pants, too. He's at the stove making hot chocolate.

"That's perfect. Thank you. For the hot chocolate and for fixing my car and for everything," I say. My head aches and I'm too tired to cry.

"Stop thanking me. I'll have to make that a new rule around here," he says, stirring, and then he looks over at me.

Dalton is a beautiful country boy. He has kind eyes and he's tall and athletic and rarely an asshole. He and Eamon played football together in high school and Dalton played a little in college, but he hurt his knee so that was that. I always felt safe when I was with both of them. Eamon, being a cop and a tall drink of water, and Dalton, being this kind, Southern gentleman. Dalton dated a lot but never had a long-term serious girlfriend, so most of the time it was just the three of us. And we took it easy whenever it was for the taking.

I like to watch Dalton move. I was the same way with Eamon, only it was different because I never noticed how Dalton moved until Eamon was gone. But now I notice. Now I see. I'm a woman and I love men, and Dalton is such a man. And so was Eamon. That's what I loved so much about Eamon.

He was a man's man. He and Dalton read their Bibles and would fish and hunt and break things and fix things. I thought about Eamon a lot before he asked me out. I thought about what it would be like to kiss him. I thought about what it would be like to sleep with him and to have his arms around me and to hear him breathing heavy and low when he was kissing my neck. I still think about those things and sometimes it makes me feel worse and sometimes it makes me feel better. I've thought about Dalton that way once or twice since Eamon was killed. And I've felt awful about that. And I've felt confused. I've felt everything. There isn't one emotion that's been left off of the list and that's why I'm so tired all of the time. It's because I feel everything, all the time and too much.

But it's easy for Dalton and me to have our separate space here in the house together. He puts his shirt on when I come home, and I never catch him looking at me in a way he shouldn't be. And what does that even mean? And I'm sure a lot of people assume that's what's going on. That we're sleeping together and playing house with Noah, but we aren't. I don't know what we're doing, but it's not that. But we're trying to make something. We're trying to figure out what to do next. We're taped together with the love that we have for each other and for Eamon and for Noah and yes, it's a crooked life. It's at once rickety and ramshackle and brand-new, but it's something, even when I don't know what. I know I'm loved. And I know that the good that's coming to me is going to come from that. And I have to believe that there's good coming. I am too scared and stubborn to ever let that go.

. . .

Dalton's cell phone is on the table and it starts vibrating, but I don't look to see who's calling. He asks me to hand it to him, and I still don't look. I give it to him and go to the cabinet to get two mugs, a red one and a blue one. Neither of us drinks out of Eamon's U of L mug. I haven't touched it since.

"Hey," Dalton says into the phone.

I put the mugs on the counter and turn on my iPod and the speakers. The first song is Otis Redding, and I know how much Dalton loves him and I do, too, so I leave it. Dalton's cradling the phone with his shoulder and pouring the hot chocolate from the pot into our mugs. And before I can say thank you and grab mine, Dalton takes my hands and slowly starts swaying back and forth. So I put my arms around him and he sometimes says *mmhmm* into the phone and I press my ear to his chest and listen to his heartbeat and we're swaying and listening to the song. And he's talking to whoever he's talking to about whatever they're talking about and then he tells the person, "Okay, I'll give you a call back then," and says bye and beeps his little phone off. He steps so he can put it back on the table. I grab my mug.

"You all danced out?" he asks, tilting his head.

"Never," I say and smile, taking a sip.

I want to ask him who he was talking to. I want to ask him more things, but I'm scared that he'll want to know why I want to know. And I wouldn't know what to tell him if he asked me that. I'm jealous and I worry that he'll find someone soon and he won't be around anymore and I'll be alone. But that's not all the truth of it. I think about how maybe one day we could be a real, normal family. Maybe he feels the same way I do. And maybe when we're ready, we can do this. We're best friends, and he loves Noah. I know he'll always be in his life. But maybe that'll change when he has his own son. I hate thinking about it I hate thinking about it I hate thinking about it so I try to make myself stop. I go to the freezer for the bottle of whiskey.

"I didn't know it was that kind of party. Yes, ma'am," he says, holding out his mug so I can add some whiskey to it.

I glug some in mine. I glug some in his.

"To whiskey and ribbons," Dalton says, tapping his mug gently against mine. That's what Eamon used to say whenever we drank together.

Dalton smiles at me and the thought of kissing him is there snapping back and forth like a clean white dishtowel hanging on a clothesline in the wind of my cluttered mind.

. . .

We're close to raging drunk now, playing basketball with wadded up balls of paper and the office garbage can and every now and then we use a pencil for batting at the balls even though those aren't the official rules.

"Was that your girlfriend, Cassidy, on the phone earlier?" I'm brave enough to ask now. I only had one glass of whiskey, but finished off the rest of the red wine so I'm still a happy drunk.

"My girlfriend? Quit it, Evi. Quit that," he says.

"Was it?"

"Yes. It was her but she's not my girlfriend. Not even close," he says, getting up and tossing the last wad of paper in the basket. He sits down behind the piano and starts playing the jangly middle part of "Piano Man."

"What did she want?" I ask and scooch next to him on the bench.

"She asked me if I wanted to go to dinner," he says.

"I told you. I told youuuu," I say loudly and punch him in the arm.

"You didn't tell me that," he says, swatting me back and we're both punching each other but I hit him hard and he only bats at my shoulder.

"I told you she liked you. And I was right."

He shakes his head and starts playing piano again. I ask him if he likes her, and he keeps playing and doesn't answer.

And then I ask him again and my eyes must look so sad because he stops and looks at me and doesn't say anything. Then he looks down at his hands and so do I. I climb into his lap and face him and put my legs around him and sit there and hug him and smell his neck.

And when I pull back and look at him, I kiss him on the mouth. We've never kissed on the mouth before. He kisses me back quickly and pulls away and I kiss him again this time, harder. And he kisses me back and pulls away and says my name. I kiss him again and this time he loosens up a little and kisses me for longer. All I hear is the house settling and the two of us breathing and I can feel his heart beating quick and steady with mine. And then my phone rings.

. . .

I climb out of Dalton's lap and go to the kitchen and answer it. It's my mom checking in on me. I use my soberest voice and ask about Noah. I've talked to her once since I left him there. She says he's sleeping. She also wants to know if I need anything. She wants to know if I'm okay and I tell her that I am. I tell her that Dalton and I are hanging out and talking. I worry I'll slip and say the word 'kiss' or the word 'tongue' or the word 'mouth.' I thank her and tell her I'll call her in the morning. She says that the roads are getting icy and not to go out and maybe I should take the rest of the weekend off and leave him with them until Sunday night.

"Okay. That probably works. But I'll call you in the morning. Thanks, mama," I say.

And she tells me to get some rest.

. . .

Dalton's in the kitchen now, and I hang up the phone. He

turns the iPod back on and plays the Otis Redding song again. He grabs me so we can dance again in this kitchen lit by one lamp tonight. His t-shirt is a blue-grey color that seems to get darker the longer I look at it. I don't know what to do. I don't know what I'm doing. I get on my tiptoes to kiss him again, and he leans down and puts his hand behind my head. When the song ends, we're kissing against the countertop and Dalton puts one hand flat against it and the other arm is wrapped around my waist. And when a new song starts, we're still like that and here comes all the feelings I've ever had, flapping like erratic moths fighting for room around the pulsing yellow light of my heart.

"I don't know what to do," I say aloud and turn away from him. I put my fingers to my warm lips. He puts both hands flat on the counter now and hangs his head.

"Me, either," he says.

"I miss Eamon sooo fucking much," I say, making fists with both of my hands and then I bring those fists up to my temples and push until it hurts.

Dalton puts his hand to his heart and there are tears in his eyes and he says, "I do, too."

"I miss how he smelled and I miss his voice and I'm afraid I'll forget everything about him and everything about us," I say, sobbing now. I'm trying to catch my breath. I take a seat on the cool kitchen floor and Dalton sits down across from me, with his back against the dishwasher door.

"And you're going to feel trapped by this. Eventually you're going to want your own family and you'll fall in love and leave and I'll be alone," I say. I keep pointing to myself while I'm talking and sometimes my eyes are closed tight.

"That hurts my feelings."

"What?"

"That you'd think I'd leave. That you don't trust me," he says. His voice is low and he reaches up to squeeze his nose.

. . .

Eamon was killed early in the morning when I was still sleeping. I remember crying *what happened where is he where is he where is he what happened.* My mom rubbed my back and made the quietest shushing sound. Since then I've been stained with grief. Like I have a permanent watermark. Like if you say the right or wrong thing or hold me up in the perfect light, you'll be able to see it.

The days following the funeral, after I'd spent lots and lots of time with Eamon's family and after I'd spent lots and lots of time with my own family, I came back to our house alone, and Dalton was on the front porch swing and I let him in and we didn't speak to each other for two days, but we didn't leave the house. There was no sound at all. We didn't listen to music or watch television. I read the dictionary a lot. I hated the word 'widow.' It sounded so ghostly and empty. I looked up the definition that I already knew. It also listed 'grass widow:' a woman whose husband is temporarily away from her. Adding the word 'grass' in front of it made it sound better. More natural. Made more sense. I couldn't stop thinking about it.

And then on the morning of the third day, Dalton started playing the piano, and I made a pot of decaf coffee and asked him if he wanted some. My voice, delicate and sleepy because Noah had kept me up all night squirming and stretching inside of me like he knew how sad I was.

After that, there were afternoons when Dalton would drop by and find me wandering outside in the backyard, in the same bright turquoise maternity dress and brown cowboy boots. I would walk around thinking the same obsessive thoughts. Was Noah's soul up there somewhere with Eamon? A glowing, airy ball of light that Eamon was holding in his hand until the day Noah was born? And then would he lean over and let it roll down and away... until Noah was out of me, screaming because maybe it hurts when your soul went in. Maybe it burned and ached all over. Maybe it was too hot or too cold or too much or too beautiful or just awful.

Come on in, Dalton would say and take my hand. *A glass of water sounds good, don't you think?* He'd open the back door leading into the kitchen. *I think we have lemons. I'll put some lemons in your water.* He'd pull out a chair for me and set me in it. *You're holding up really well, Evangeline,* he'd say, but it sounded like he was far away or like I was sleeping and dreaming and he was awake.

. . .

Two years ago when we were first married, I pictured Eamon dying a lot. Maybe all wives of policemen and firefighters and soldiers do. Coal miners' wives. Mountain climbers' wives. The wives of the men who build bridges. The wife of the man who puts his head in the lion's jaws to a chorus of sharp gasps at the circus every night. And what about the guy who works in the tiny gas station all night by himself? I'm sure his wife spends a lot of those nights, pacing the kitchen floor, drinking cold coffee and whiskey.

Either way, it's not one of those things I've ever bothered to say out loud to anyone, so I don't know. But I let it play out completely in my head. From the police chaplain coming to our door to all of the fully uniformed officers who would be at the funeral. I thought about how they'd help me walk to my seat in the front row. How I'd go home and everything would feel emptier. Like someone had let the air out of something we didn't even know had air in it to begin with. How all of his clothes would still be hanging in our closet and how I'd smell them and leave them there. For months. For years, maybe. Maybe what was left of them would still be hanging there when I'd been a widow for twenty years. Or maybe I'd get remarried one day down the road, and my new husband would ask me if I wanted him to box them up for me and I'd nod without looking up at him. I don't know. But I made myself think about it. But none of it mattered because it didn't help me when it really happened. Everything felt like it was beginning and ending at the same time and there was nothing I could do about it.

Sometimes people stop me on the street or in the grocery store. Kind old women reach up to pat my face and say they're sorry. Practically every uniformed worker in this city knows my face and story because everyone knew Eamon. Sometimes I am startled and I don't want to talk and I want to be alone. On days when I'm feeling particularly lonely, I welcome the attention. Noah provides a good distraction. People love to tell me how much he looks like Eamon and he does and I'm glad. It's comforting. It reminds me that he was real. That we were real and together once here on this Earth. That people both do and don't disappear.

. . .

"Dalton, you're a totally normal guy. I'm sure you've slept with someone since you've been living here. I don't like thinking that there are all of these secrets, even if it's none of my business," I admit, wiping my eyes. I want a glass of water. I need a glass of water. I stand up and go to the sink. My head spins so I hang onto the counter for balance.

Dalton doesn't say anything. He's tracing the grooves of the linoleum with his finger. Then he scratches at his beard and gets up off of the floor and goes into the drawer where we keep the cigarettes we try not to smoke too much.

"You had sex with her. I know you did. And I have to admit I'm jealous. I know it may sound crazy but I don't care.

I am," I say, filling up a glass with tap water.

"I don't know if we should talk about this stuff when we've been drinking and it's so late and you're exhausted and I don't know what to say yet," he says, coming over and leaning to take a drink of water right out of the faucet. And then he slips a cigarette from the pack and offers me one. I take it.

"Does it freak you out for me to say that I'm jealous?"

"Why would it?"

"Don't ask me a question when I've asked you a question."

"Okay," he says, holding his hands up and walking to the door. We always crack it a little bit and smoke inside when it's this cold.

I keep thinking about the kissing. I keep thinking about his body pressed against me like that.

"I hate feeling like this," I say as he lights my cigarette.

He puts his arm around me after he lights his own cigarette and we stand there and smoke as the tree branches turn to ice.

. . .

When we decide to go to bed it's well past two. I tell him no funny business and he makes a crooked face at me and says, "What do you mean, no funny business?"

"I wanna snuggle with somebody. I wanna snuggle with you. I want you to sleep in my bed tonight. But no funny business," I say, shaking my finger at him. I'm only barely drunk now. I need to pee and brush my teeth. I look in the bathroom mirror and stick my tongue out at myself. I leave my eye makeup like I always do since I love how it looks in the morning, all smudgy and black.

"You look beautiful," Dalton says.

"No funny business," I say again.

He raises his hand as if he's making a precious, solemn

vow and laughs.

And then he says, "I promise."

And I'm the good kind of nervous as I crawl in between my sheets.

He gets behind me and puts his arms around me. I can feel that he's still wearing his t-shirt, his pajama pants, his socks. I can't hear the ice falling anymore. Now it must be snow. We are quiet in my dark, ticking bedroom and I tell Dalton that I'm sad but even when I'm not sad, I get sad because I feel guilty. And I tell him that Eamon never made me cry because he didn't. Not once.

I turn to face him. He puts his hand on my cheek and tells me he'll never leave. And then he tells me that he didn't have sex with Cassidy but they made out in his truck the other day. But he couldn't do anything else because he thought about me.

"Why?" I ask and let my eyes close.

"I think about you and Noah all the time. Sometimes it's all I think about," he says.

I fall asleep while he's saying it and I can hear his voice while I'm half-dreaming. I remember waking up in the middle of the night when Noah was only a couple of weeks old. I stumbled into the hallway and didn't remember that Eamon was dead until I saw Dalton in the soft blue lamplight, holding Noah's little body in the crook of his arm. I saw the top of Noah's head and the dark tuft of wild black hair he was born with. Dalton was holding him and looking out of the window, and Noah was making gentle sleepy noises. I leaned against the doorframe and watched them. I listened for it then and I'm still listening for it now. I am always putting my ear down to the railroad tracks, waiting for the distant, low rattle and rumble of something coming to heal me.

LEESA CROSS-SMITH is a homemaker and the author of *Every Kiss A War*, *Whiskey & Ribbons*, and the forthcoming books *So We Can Glow* and *This Close to Okay*. *Whiskey & Ribbons* was longlisted for the 2018 Center for Fiction First Novel Prize. Visit LeesaCrossSmith.com.

INTERVIEW WITH
LEESA CROSS-SMITH

January 2019

CARVE

Last fall, we launched online fiction-writing classes based around stories from *Carve*'s archive. "Whiskey & Ribbons" is included in one of the lessons, and one of the students in the class loved the story and made a comment about how it should be a novel. So I commented back, "Great news. It is!"

The short story belongs just to one perspective, Evi's, and the novel belongs to three different perspectives: Evi's, Eamon's, and Dalton's. I wondered about your process expanding the story into a novel and embodying all three of these characters, and also building out Dalton's and Eamon's stories beyond the scope of the original story.

LEESA

First of all, thanks—that's really kind of the students to read and be sweet about it. Really, I found I couldn't stop thinking about the story, so it was as simple as that for me. When I was first getting things published it was always short fiction. I love short fiction, I love writing and reading short fiction. And there are some stories that are just short stories and that's all they can be—I'm not even interested in expanding them in any way. But "Whiskey & Ribbons" is special, because I couldn't stop thinking about it for years and years and years. I don't even know how many years. I think I got the original idea back in late 2000/early 2001.

I didn't end up making it a completed short story until 2010, and then I still found myself thinking about it, wanting to "finish" the story, elaborate on what was going on, what had happened before, what happened directly afterward. It came pretty easily for me, that I wanted to make it longer, that I wanted to write about it some more. It just wouldn't leave me alone.

I don't like to speak in just magical ways and not give practical ideas for craft, but it really was just sort of magical and I couldn't stop thinking about it. I tried to write an entire book just from Evangeline's point of view, but I felt really claustrophobic. Her point of view is already a little claustrophobic. She's trapped in a circle of grief that's still so recent, and she has also had a baby, so she can't separate those things and won't be able to for a while. So I wanted to let her be claustrophobic and trapped—literally and figuratively trapped, because they're snowed in and she's also trapped in this *Groundhog Day* feeling.

To give the reader a little breathing room, it was important to be able to see what the guys were doing, to hear from the other people in her life about how they make a life together. How they made a life together before and how they make a life together afterward, when Eamon is gone.

Life is really hard, so I try to make things as easy on myself as I can. It was easier on me to write from all three points of view. So that's the reason I expanded it and why I expanded it the way that I did.

CARVE

I think this technique makes the reader's experience of the story so devastating and holistic. Realistic too, though. It shows how complicated and multifaceted and basically human the intimacy shared by these characters is when we can go into Eamon's head for a while and see Evi from his perspective.

I was also struck by how the scene that is in the *Carve* story actually happens toward the end of the novel. There's so much that builds up to it, so much history. Even in meeting Frances and Cassidy, these women who were important to Dalton—Frances is a huge part of the novel, and Cassidy is more present too. Is Frances in the story? I think only Cassidy is, and only on the edges of it.

LEESA

Evi definitely has Frances in the back of her mind. It's funny that I don't remember exactly, but the threat of Dalton's other women is there, and that's what's driving her.

CARVE

Yeah. How much of this backstory did you know when you wrote the original short story, and how much of it came later?

LEESA

I would say half. Maybe that's a weird answer, but when I dig into a short story with more than one major character I am always creating this life for them, whether it goes on the page or not. That's the only way I can decide what they have on, or what music they listen to, or how they take a coffee. There's that Anne Lamott quote, something like, "You should know what is in your character's pockets."

When I wrote the short story, I already knew how Dalton was with women. In my head, I thought that he probably had an on/off girlfriend, a complicated relationship that had something about it that he would find comforting. Even though I might not have it in the story, I knew it. I also knew his effect on women. Women just love him. That is easy for him. So Cassidy, the girl at the bike shop—in the short story, she's like, "Can you give me a ride?" And he says, "Of course," and then of course she falls in love with him on the way home because that's just how he is.

I had the foundation for a lot of those details, but since I wasn't writing from the boys' perspectives it didn't really go into the story. But when I couldn't stop thinking about the story, those were the things I couldn't stop thinking about. I wanted to know more about their relationship to Evi, and what the boys were like growing up, their relationship to each other, which I love. That relationship was an important part, a huge part, of the novel. I want to show their deep, crazy, wild love for each other, too.

I mean, in no way could I have written a novel about that story in 2011. I wrote about a hundred stories in between, and another novel. I avoided writing *Whiskey & Ribbons* the novel for a while because I didn't have a structure. I wasn't mature enough as a writer to be able to write it, so it took the time it needed to take.

CARVE

When did you begin writing, and what was your path to where you are now?

LEESA

I always wrote stories when I was a little girl. I used to look at my mom's magazines and there'd be a family in a picture, an ad for a washing machine or something. I would think about who they were. The dad, where he works. If they have a dog. Do they want to have another baby? Does the kid play baseball? That's where my writing started.

I have always been a voracious reader. And I wanted to be a writer, but it's hard to feel like that's something someone can really do. It sort of feels like a hobby, I think. Or maybe it's safer to say it's a hobby, that I have a real job and I write sometimes when I can find the time. But I still took creative writing classes in college and majored in English. I got a practical job using my writing skills when I got out of college and wrote obituaries at the newspaper. But then I thought, what if I wrote something and tried to get it published? What, then? So, I started there, in 2010.

CARVE

Carve posted a Q&A with you on the blog in 2013, and you talked about how winning the editor's choice award in the Raymond Carver contest was the first time you received money for your creative writing and it helped you start taking writing seriously. It made me smile to see the contest on your website under the heading "Special Things."

LEESA

It's a very special thing. I specifically remember that moment. It's so funny, because it was not fancy at all. I was sitting on my computer, eating. We don't have a microwave so whenever I cook something microwavable I have to actually cook it for a really long time in the oven. I had a microwave burrito, but I cooked it in the oven, so it took like an hour.

Anyway, I was sitting on the computer watching *Luther*, with Idris Elba, eating this burrito that had taken like an hour to cook, and then the news about the contest came on Twitter. *Carve* used to tweet out the winners and it said, "Leesa Cross-Smith, Whiskey & Ribbons." And I seriously had an out-of-body experience. I almost felt like someone was watching me eating a burrito, watching *Luther*, learning I'd won a prize. It was weird.

CARVE

That's amazing.

LEESA

It is, because I was embarrassed to enter in the first place. I didn't tell anybody that I'd entered, because if I don't tell anybody then I don't have to talk about it.

CARVE

So what happened after the contest? You published a collection, but did you keep submitting to journals? Did you start pitching agents?

LEESA

Yeah, I did get an email from an agent after the contest. At that time I was still working on my short story collection. I only had a young adult novel written and the agency wasn't interested in a young adult novel. I knew absolutely nothing about how any of that stuff worked, so it was super cool for them to contact me and ask me to query. But I didn't have anything, so I kept submitting stories and slowly putting my collection together. But feeling like "Whiskey & Ribbons" was a really solid story that people wanted to read helped propel me to feel like I had something worthy in that collection—something that someone could potentially want to publish, that people would want to read.

CARVE

Absolutely. Okay, so tell me about these pictures on your website of the Avett Brothers holding your collection.

LEESA

The artist who designed the cover for *Every Kiss A War*—I sent him pictures and ideas. It's my mouth on the cover, he painted an image of my mouth. His name is Jeremy Okai Davis, and he's best friends with Seth Avett. They've been best friends since college. I found him through some Avett Brothers posters or something like that, and we connected online. He is so awesome and talented.

I mention the Avett Brothers on the first page, and their best friend painted the cover, so I knew that they would be interested in at least seeing the book. And I knew Jeremy was going to be with them that weekend at a show, so I was like, "If you see them, take a picture of him holding my book and also his brother holding the book, pretty please." And he did.

CARVE

That's really sweet.

LEESA

He's awesome, and I was really lucky to connect with him.

CARVE

I read that this collection had the title *Everyone Breaks Everyone's Heart* at some point, but it was published under *Every Kiss A War*. What was the evolution of the title?

LEESA

When I first started putting it together, it was *Everyone Breaks Everyone's Heart*. It came from a line in one of the stories, a story called "Hem." The story is about a guy who is trying to get over a breakup and he's really depressed. He makes friends with another teacher at his school and one night they're out, and they end up sitting outside of his ex-girlfriend's house having a discussion about relationships and how hard it is when people break up. One of them says, "Everyone breaks everyone's heart."

That's the thread that goes through all of the stories in that collection—they're all about men and women and relationships, and I was thinking on that fact that everyone breaks everyone's heart, really, in a way. I mean, we all hurt each other. Forgiveness holds us. We need forgiveness.

The man who runs Mojave River Press, the publishing

company that ended up publishing *Every Kiss A War*, asked if I had any other titles. He thought we needed another title that stood out a little more. I still really loved *Everyone Breaks Everyone's Heart*, but I'd written another short story, published at *SmokeLong Quarterly*, that had a line about another relationship that was falling apart, a girl who was thinking that every kiss was like a war with this man in her life. So I suggested *Every Kiss is a War*, maybe? We dropped the "is," and it became *Every Kiss A War*, which kind of says the same thing as *Everyone Breaks Everyone's Heart*. It has that same feeling for me.

CARVE

Sure. I love "everyone breaks everyone's heart" as a line of dialogue, too.

LEESA

Yeah, me too.

CARVE

You have another collection and a novel coming out. What can you share about those projects?

LEESA

My short story collection is called *So We Can Glow*, and it's set to come out from Grand Central Publishing in spring 2020. It's a collection of stories all narrated by and focused on women, teenage women and older women and women of all different ages from all different backgrounds. At the heart of it, it's about women at crossroads, women having to make difficult decisions, women making the worst decisions of their lives and struggling with the men in their lives and the women in their lives and their relationships, being mothers and being wives and wanting to be alone, and at times being manipulated by men and at times trying to break from men completely or figure out how to live their lives beside men. That's the thread running through that entire collection.

I also have a novel called *This Close to Okay* that's set to come out in 2021 also from Grand Central. It's about a therapist who encounters and interrupts a man attempting to choose suicide. There's an element of suspense as the story unravels over a rainy Halloween weekend.

CARVE

I can't wait to read them. I apologize if this is an awkward way to ask this question: Do you still have a practical day job writing, or do you write your books full-time?

LEESA

You asked it just fine! No, I worked a practical day job from 2002 until early 2004, eight days before I had my daughter. I haven't worked a practical day job since then, and I was a homemaker. My husband has a corporate day job. He works and makes the money that allows us to eat and have a home, and I write.

CARVE

In your author bio, you identify first as a homemaker and then as writer. I was thinking about this in the context of the family throughline in your novel, how essential family is to your characters, and also how your work is getting a lot of really well-deserved attention. How do you balance that attention with your family life and your private writing life?

LEESA

My kids are older now, and I didn't even really get started submitting until both my kids were in school, once my daughter was in kindergarten and my son started going to a two-day-a-week preschool program at the church. I didn't get started writing seriously and submitting until I didn't have little babies in the house. I talk about this a lot, because I hear from new mommas that want to write or do write and/or read. I tell them, "You can always email me for encouragement and I'll tell you about how I didn't read a book for years. For years after my daughter was born, I did not read a book." And they'll say, "You mean write a book?" And I'll say, "No, read a book. I did not read a book, because I had two little ones." They're only two-and-a-half years apart, so I had two little babies and that was my job during the day, and that was fine. I didn't have time to do anything else.

Now, it's a lot different because my kids are older. My daughter's in high school and my son's in middle school. I have a lot more free time. I have a lot more time during the day and even in the evenings to work. When I was traveling on book tour, a lot of times my family would come with me, so we would get to do things together as a family. My kids could actually get school credit for a couple weeks, and we would go and do other things together too. We're big American history buffs, so if I had an event in a city that had something related to the Civil War or something else that interested us, we'd go see it. And then I could go do my event. It's easier for me now. I would not be sitting here saying the same thing if I was nursing a baby right now, if I had two little ones. But my kids are old enough to dress and feed themselves, so it allows me a lot more freedom.

But I really like the word "homemaker." I started putting it in my bios because I don't have an MFA, I chose not to get an MFA. And I wanted to be able to represent all the other moms out there—the women who are moms, and they like to do other things too. So, I'm a homemaker and also I write books. Since Eve, women have all been doing this—we're all more than one thing. Everyone is more than one thing, and we contain multitudes. I do like keeping that in my bio because I like the word. It's also my job. It's one of the jobs that I have.

CARVE

You also love baseball, I found out from the internet.

LEESA

I do.

CARVE

Where does your sportswriting live in your life?

LEESA

That's something I do just because I love it. I love reading about baseball. It's poetic and romantic and I just love the language of it. I love the game, and so I love reading about it. Every now and then I try my hand at writing about it, I get asked sometimes to write about it, and I jump on that as much as I can. But a lot of times, I just write it for myself.

A couple of years ago I kept a baseball journal. I would write about the baseball games I watched that week, what I was doing when I was watching the game, and put it up on Medium. When it's baseball season it's a huge part of my life, and I watch or listen to at least one game a night. I find it really soothing. I love the history behind it, how it's tied to American history and the Civil War. I have a pure joy for it.

CARVE

You've spoken a little bit about how it's not necessary to get an MFA to become a professional writer. There are so many other ways to learn and to develop community. I also see your work in conversation with other writers—you have a blurb on Kem Joy Ukwu's book—another *Carve* writer—and Roxane Gay and Alexander Chee have blurbed your work. Who have these writers been for you? And what has community looked like in your career?

I was really blessed to meet Roxane early on—in 2010, I want to say. I connected with her online, when she was editor of a literary magazine called *Bluestem Magazine*. I sent a story over there. I don't believe I knew who she was yet. Maybe we were friends on Twitter, but this was back when Roxane had like nine hundred followers and now she has over half a million— this was back in the day. I'm always out there looking for black women writers, and I loved everything that she wrote.

So I sent the story to her. She loved it and published it. And then I just started emailing her, basically, and asking her all kinds of questions about agents and putting collections together and stuff like that. To this day she has never been anything but super kind to me. I think that she represents so much, especially for black women and black women writers. She is so generous with her time, money, and energy. The first time we met, she took me out to dinner. Her kindness really blows me away. I really can't praise her enough. But I was nervous to ask her to look at my collection, because she's so busy. This was *Every Kiss A War*—I said something like, "Maybe if you have time to take a look at my collection..." But she just knocks stuff like that out. She's happy to help out emerging writers when she can. She's exceptionally generous and I adore her.

But again, I feel very fortunate I met her so early. She's just a gem. Alexander Chee and I also connected on social media. His writing is so elegant and lyrical. He's New York literati, so really it was a dream to have him blurb my novel.

When I first started submitting I also wanted to dig into the online writing community, and I made those connections through Twitter. I started reading the journals I wanted to be published in and then I looked at the writers' bios, clicking on their Twitters and websites and reading their stories, wherever they had been published. Then I started writing them either emails or tweets, tweeting at them about how much I loved their work if I found something I really loved. I still do that now. I love to talk about things that I read, that I love, what someone's doing on a sentence-level, or the story in general—whatever I love about it. I like to tell people specifics about what I love about what they're doing. I'm not a natural hater. I'm a lover! Doing that provided an easy way for me to dig into the community and to get to know people.

Then my husband and I started a literary magazine of our own, *WhiskeyPaper*. That was a great way for me to connect with a lot of other writers. At this point, we have published hundreds of stories, so that's a lot of writers. That's a lot of writers' connections. And it's something I truly, truly enjoy. The community that was born from that was extra icing on the cake.

CARVE

How did *WhiskeyPaper* come about?

LEESA

It was me sitting on the computer thinking, "I think I have good taste. Let's see what we can do." It was as simple as that. We opened submissions to short stories, and then we tightened it up and started asking for even shorter stories because I knew I'd be able to get them back quickly, if I was reading thousand-word stories. We wanted to have a quick turnaround and publish things that were a little lighter. A lot of writing is really, really dark. Even if the writing's dark, I like some light in there. So we focused on stories that were sweet, that had a little bit of lightness in them, and were short, so that I wouldn't get exhausted reading them. The rest of it just came together. I had no idea whether anyone would even submit, but once we got it going we were getting fifty, seventy-five stories a week.

CARVE

Faith and family are so much a part of *Whiskey & Ribbons*, and so much a part of your life too. What is the relationship between your spiritual community and your writing life?

LEESA

People can go different ways when they write Christian characters or characters with faith, but so often it's grotesque... as in, characters using Christianity as a weapon. You know what I'm saying?

I write characters who are Christian and they also live normal lives as well, or characters who are struggling with their faith but not completely rejecting it. They're trying to figure it out or figure out how it works in their lives. With *Whiskey & Ribbons* in particular, Evangeline and Eamon meet at church. Evangeline teaches the little ones in Sunday school and is a member of the church, but Eamon only works security there. He's not there because he's a member, but that's where they meet. And then she really has nothing else to lean on when she loses her husband when she's nine months pregnant. She just has Jesus. And in her eyes, what else can hold her up then, but a supernatural God? She has faith, and it's not perfect. It doesn't mean that she has an instant cure-all or a time machine. It just means that's how she's coping with life and the hand that life has dealt her.

I'm always trying to write about flawed people and real people, people who aren't trying to be preachy at all. I'm not interested in writing anything preachy or trying to make anyone feel bad. I am interested in how people are human, and faith is an important part of life for me and for a lot of people.

CARVE

Yeah, absolutely. For me, this thought is recalling your mention of touring with your book. I read your essay from last February in the *Oxford American* about speaking and reading and noise and quiet and gentleness. And I wondered what the relationship between gentleness and quietude and writing is for you.

LEESA

I wrote an essay for Poets & Writers about quiet books and writing quiet fiction, how it could be the kiss of death if a writer is querying and mentions "quiet."

CARVE

"A quiet story."

LEESA

Right. But I take "quiet" as a compliment, because it means what I set out to do is coming through. If someone says, "It's a quiet story," I'll say, "Thank you." Even if they really mean it like, "Grr."

I love reading about intimacy and tenderness, gentleness, like you were saying. So those are the things I like writing, too. In some books there's something hard on every page—there's a car crash and then the car explodes. That's fine. There are people who write that kind of stuff, there are movies geared toward those people. But I really like purposely slowed-down books, stories where you get to know the person, have breakfast with the person, have 2 a.m. conversations with the person. That's what I love to watch in my movies and that's what I like to read in the books I read. And that's what I like to write.

The world is really noisy and scary and bloody and violent and loud. As much as I can, I lean toward peace and quiet. Because I'm easily startled and I don't like a lot of noise. It's as simple as that.

CARVE

The Glimmering Hush is the title of that series, your column in the *Oxford American*. What is the glimmering hush?

LEESA

My editor there, who's really great, said we needed to come up with a title for it. I immediately thought The Glimmering Hush because I was thinking about a dreamy sort of quiet out there. I'm thinking, even when the world is loud, I can still look for the glimmering hush. Look for quiet, look off into the distance. Dream about a place and time where I can be away from all this and see, almost like an illusion, a shimmering quiet that has its little cartoon finger swirled at me, saying, "Come over here. It's quiet over here."

CARVE

I love that image. It reminds me of a review of your work that I read, which talked about the nostalgia of memory and the magic of place in your writing. For me that begged the question of Southern-ness, which I've seen mentioned elsewhere in relation to your work. How do you perceive that term? How do you think about place?

LEESA

As with faith and religion and Christianity, a lot of times in literature and on TV you'll see the South portrayed in a way that is cliché or stereotypical or grotesque. Like, TV only wants to talk about certain things when it talks about the South, like exaggerated accents or racism. Things that are, yes, a part of the South and the South's history. But there are also a lot of other things too.

As a black girl from Kentucky, it's already a conversation. People are like, "I didn't know black people lived in Kentucky." A lot of black people live in Kentucky! A lot. There's a lot of us here. And my husband is white. Look at that! There are mixed families in Kentucky. A lot of them!

The rest of my family's from Alabama, so I grew up in the South. I love the South, but thinking about trying to represent it in my writing—it's really just normal, because that's where the characters live. But it's set in Kentucky, so it's a Southern book to a lot of people.

Writing books with Southern elements is a natural result of my life in Kentucky. I set my stories here because I want to read stories about all kinds of people in Kentucky, because that's where I'm from. Everyone likes to look for books that they can connect to—like, "Oh, I'm from where this book is set, or my mom's from there." People love that sort of thing.

So *Whiskey & Ribbons* is set in Louisville, Kentucky. Now, if someone wanted to read a book about Louisville, they would be disappointed in that book because my characters are snowed in for a lot of the book, so they stay in the house. So that part really could be set anywhere, I guess. But it's not. It's set here because I wanted it to be set here, because that's where I am.

Also, all of my books have Kentucky roots but of course, I love writing about other places, too. I write often of California and the desert because those places hold a special spot in my heart forever. But Kentucky is where my characters make their homes.

CARVE

Do you have any sense of who reads, or who you hope will read, your work?

LEESA

I don't know if I know the answer to that. If my work is categorized as women's fiction, I'm a hundred percent okay with that because I love women and I'm writing stories about and for women. Also, as a black woman, I didn't see myself represented that much in the books I read when I was younger. I would always be really excited for black women to pick up my books and feel like they were represented in them, in a way they would like to be represented. That would be really important to me.

I would also say, Christians who are living normal lives. Christians who aren't necessarily Republicans. People who contain multitudes in general. And also, people who are looking for hope.

I'm a writer who really wants to take care of her characters. There's a Jane Austen quote, "My characters shall have, after a little trouble, all that they desire." I've always kind of thought of myself as a writer like that. I'm here to take care of my characters. I feel like I'm a safe writer when it comes to that. And that's another thing that, like the "quiet" stories, could be a kiss of death. But I like those things, quiet and safe. I mean, who doesn't want to be quiet and safe?

When people tell me that they read one of my books and it felt like curling up with a blanket or a cup of tea—those are my favorite things. That's how I feel about some of my favorite writers, like Maeve Binchy and Jane Austen. There are so many different kinds of books and so many different kinds of ways of being a writer, but that's my favorite way of being a writer, and those are my favorite books.

CARVE

I read *Whiskey & Ribbons* in an afternoon, curled up on the couch. It is the kind of novel that you can fall into, even though it deals with difficult feelings. There's jealousy and there's grief. But I think that your gentleness and care as a writer makes it possible for the reader explore those feelings without just feeling devastated.

LEESA

Thank you. That's such a compliment, one that I always appreciate.

CARVE

I am also in love with the voice of your author website—how you have all of these lists, things that are included in your work or that you're inspired by, things connected by ampersands. For example, your first book: "Twenty-seven little stories about love & light & boys who listen to Neil Young & girls who listen to Liz Phair & Kentucky & whiskey & fireworks & fights & baseball & cowboys & complicated feelings & kitchen kisses." And you have a huge, comprehensive list on your homepage.

LEESA

I add to that list probably once a week.

CARVE

It has links in it, too. I could spend hours going through that list and clicking on things.

LEESA

Thank you! I'm starting to think it's getting pretty long, but people can read whatever part they want. The list you just read, about *Every Kiss A War*—that's how I think. Bless my agent's heart—that's how I write her my ideas. When I first sent her my new short story collection, I was like, "It's about kissing & high school & teenage girls & moms & summer & pink & nostalgia & best friends & sex & boys, etc. " That's how I frame things, what's jumping out to me. It's sort of the way I outline. That's how my brain works.

CARVE

What mantra is guiding your recent work?

LEESA

My manuscripts are due very soon, so right now my mantra is, "Get it done." That's not very artistic or whatever, but it really is such an important part of the process. The fun is in starting a story, having an idea for a story, but if you don't get it done it doesn't really matter. So whenever I talk to people who ask me for writing advice, I tell them—and I say the same thing to my daughter, who's a lovely writer—"You have to finish your story."

Finish your story. Finish your book. You have to finish it or you don't have anything. When you want to query, you have to have something that's finished. When you want to submit a story, you have to have something that's finished. Going back to your previous question, the lists I have about the stories—a list is not a story. That is an idea, those are elements of a story. But you have to actually open the file, start at the beginning, or wherever you wanna start—and then finish it. Have a completed project.

So definitely, "Get it done." It's the same as with any aspect of the literary community, whether you're putting a magazine together, reading submissions, writing, doing a blog post. At some point, you have to actually get it done. And that's the part that I think is lost sometimes—you know #AmWriting on Twitter, which is a nightmare anyway... if you're actually trying to get something done you can't be on Twitter at all. Or at least, I can't. Too distracting. I delete all that stuff from my phone and get to work so I can get it done.

When I was finishing up one of the earliest drafts of my forthcoming novel, I wrote almost 30,000 words in a month because I had to get the book done. I had to get the book written, then we could do all that other stuff. The hard work is actually sitting down at the computer for hours and hours and hours. It's not nearly as fun or as pretty or as exciting as taking a picture of the book and putting it on Instagram or tweeting about it, but that's the part that has to get done to get you there.

Demetrius

KEM JOY UKWU

December 2011

I turn twenty-five today. My birthday party will start later this evening. If my mother were here, this party would be in her honor as well. I was born on her twenty-fifth birthday.

I was her gift, wrapped in blood and goo. It was the twenty-fifth of September when the nurse handed me over to her. She held me, looked down at my face, and shook her head. That's how my older half-sister, Chioma, recalled it. She didn't tell me about her not wanting me. That part I figured on my own after I learned that my mother left my father, my half-sister, and me the next day with a written note that said, "I'm sorry," placed on top of $10,000 in cash. The money was her gift to me. I have yet to spend it.

It currently sits in a savings account, collecting dust and interest. My father opened the account the following day after reading that note. Chioma told me that he sat in the living room on the green fake-leather couch we still own, reading that note for the first time as if it was one of his students' term papers. He sat on the couch for hours, Chioma insists, holding the crinkled white piece of goodbye with both hands.

"He wasted time with that note," Chioma said years ago to me. "Like he wasted time with that woman."

She sat down next to me on the same couch after we had returned from his service at the funeral parlor a few blocks away from St. Cornelius College, where he'd taught English. He wanted to be cremated. I insisted this to Chioma after she commented on the shame of the situation.

"The only reason, Obi, that he wanted to be cremated was because he knew there was no one back home to collect him properly."

As far as Chioma was concerned, home was Nigeria. She was born and raised there. She referred to the fact that our father had no siblings, no parents, and therefore no aunties nor uncles nor cousins. He had his first set of in-laws and then lost them when he married my mother only one month after Chioma's mother's death. The falling in love part with my mother happened before Chioma's mother passed away. That's how Chioma likes to remember it.

We sat there on the couch, talking. Chioma said one thing and I countered. Chioma always wins. She has a beautiful talent with words. She uses them with the grace of an eagle and the ruthlessness of a dictator. She's an attorney.

"Things will be different now."

"How so?"

"Well, I had planned to move back to Lagos and live with Aunty Grace after graduation. That is no longer my plan. Someone needs to be here with you."

"I'm eighteen."

"And?"

"I'm old enough to take care of myself."

"Rubbish." One of Chioma's favorite words. "I have connections from Swade & Marks. I can surely land a position in their New York office after I graduate. That firm is not the best, but it will be suitable for me. In the meantime, you need to work on your college applications. Which schools will you apply to?"

"St. Cornelius."

"Rubbish. You will apply to Cornell, NYU, and Fordham."

"I can't get into those schools."

"How have your grades been?"

"I am a proud B student."

"Daddy did not push you with your schoolwork?"

"My grades weren't everything to him."

"They should have been *something*. The first question Daddy always asked me, even before he greeted me, was *how are your studies*?"

I didn't share this with Chioma—and I don't think I ever will—but I knew why he asked her that question and why his first question to me was *did you eat*? He knew that she was, as they say, destined for greatness.

As for me, I didn't know what I was destined to do, who I was ordained to be. I still don't. And my father knew that I didn't know. And I think he believed that I would never find the answer.

"You're good with school stuff," I noted.

"Well, you should be too. You need to figure out what you are going to do with your life, Obioma. I will not be here with you forever."

I knew that to be true. And seven years later, sitting here on this green couch waiting for my party to start, I know it now. My sister's family's luggage waits by our front door.

. . .

I remember Chioma's wedding. The church ceremony took place in Lagos. The event was a bright collage of yellows, purples, blues, and oranges showcased by long shirts and pants, dresses and tall headscarves that belittled gold and diamond crowns. It was, I knew, the happiest day of Chioma's life. And not-so-ironically, the saddest of mine.

I was one of her bridesmaids. It was a special honor to wear the dark purple sundress. She sternly lectured me in her

Aunt Grace's dining area a few days before her wedding as she drank a cup of her Earl Grey tea. She sat up straight, looking through bridal magazines she'd brought from the States, even though she finished her wedding planning long ago.

"When it is your turn, you will understand."

I laughed in response.

"Ah, that is right, no wedding for Obi. She will get married by a justice of the peace."

"It would be cheaper. More practical, don't you think?" I argued.

"More selfish. How could you do that? How could you not involve your family, your community?"

I shrugged and said no more. I stood, ninth in a line of ten bridesmaids and her matron of honor, looking over at her inside the church. As the sun shined at her through stain-colored windows, I knew that I was losing her, even though she was never fully mine. I only had half her blood and not even half her time.

Chioma has always been quite the independent. Soon after I was born, she returned to Nigeria to live with one of her mother's four sisters. She attended a top-notch boarding school, staying with her Aunt Grace during vacation intervals, keeping in contact with our father by phone while he was here in the States raising me alone. She came back to the States once every couple of years to visit our father and me. She moved back here semi-permanently to attend college, but not at St. Cornelius as our father originally wanted.

She chose Fordham and often snickers with regret about not choosing Cornell instead. That was one of the many sacrifices she made to be close to her family, she laments, moving to the Bronx instead of to the land of Ivy. After graduating *summa cum laude* in three years instead of the classic four, she moved to Ithaca to attend law school at Cornell, making up for her unforgivable error of passing it up for undergrad.

She accomplished this almost all on her own, rarely asking our father for money, even though he was always ready to provide it.

Two months after our father passed, she agreed to marry Kenechukwu Agbochukwu, a fourth-year medical student at Johns Hopkins. They met through his parents, who are friends with Chioma's aunts. It only took a few months for her to accept that he was the one. He traveled from Baltimore to our father's service to support Chioma, which she appreciated.

I asked Chioma if she loved him the same day I received her bridesmaid lecture in her Aunt Grace's large estate in Lagos.

She said yes, of course.

"What about him do you love?"

"Sense," Chioma answered simply. "The man has it. Many men waste time. Ken does not."

Chioma was correct, Ken didn't waste time. He proposed to Chioma only after knowing her for a few months.

And there they were, the woman who gave up Cornell once and the man with lots of sense, exchanging vows before their God and 300 of their closest family and friends.

Her matron of honor, Lynne Okocha, the only attendant Chioma selected to wear an evening gown instead of the sundress, told me during their packed reception that she was proud of *her* best friend for making such a wise selection, picking Ken to be her lifelong mate.

I wanted to pointedly reply to her, "I should be wearing your gown."

. . .

I didn't realize until a few days later after their wedding that I wasn't going to lose Chioma altogether just yet. She and Ken decided to move into our father's house. Both Chioma and Ken had finished their graduate education, and it would benefit them both to begin their respective careers in law and medicine in the States, specifically New York, where they could make connections that would serve them in the long run. And most sensibly, they could live in our father's house in White Plains and save money by not having to pay rent. That was how Chioma explained it to me at the Murtala Muhammed Airport in Lagos, during her third day as Mrs. Dr. Ken Agbochukwu.

"It makes sense," she concluded, before we said our goodbyes.

I flew back to New York after that news and waited two weeks for Chioma and Ken to move in after they returned from their honeymoon in Italy. I geared up to start my college life at St. Corn's. They offered me a full tuition scholarship to matriculate there (a sympathy token for my father's death) and I couldn't say no, which is what I explained to Chioma over the phone, weeks before her wedding.

"Congratulations," she said. "Did you hear back from Cornell or NYU? Fordham?"

"No," I lied. "Haven't heard yet."

"Call their admissions offices and follow up."

"I will," I said, knowing very well that I wouldn't. They had all rejected me, which didn't hurt at all as I only saw myself at St. Corn's. But I couldn't lie further to say that I actually got in. She would've slapped me with her sandpaper palms if I had been accepted to any of those schools and didn't go. I hoped she would forget eventually, with all of her life-planning going on with Ken. But I knew better. Chioma forgets nothing.

We had one week of shared time after they returned from their honeymoon and before I moved half of my belongings to my dorm at St. Corn's to start my freshman year.

"You living there is pure rubbish, Obi," she said to me as I packed up my clothes in my bedroom. She stood against my door, folding her arms. "The campus is walking distance from here. What? You cannot walk to your classes?"

Of course, I could have. I walked to their campus at least every other day after our father passed, hoping to find him walking around, carrying his books by Márquez, Achebe, and his personal favorite, Austen, wearing one of his colorful sweaters and New York Yankees cap (he was the only Nigerian man I knew who loved baseball). I walked around the small campus for hours, believing it would've only been a matter of time before I would catch him.

"Sure I could. I could also walk to class from one of their dorms."

"You would save money by living here."

Save money or save sanity? I picked the latter. I zipped up our father's suitcase and hauled it out of the room, bypassing Chioma and her floral perfume. I walked down the stairs and encountered once again their boxes and luggage, reminders to me of the true reason I wanted to live far, far (all of ten minutes) away.

I knew that I would stop by once or twice a month, not to say hello or to do laundry, but to show my face. To remind her that I existed. That this house was also mine.

. . .

Chioma has an eye for redecoration. She rarely allows herself to watch television, she disdains the uselessness of it, but on the very few occasions she has turned on the flat-screen in the living room, the channel always featured a show about home makeovers. She and Ken wanted to renovate the entire house to reflect their style. They started with their bedroom. Then the kitchen.

Our kitchen was in need of repair. Cracks decorated the tile floor, and the chipped white paint on the walls was friendly, always greeting me after entry. Chioma always complained about them to my father during her visits when he was alive and then to me after he passed. It bothered her enough to offer snippy comments but not enough to do something about it. Until she got married.

I came to visit one weekend during my freshman year and entered the kitchen and got lost.

"Welcome!" shouted the mahogany cabinets and granite countertops. The old appliances were now brand new concoctions that looked too beautiful to be actually defined, let alone used. I stood, trying to convince myself that I was standing in my house.

"Beautiful and clean. That is how everything should be," Chioma stated as she entered the kitchen behind me, startling me.

"It's quite lovely," I said. "How long did it take for you to do this?"

"Two weeks. It should have taken three, but we paid extra for less time."

"Very efficient."

"You know me well."

Chioma left. Still stunned, I smiled. I felt like I had won something without playing.

I decided to sleep over that evening and after waking up the next morning, strolling down the stairs to the living room, my eyes caught a wall. I had never seen that blue wall bare. Dust and lint outlined the shape of a sofa. I paused and then continued my steps.

I walked into euphoria where Chioma and Ken were eating French toast and scrambled eggs on plates I had never seen before. Perhaps new china.

"Good morning, Obioma," Chioma greeted. Ken looked up from reading *The New York Times* and nodded towards my direction, his usual hello.

There was a time that I resented her calling me Obioma. That's my middle name. It means "good heart" in Igbo, Chioma's native language that I have yet to master (or learn).

"Chioma" means "good God." Chioma has often joked to me that you can never have a good heart without a good God. I have repeatedly wished that she would address me by my first name, Colleen. After time, it has annoyed me less and less. I think it's because I'm grateful that she addresses me at all. But when I heard "Obioma," after not seeing our couch that morning, my heart didn't feel good—in effect, it burned.

"Where's the couch?"

"We gave it away this morning," Chioma answered, taking a sip of her orange juice. "It was too ugly to sell."

"Why did you do that?"

"Ken is going to renovate the living room."

My arms began to tremble. I wanted to grab her shoulders and shake her like salt over those perfectly assembled eggs on her unblemished china.

"I want it back."

"You want that old thing? What for?"

"Doesn't matter," I said. "You should've asked me first."

"Ken knows what would look good here."

My hand shot up, my pointer finger pointing at Chioma's doctor-man. And then, it came out.

"This is not his home!"

Ken folded up his newspaper. He stood up from his stool by the counter and walked out of the kitchen.

Chioma is the most beautiful when she looks like she wants to kill someone. Her dark chocolate skin and thick lips—gifts from her mother—look nothing like my light cappuccino-colored face, sprinkled with the lightest of brown freckles: gifts, I assume, from mine.

The only features we share are our father's eyes—big, dark brown saucers. And at that moment, they were paper-cutting me in two.

"What is his is mine and what is mine is his," said Chioma, her voice low and even. How I wished she had yelled instead. I could've charged her next delivery to pure frustration, rather than an icy, numbing truth.

"If you had a husband, Obi, you would understand that."

She meant to say if I had someone, anyone.

The next morning after I said the un-say-able in their new kitchen, I noticed the couch had returned. I knew it wasn't Chioma's doing. She doesn't believe in take-backs.

I thought Ken brought it back because I scared him with my *to-hell-with-you* statement. I think what I said, despite my callous release, made sense to him. He knew this house wasn't his place of permanence. It was just somewhere to live for the time needed. Why waste money on additional renovations when it was only a matter of time when they would move back to Nigeria? He probably wanted to thank me.

I entered the kitchen, where he sat by the counter on the same stool from the previous morning, reading *The New York Times* again, Sunday edition. He nodded towards me. I nodded back. I noticed there was no cup of coffee by him, so I decided to pour him some. I grabbed a Cornell mug from the brand-new cupboard and the pot with already-brewed coffee resting in it. I filled the mug slowly, wondering what he was thinking.

I placed my caffeinated apology on the counter next to him.

"I already had some, thank you," he said. "You can leave that for Chioma, she should be downstairs shortly."

I left the mug and walked out of the house, through the back door at the other end of the kitchen. I didn't want to see Chioma kiss her husband's cheek, ignoring the Cornell mug with steaming wake-up juice.

. . .

During the spring semester of my senior year, I called Chioma to wish her a happy birthday. It was then that she told me she was five months pregnant.

"Twins. Boys. Such a blessing," Chioma said.

"Congratulations," I said. I think I had an idea she was expecting. Last time I saw her, two months before, she looked a bit heavier and was annoyingly joyful.

"You are going to be an aunty of two. Praise God."

"Really, Chioma," I said, trying to pitch my voice higher. "That's wonderful."

"I do not know how this will affect my chances of making partner." It was Chioma's goal to move back to Nigeria as a full-fledged partner at her firm and start up an office there. Oil production and such, lots of opportunities, she said. She would make that firm global, she insisted.

"You do good work, I'm sure," I said.

"With twins, I will have to cut back in hours. Unless I find suitable daycare by the time they arrive."

"I don't have a job lined up yet, I can watch your babies until you make daycare arrangements."

Chioma waited a beat. "Thank you, Obi. That is a fantastic idea. Your help would be very much appreciated."

"My pleasure. Happy birthday," I said. I thought I was an idiot then after I said I would care for her newborns. I realize now why I offered my gift. Time is such a wonderful present. The value is only noticed when it's lost.

On and off for almost three years, I cared for her sons. I wiped their bottoms and changed their diapers. I fed them, bathed them, soothed them, and taught them how to give high-fives. Anytime Chioma or Ken was at work, building their careers, setting up bricks for their empires, I held down this half-renovated fort.

And I loved it. Much to my own surprise as I'm usually not a fan of children.

With the exception of a part-time babysitter who watched them while I worked at my part-time job at a local bookstore three days a week, I was here. I like to think that I left a mark on my nephews but now I'm sure they'll forget me. I'll become that Post-It note on a cover of a book, there but not a part of the story.

Aunty Miscellaneous.

I try not to think of my nephews when they're not standing in front of me.

. . .

My birthday party will start soon. I realize this after I look at the time on my outdated cell phone, one that doesn't have a camera and doesn't flip open. It's quite old, but I haven't yet found the desire to upgrade it.

Chioma is excited about this party; it was her idea and she planned it. Invitees include Ken and the twins and a few of her friends from her days at Fordham.

My three college friends are also on the invite list, but can't attend. I don't take it personally as all of them live far away: one's in Arizona, another lives in England, and the other lives in Philadelphia.

Chioma stressed to me that I should create a Facebook page to help me keep in contact with them. "The application is highly useful," she told me two months ago after she announced that she, Ken, and the twins were moving to Nigeria permanently.

We were in our kitchen. She manned the counter by the stove, preparing dinner. I sat by the kitchen counter island in the middle, flipping through a beauty magazine, pretending that I wasn't fully present in the conversation.

"It will be a wonderful way for us to keep in touch. You would know everything that is going on with the boys, Ken, me," Chioma said as she chopped onions.

"Everyone else would know too," I countered.

"Yes. That is why it is efficient."

I remained silent, choosing to focus on the comforting, enticing smell of the stew she was preparing. The aroma, fresh and stout with basil, oregano, and curry, filled up the kitchen. I promised silently then that I'd tell her how much joy eating her stew gives me before she leaves for Nigeria. Now, I don't know. Maybe I'll let her know on Facebook.

"I'm going to sign the house over to you," Chioma said, placing the onion slices in the pot. A declaration. As if she was going to pass on a mantle or a crown.

The house was already mine. Mine and hers. But now, it would be just my own. I should've had a celebratory thought about that, but I didn't.

"When are you leaving?"

"We bought tickets for the twentieth but we are changing our flights for the twenty-sixth."

"Why?"

"Do not be silly. We will not leave before your birthday," Chioma replied. "Actually, we are going to throw a party for you."

My next question was going to be a repeated "Why?" but I dropped it, not wanting to sound ungrateful.

I do feel grateful, sitting here in the living room, looking at all of the decorations. Purple balloons filled with helium, tied with white strings, float by the entryway into the kitchen and the stairs. My eyes make my way back to their luggage, waiting idly by the front door.

They'll leave tomorrow morning. I decide to leave now.

I stand up, grab my keys from the end table, and walk to the front door. My steps have always been light. That's why I don't worry that Chioma, Ken, and the twins, all upstairs, might hear me. They won't. And all's well.

. . .

I walk to St. Corn's. In late September, there is much buzz and restless activity on campus. The academic year has recently started and students are walking about. Two students are throwing a football around on the main quad. Daylight is ending, and the sky is layered with stripes of orange and purple. The air is still warm, as if summer is a houseguest and doesn't want to leave quite yet.

I grow jealous. It's been three years since I've graduated and that should have been enough time to get over that I'm no longer a student. I want to walk around here as if I still have options, possibilities, friends that I see every day, an active social life, excitement about my future. I remind myself that twenty-five is not old.

I walk to Crest Hall, my dormitory during my last two years there. It's also the building where a plaque was placed in the lobby, one that honored my father. He was a superstar of sorts here. His colleagues adored him. I knew this because many of them, who taught me in several classes, told me. As I walk, I now realize why he loved and needed this place. It was because it loved and needed him back.

I wonder if he ever felt that way with anyone outside of here. I guess he hadn't. Maybe not even with me. Perhaps I had reminded him too much of my mother. I do share her first name. I never asked him why he named me after her. And I would never ask Chioma now that he's dead. Her response— I'm certain—would be, "Because the man did not have sense."

I wonder if I should be brave and ask her when I return home, just to see if I'm correct. I change my mind, knowing how she reacts whenever the topic of my mother comes up.

Chioma's mother was perfect. I know this from the large portrait of her that hangs on the wall above the stairway. Chioma placed it there after she and Ken moved in, along with photos of her aunts and cousins, pictures of Ken's immediate and extended family, and photos of the boys.

Chioma's mother wears a red collared blouse in the picture. Her small, round afro caps her round head like a glove. Her blood-colored lips match her blouse and they are smiling. Not widely, just enough to show satisfaction. Just how Chioma smiles.

As I open the door to Crest Hall, I wonder if I should steal our father's plaque to hang it next to Chioma's mother. I decide against it as I see a security guard sitting behind a desk. He asks to see my student ID.

I balk. We never needed to show our IDs to the guards when I was a student.

"I just want to hang out in the main lounge, watch some television."

The guard waits.

"I'm alumni."

The guard shrugs.

I leave the dorm. As I'm walking, I think about my father. I think about Chioma. A realization hits me, overwhelming me. I know what I want to do. My decision is a surrendering, but also a step—or leap—forward. As I reach the brick campus gates, I know where I'm going next. I hope that I'm not too late and that their doors are still open.

. . .

It's one o'clock in the morning. I step inside the house and the kitchen light is on. Fear hits me. I walk towards the light and much to my relief, no one is there. Just presents on top of the counter. I take Chioma's gift. I recognize it right away because it's the only box perfectly wrapped with purple ribbons. As I bring it upstairs with me, I notice that all of their hanged photos on the stairway wall are gone.

. . .

I wake up. I look over to my alarm clock. 6:15. Their cab will arrive at ten. I close my eyes and nestle my head further onto my pillow. I let Chioma believe that I'm in a deep slumber when she opens the door an hour later to check in on me. I wonder if she knows that I know that she has been doing that for years, at night and in the morning, opening my door slightly to see if I'm resting. I always hear the creak of the door and even when I'm sleeping, it always wakes me. And I always keep my eyes closed.

She closes my door. I hear her say to Ken, "Obi is sleeping, I do not want to wake her."

"She knows that we are leaving today," Ken replies. "She should be up."

"She will rise soon," Chioma asserts. "She is not daft."

I hear my nephews squealing, being their jubilant selves. Their noises remind me of when Chioma and I discussed their names when she was eight months pregnant. It was the day after my graduation from St. Corn's. I was sitting on the couch, watching television. When Chioma sat down next to me, I immediately changed the channel to some show about first-time homeowners.

"Ken wants to give them American names," she said as she nestled her butt on a cushion. "Matthew and Paul."

"They're also biblical names," I pointed out.

"Yes, they are. Well noted."

I nodded. After a few moments of silence, an idea landed in my mind, softly like a feather. This idea, I knew, was beautiful.

"Why don't you and Ken name one of them after Dad?"

"Dee-mee-tree-us," Chioma said, as if she was trying on the name like a pair of jeans, to see if it fit. Then came her verdict.

"I do not prefer it."

Matthew and Paul were born a month later. And three years later, they have grown into mini-men, with minds as strong as their mother's and as whip-smart as their father's. They know how to read, how to use the toilet, and of course, how to say "No." Only to me, of course. Dare they say no to their mother? No one says no to Chioma.

I would've broken that rule if she asked me to move with her to Nigeria when she first told me they were leaving. I would've said a long, drawn-out, humor-intended "no."

She didn't ask. And I didn't want her to. I wanted a threat instead. I had hoped she would order me with her voice, iced with a snarl, to pack my stuff and move with them. She would've done so to Ken and her boys if they indicated in any way that they had no interest in moving. And she would've done this rightfully so, for they belong to her. As I remove my comforter from my body and sit up on my bed, I allow myself to accept, like a failing grade, that I don't.

But that doesn't matter, not anymore, because I have also allowed myself to accept that I still want to be close to them, even if by physical space alone, even though they no longer need me, or may have never needed me.

My hardwood floor is cold. My feet tell me that they're unhappy as I stand up and walk over to my bedroom door. I open it and Chioma stands there, waiting.

I expect a comment about last night. My disrespectful no-show. My rude absence.

"I prepared breakfast," Chioma says. "We will eat when you are ready."

I want to tell her what I did yesterday. Instead, I say, "Your stew is wonderful."

Chioma raises an eyebrow. "I did not make stew," she says. "I made eggs."

She turns around and walks down the stairs.

. . .

Five minutes to ten and the cab is full with their luggage. Chioma and Ken decided not to take any of their new furniture with them. They, with their sons, are moving to a house Ken's parents built for them in Abuja. The house is fully furnished and there's no need to bring anything more than clothes and other essentials, Chioma told me some time ago. They'll travel to Lagos first to stay with her Aunt Grace and then they'll make their trek to Nigeria's capital.

I'm dressed with the clothes I had originally planned to wear for my party the night before, black pants and a dark green V-neck sweater with gold fringes on the sleeves. My black high-heeled shoes complete the ensemble. I'm ready for a party but right now I'm not going anywhere but the front porch. I welcome this irony.

The boys are nestled in their car-seats in the backseat of the yellow mini-van cab. I choose not to hug them good-bye. I tell myself that I will see them very soon.

I wave to them and smile. I say, "Be good."

Ken stands by the cab. I really don't know what to say to him. I could say, "Take care of Chioma," but he already does that. Even "goodbye" seems disingenuous. All I say to him, as I stand on the porch and Chioma stands beside me, is "Good luck."

Another useless thing to say, he doesn't need it. Neither does his wife. I know this as I look at her. She turns to face me.

Her straight-permed hair offers a hilarious contrast to my never-say-die reddish-brown afro. I should laugh out loud from this observation but I don't feel like it. I notice the air suddenly becoming cool, and I place my hands in my pockets to warm them up. I recall yesterday's warm weather and wonder why Mother Nature made this change now instead of later today or tomorrow.

"I plan to wire $500 dollars every month to your account, starting in October, when we're settled in Abuja," Chioma says to me.

"Why?"

"Do not ask me that rubbish question. It is not much, but hopefully with your income, it will suffice to assist you with bills and other expenses."

I want to tell her to keep her money, that I don't want it. But saying no wouldn't change anything, she'd do it anyway.

"The money will be wired to the bank with your first savings account," she says.

"I don't use that account."

"You will start."

I shrug and accept my defeat. I try to keep my mood light by admiring the orange leaves falling from the tree by our porch. Their varied shades are bright, vibrant, hopeful.

"Thanks."

"No gratitude is needed. It is the right thing to do."

I nod and wait. Her face changes. She inhales and then exhales. Her cheeks perk up and she smiles at me.

"I love you," she says.

I freeze. It's the first time she says it to me. She knows that I know this.

I relax my shoulders and return her smile. "I bought a ticket for a flight to Lagos leaving next week."

Chioma maintains her smile. "It would be fantastic to have you visit us."

I clear the fear dangling in my throat. "It's a one-way. I was thinking that I could live with you. Help you with the boys. Or I could move into an apartment close by. I would come back here eventually to sell the house but living in Nigeria close to you would be good for me. Don't you think so?"

Chioma's face returns to the one I know. "No, I do not. It is not a smart idea. We will discuss it later. Call me."

I feel like scalding hot water has spilled on me. Pain stops me from offering a rebuttal.

Chioma turns and walks to the cab, where Ken is standing, holding the door open to let her in. I watch Chioma step into the cab and seat herself next to her boys. Ken shuts the door and walks around to the front passenger seat. He gets in and shuts the door, and the cab drives off.

I turn around slowly to face my house. I enter it and close the door. I take off my shoes and walk to the living room. I see Chioma's wrapped gift sitting on my green monstrosity. I brought it downstairs earlier this morning, hoping I would open it in front of her.

I take the box and rip off its shiny wrapping. I open the box to find a phone, one that you can type with. One of those elite, fancy types. Also in the box are a charger and a manual. I nod and think to myself, she *is* efficient.

I still feel the burn from Chioma's last words to me, though the sting no longer hurts. It's as if the sharp pain is freeing me from something I never knew I was trapped in. I can't pinpoint the feeling and I don't care to. I run with it.

I will go to the mall to have my present activated with my phone number. Before I do that, I will return to the copy center there to use one of their computers, perhaps the same one I used to purchase my flight yesterday after I left St. Cornelius. I will cancel my ticket and cancel my Facebook page that I created last night.

Then, I will go to the furniture store. Using money from my never-touched savings account, I will re-decorate this place—my home—and all of the rooms in it.

Except the kitchen. I will leave it alone. If I never see my half-sister again, I have decided that the perfect mahogany cabinets and shiny tiled floors will efficiently act and serve in her place.

KEM JOY UKWU's debut short story collection *Locked Gray/Linked Blue: Stories* was published by the Kindred Books imprint of Brain Mill Press. Her fiction has appeared in *Auburn Avenue, PANK, BLACKBERRY: a magazine, Carve, TINGE, Blue Lake Review, Jabberwock Review, The Brooklyn Quarterly,* and *Day One.* As an Institute Scholar, she led a workshop each for the 2016 and 2018 Writing from the Margins Institute at Bloomfield College. Born and raised in the Bronx, she currently lives in New Jersey with her husband.

INTERVIEW WITH
KEM JOY UKWU

January 2019

CARVE
What do you recall about your process writing "Demetrius"?

KEM
In terms of my writing journey, "Demetrius" was my second short story that was published in a literary magazine after I made a commitment to write more stories on a consistent basis. I was very proud that "Demetrius" was published in *Carve*.

The beginnings of "Demetrius" came from a one-day intensive course that I took, and the idea was a scene with two sisters. I forget how much I wrote out at that time, but I wrote out at least a scene and then I just continued on with the story, a story about a young woman who is about to say goodbye to one of the very small number of family members that she knows and talks to. "Demetrius" included a kind of estrangement she experienced while living with her sister and her family. Her journey demonstrated how estrangement doesn't always exist just in terms of family members not talking—estrangement could exist with family members living together and talking to each other, yet still with a sense of disconnection. A lot of my work deals with the emotional disconnections between family members and friends.

CARVE
While reading your collection, *Locked Gray/Linked Blue*, I made

a list of themes that I saw recurring—this is obviously not a comprehensive list of the themes of your book—but I noticed so much about intimacy and family, trust and skepticism, and social contracts between people, like friendship or marriage or sisterhood. There's so much connection and disconnection across these stories, and also reconciliation, or not. I also pulled this quote: "Nothing, including love, is fully curable." Do these themes persist in your recent work?

KEM

Absolutely. It took me a while to realize what I wanted to write about most. When I started writing on a regular consistent basis, I basically had to learn about what mattered the most to me as a writer, in terms of the stories I would tell. I realized that the emotional experiences of people who are trying and sometimes failing to relate to those whom they care about—those were the themes and the ideas that were most prevalent to me.

CARVE

Another thing I saw happening with a number of different characters was a tension between what a woman says and what a woman leaves unsaid, and the connection between saying and vulnerability. This quote rounds this idea out for me: "Words can induce good change, but how often, how fully?" I wondered how you're considering that thought, as a writer. What is the connection between the idea that there's vulnerability in saying and being a writer, dealing in words?

KEM

That quotation is from "Speakers & Headphones," one of the stories in *Locked Gray/Linked Blue*.

CARVE

A devastating story, a beautiful story.

KEM

Thank you. I think it really stems from this notion that words matter and words are very important, but they're not the entirety of change. Words can be the start, and words can be a part of change.

In the context of "Speakers & Headphones," there is a sense that talking things out is important, but in some contexts and some situations, words sometimes aren't enough. Sometimes words can help, but words don't always solve—they can be part of a solution but not the entirety of the solution. Without giving away the end of the story, one of the characters realizes that she wanted her friend to tell her what was wrong. The friend knew that telling her would provide some help, but not enough to actually change her situation.

As a writer, I think writing words is wonderful and can be healing. Writing is so important. But as a writer, I still need to remind myself that writing words—it can be a part of someone's experience, whether they're writing or reading. Words are only a part of it, not the entire experience in various contexts.

CARVE

So this is to say reading and writing short stories, or fiction in general, creates space for empathy, but that empathy needs to be step one, not the end goal.

KEM

Exactly. Though the end goal of helping to try to make things better might be restricted by circumstances, just like one of the main characters from "Speakers & Headphones" could only do what she could to try to help her friend.

CARVE

I totally agree. Another thing that struck me is this book's multifaceted consideration of race and class in New Jersey and New York. Place is important throughout these stories. I think the only character who is on the West Coast ends up in Seattle, but there's a sense that she's trying to escape something. How are you thinking about place as you write?

KEM

That's so interesting. I think that I am more of a writer of space than a writer of place. My focus is more on the spaces that the characters exist in. Many pivotal scenes involving characters trying to relate to each other take place in kitchens or living rooms. The cities—they are important, but they're not really the center of the conflicts in my stories. The focus of much of my work tends to be on characters' emotional experiences. However, as a writer, I want to learn how to include place more in my fiction, to make place part of the focus of my storytelling. So that's something that I would like to learn even more as I continue my writing journey.

CARVE

Yes, it's so significant how your stories keep meaningful spaces—place on a smaller, more domestic scale. "Demetrius" is a good example of that, I think, because the house itself drives so much of the tension. And the main character is upset about her space changing, the couch disappearing and then coming back. How are you as a writer influenced by your environment?

KEM

I think I'm still learning that. I'm still learning about how places and spaces influence me. I think that there's something very central about spaces where people have conversations, or places where silence exists. For instance, the house in "Demetrius"—you're right, it drives the tension, the house is like a character because the house is basically the bridge between the two sisters. It's also a neutral and not neutral place for them at the same time. The house connects them, because if not for the house, how often would the two sisters talk? How often would they relate to each other as siblings?

One of the sisters moving away to Nigeria represents the expansion of their estrangement. As sisters, they're not very close emotionally, even though they live together. But one sister moving away to Nigeria and one sister remaining in the United States would increase that emotional estrangement, maybe even cement that estrangement. In my work, spaces represent where relationships—family relationships, friendships, or romantic attachments—can grow and strengthen, and/or where they can disappear.

CARVE

All of that being said, what have your recent projects been focused on?

KEM

I'm currently working on adapting a screenplay from one of my short stories, a story not in *Locked Gray/Linked Blue*. It's based on a short story that was published in another journal. I'm working on finalizing the first draft of that, and I'm really excited because screenplay writing is very exciting to me. That's another thing I realized from writing fiction—that I love writing dialogue. I'm also working on revising a novel manuscript. I've taken a break from it, so after I finish the screenplay, I'm going to go back to my novel manuscript and try to make the next draft even stronger.

CARVE

That's really exciting. What you're saying about dialogue—I'm thinking about that in the context of the tension between things said and things left unsaid. In your story, "Proposed"—this character in particular has so many lines of snappy dialogue. But then it turns out she didn't actually say those words, it's just what she was thinking, what she wanted to say. And then she'll say something more polite than what she wanted to say.

In a screenplay, you have to rely on the dialogue, what's actually being said. Do you feel that you have less internal access to your characters, moving out of fiction and into screenwriting?

KEM

Fiction allows for instances where there are things unsaid—fiction allows for the writer to write out the unsaid things, because it might be unsaid to another character, but it's not unsaid to the reader. Writing the screenplay is a little bit different because I have to make sure that whatever's unsaid is actually somewhat said in the dialogue. I have to really think about each line saying something, but also hinting at something that's not said, if that's pivotal to that scene or the story.

CARVE

Some of your stories have such a cinematic arc—it's great that you're working with a screenplay. How do you consider narrative structure? This is to ask, from what writers did you learn the form of the short story? And how are you thinking about what kind of arc a story should hold?

KEM

I read Robin Black's short story collection entitled *If I Loved You, I Would Tell You This*. Her stories are wonderful. There's emotional storytelling in her work that I've been inspired by.

Danielle Evans wrote a powerful collection called *Before You Suffocate Your Own Fool Self*. Her collection and Robin

Black's were the two main collections I read soon after I made the commitment to write stories more consistently. Their writing is amazing in many ways, including telling stories with a focus on the characters. I learned so much from reading their work.

In terms of an arc, sometimes I know how a story will end when I'm writing it. For some of my short stories, I have thought about how that story would continue after its ending, therefore making its ending not necessarily final. I write flashbacks often, which I have found constructive in writing stories where emotional experiences and consequences are not only the outcomes but also the focus.

CARVE

You've mentioned your decision to commit to writing stories. What was the path to that decision? What made you want to do that, and what did it look like?

KEM

I worked on a novel manuscript before I made this commitment to write more consistently, and when I finished that novel manuscript, I was like, okay, this is it, I'm done. And then I realized that I had much more to learn about writing. Sometimes when one is writing, it's easy to not pay attention to the actual process. Sometimes it's all about wanting to tell a story, to get a story out. I didn't know too much about literary magazines at first, but after I learned more about literary magazines and I started reading them, both in print and online—*Carve* being one of those magazines—that's when I really started to pay attention to writing styles. That's when I started paying attention to the actual craft of writing. That's when I started to learn what wonderful writing looks like.

Before I started this commitment, as a reader, I read books without paying attention to the actual writing styles.

After I started writing short stories on a consistent basis and submitting them to journals—that's when I really started to pay attention, both as a writer and a reader, to various writing styles. I started reading more poetry as well. I still have a lot to learn about poetry, but as a reader of poetry, it has inspired me.

CARVE

Do you read poetry in literary magazines also, or do you read collections?

KEM

Both. I've visited websites of literary magazines and read poetry published there. I have also bought and read wonderful poetry collections. I read Jonterri Gadson's poetry collection entitled *Blues Triumphant*, and it's an amazing collection.

I started reading short stories and poetry in literary magazines and thinking, this work is wonderful. And then I would pay attention to the reasons why it is wonderful, the specifics. I think that has influenced me as a writer. To refer to the term "reading like a writer"—when I started writing stories more consistently, I started reading like a writer, too. And I started finding myself wanting to highlight sentences, phrases that would convey so much with a relatively small number of words.

In my stories, I try to pay attention to the words I'm using. I'm a big fan of wordplay. If there's a way that I can write a sentence using a word that can have more than one meaning and have both meanings apply to the actual story, I'll write it.

CARVE

Considering the architecture of your collection, the title has a slash and the book has two sections, each with half of the collection title. What inspired you to structure your book that way?

KEM

It began with thinking of the title of the book, and then the architecture came later. Once I decided on the title of the collection, that's when I started to fully realize what *Locked Gray/ Linked Blue* actually meant. The meanings of the title apply to the emotional experiences of the characters in the stories. *Locked Gray* is about an idea that a person could be connected to another person in a way that seems permanent but is ambiguous or uncertain. The color gray represents that—in some contexts, the color gray could mean something is not clear. *Locked Gray* represents a person caring about someone and their love for someone is permanent, but their actual connection might not be permanent.

Linked Blue has a similar meaning—"linked" represents connection, and the color blue represents sadness. People can be connected to each other and that connection can be strong, but it could also be rooted in melancholy. Blue is my favorite color, yet in some contexts, it represents melancholy and sadness.

Once I finalized the title, I realized some of the stories had the certainty that a family connection was strong, but there was uncertainty about how permanent those connections would be. "Demetrius" is an example—"Demetrius" is from Colleen's perspective, and she does feel locked to her sister in a way. But there is a sense of uncertainty when she realizes that her sister and her family are going to move away. The last story of the collection, "Her Mother, Nneka"—spoilers—is from her sister Chioma's perspective.

CARVE

I was so excited to get to that story and realize that it was in conversation with "Demetrius"!

KEM

It's from Chioma's perspective, and it's in "Linked Blue" because her connection to her sister is rooted in sadness. Her sister, in a way, is a reminder of the loss of her own mother. So in terms of the title, a number of the stories were rooted in "Locked Gray." And then the other set of stories seemed more rooted in "Linked Blue."

CARVE

The collection also has a certain symmetry to it. I noticed that the last story of the first section is in the second-person, and so is the first story of the second section. And "Demetrius," as you said, is the first story of the collection, and the last story retells it from the sister's perspective. But "Demetrius" is told in the first-person, and "Her Mother, Nneka" is in the third-person. I thought was really interesting, and over the course of the book you move so fluidly in and out of first-person, second-person, and third-person narratives. How do you consider point of view and perspective when you write? Is it something that arises naturally out of the needs of the story, or is it something that you know you want to impose on a story as you sit down to begin it?

KEM

It's the former, it's more natural. When I started writing "Her Mother, Nneka," I really wanted to answer my own questions about Chioma's perspective. My way of answering those questions was to basically write out her side of the story. I think when I started writing it in third-person, it was really natural. I wasn't purposefully thinking I would write it in the third-person—it was more like, let me just start writing out the scene before her sister's party. What does that look like to her? And when I started writing it, it was in the third-person.

For a lot of the stories in my collection, I didn't decide

what point of view or perspective I would write from. It just happens when I start writing, and then in the revision stages, that's when I can make decisions about keeping or changing the perspective. In the revision stages, I am more intentional about things like perspective and structure and plot.

CARVE

What was your process compiling stories for a collection like, and deciding what shape the collection would take?

KEM

When I first wrote "Demetrius," I didn't know that it was going to be a part of a collection. I figured I was writing a story, I would submit it to journals, maybe it would get published. It wasn't until after I wrote a number of the short stories in the collection that I realized they could form together as a collection. That's when I realized the thread that connects all of the stories together, and the thread is a kind of storytelling where emotional experiences are the centers. All of the characters have different backstories, and I think the thing that connects the stories together is that they feature characters who are dealing with trying to connect to someone whom they care about, and they're trying and sometimes failing to relate to them. Once I realized that, and then as I wrote more stories, that's when I started to ask myself if the following stories I wrote would fit into *Locked Gray/Linked Blue*.

"Her Mother, Nneka" was the very last story that I wrote that I included in the collection. When I wrote it, I wanted to answer my questions about Chioma's perspective, and once I did, I realized the story could fit into the collection. I've written other stories that I didn't include in the collection because I thought they didn't connect to many of the themes that are present in *Locked Gray/Linked Blue*.

CARVE

What has your experience of touring with this book and giving readings been like?

KEM

They have been wonderful. There's something about reading stories aloud that has given me the opportunity to receive immediate feedback about my work. Not only in what listeners tell me after the reading, but also in terms of noticing some of the audience's reactions as I'm reading. The experience of people providing amazing feedback immediately after listening to one of my stories has been very helpful and inspirational. It's a bit different than receiving feedback in writing. I think there's a bit more nuance, for me, receiving feedback in person from someone telling me their thoughts about one of my stories that I read aloud. Even so, receiving written feedback has been pivotal in my writing journey.

CARVE

Is that something that has carried over into your writing process, since you've started receiving that type of feedback? How does receiving verbal feedback manifest in your writing life?

KEM

Excellent question. I'm not sure if that has affected my writing of stories. I think it might have affected my reading of stories. When I've read my stories aloud, I've been inspired by the reactions of audience members.

However, moving forward in my writing, I might start thinking about reading it aloud and what I would anticipate the reaction would be from people listening to it. That's something I could definitely think about more when writing. It's hard though, because when writing, sometimes you don't want to think about future feedback. I'm not sure if it would be productive for me to think about future feedback as I'm writing stories in the first draft. In the first draft, for me, it's about getting the story out. However, in the revisions, I might think more about ways in which the story could be consumed, whether it's through reading or through listening.

CARVE

I think that's wise, not to have so many voices inside your head while you're writing. But when you are working through your process of revision, do you have people that you share your work with or do you like to keep it private?

KEM

I have shared my work with amazing readers, many of whom are also writers. Usually, the first person that I will share my story with or ask for feedback is my husband. When I first started writing the stories in this collection, it was all about getting feedback from almost anyone who would read it. I'm always grateful when people read my work and provide feedback, because time is something a person can never get back.

CARVE

You've also led workshops over the last couple of years. What has that experience been like?

KEM

I led one workshop each for the 2016 and 2018 Writing from the Margins Institute at Bloomfield College. Those experiences were amazing and they were community-focused, providing free-of-charge seminars and workshops to the community. I also gave a reading and led a seminar at the Bloomfield Public Library in 2018, and that was a great experience as well. I also organized and coordinated a panel for the Montclair Literary Festival in 2018, and that panel focused on writers who published work without or on the way to an MFA. All of the panelists had published stories, essays, articles, and/or books without an MFA (at the time of the festival), and that was very inspirational. Earning an MFA, from what I've heard, is very helpful, yet it's not the only way to become a strong and productive writer. It's one path, but it's not the only option. I hope that panel was inspirational to attendees, and it was definitely inspirational to me.

CARVE

What mantra is guiding your recent work?

KEM

I try to remind myself that as I am writing, I am moving forward, even during times when it might not seem like it. Writing is a both a joy and a challenge and all vitality.

The Eternal Youth of Everyone Else

ADRIENNE CELT

June 2012

We have a secret in our family, and Bendida is it. She has been nine in body and spirit for as long as I can remember, though my memory's not good enough to do her justice. Sometimes we'll sit quietly in a room together, reading, and she'll startle at a face in her picture book, looking for all the world as if she's seen a ghost. When I ask her what's wrong, she brushes me off.

"What's the matter, Benny?"

"Nothing."

"Come on," I'll coax. "Tell me what happened." She'll eye me then, as if to let me know that I can't understand the enormity of what I'm asking.

"I was just remembering something, is all."

. . .

Modern science, with its affinity for EKGs and endless blood-work, has never been given a chance to explain her to us—if nothing else, we can protect her from an eternity of testing. Still, we integrate its language into our lifestyle, wielding misdirection like matadors. People are uncomfortable with the idea of a healthy little girl being tucked away from the world at large; they imagine dark eyes peeping over windowsills, ears trained fearfully for the falling of footsteps. But most inconvenient questions can be parried away with the words "congenital disease" and a plea for privacy. Everyone is susceptible to the sympathy of a sick child.

A recessive gene, we say, kicking the dirt with the tips of our toes, concentrating hard on furrowing our brows. If present in both X chromosomes, it heightens the susceptibility to disease in the young women of our family. People bow their heads when they hear this, as if we're talking about the recently dead, and not the potentially infirm. It makes them fragile, we say, and our interlocutors puff out their cheeks, aware that their mere inquiry is shaving minutes off of our time with her. Such hard luck, they reply, to see so many lovely girls pass away before their time.

In fact, Bendida's never died, and as far as anyone can tell, she never will. I sit in her room playing card games—gin rummy, crazy eights—and watch her skin pulse with activity, gaze at the tangled mess of her dark and unbrushed hair. It's hard not to look for a weakness, to try and catch time standing still for the glory of seeing it pick up again. But Bendida just sighs when she's bored and rolls onto her back, announcing that she's ready for bed.

. . .

Benny has lived with my branch of the family for almost my entire life, so in a sense we grew up together. For a long time she stayed with my Uncle Len and Aunt Maureen, about two hours south of our house in Eugene, Oregon. They treated her with open arms, like the honest daughter of a simple man and wife. I can barely remember our earliest interactions; it wasn't until my tenth birthday that I ever stopped to wonder about the skinny girl I called my cousin.

We were driving south for a belated birthday party, in my honor. As the landscape shifts from townships to farmland, the speed limit on I-5 lifts from sixty to seventy and we were barreling steadily down the road when I became bored with the view out my window. Up until that point, the spectacle of flooded grazing pastures held my attention, a haunting vista of great gray lakes run through with the bony limbs of trees submerged. But we'd reached higher ground, and here the cows had found a dry patch for their lazy browsing. Lacking in potentially competitive siblings, it wasn't any fun to count them, and I turned inward, struck by a thought.

"When's Benny's birthday?" I asked.

In the seats ahead of me, my mother frowned and my father stayed silent, his eyes trained on the road as if we were driving through heavy rain. It's not that Bendida doesn't have a birthday, she must have, sometime, or so we assume. But she long ago stopped being interested by it, since it doesn't foretell change or measure distance like it should.

It was one of those rare moments when the silence in a space really does seem palpable, a thing that can be brushed aside. My mother tried a simple false start first.

"Well," she said. "Maybe there's something you should know about your cousin."

I sat expectantly, waiting for her to go on. I wasn't yet at an age where statements of that kind seem weighted with foreboding, and though a chill would surely go down my spine if I were to live through those few seconds again, I remember being thoroughly nonplussed, watching a speckled cow approach and disappear. I almost forgot what we were talking about before my mother took a deep breath and tried again.

"It's hard to explain," she said, slower than she usually spoke to me. I didn't like being talked down to by adults and leaned forward to pluck irritatingly at her sleeve.

"I'm smart," I sniffed. "It can't be that hard."

From the driver's seat, my father laughed, the same wry snort he always made when I used my Serious Adult voice. My mother shot him a look, then returned her eyes to the rearview mirror, where my own reflected back at her.

When we arrived, Bendida ran out to greet me with a bouquet of Mylar balloons wrapped around her left wrist. She pulled me into the house and showed off the decorations, streamers and banners splashing color across beige walls and windows. I hung back, trying not to be rude. But I was a child and I couldn't help staring, trying to burrow into the mystery that had, until recently, just been Benny. She continued to bounce around the room like a regular nine-year-old, an unstable atom, until suddenly she noticed what I was doing, and being a child herself, stared back. We both stood there for minutes, boring into one another, trying to figure out just what was going on.

My mother walked into the room, laden with brightly wrapped gifts and a casserole tray of half-frozen lasagna, and I happened to catch the look on her face the moment that her gaze crossed Bendida's. It was something I'd never thought to look for before—but what did she think? I wondered. What could she possibly? In the car, we'd stuck to the basic facts, perhaps in an attempt not to upset me. But I was adrift in an open sea, and I wanted to know where everyone else was.

My mother's eyes were bright, a young girl's eyes, full of fierce love and something that looked to me like pity, as they bounced between Bendida and myself. They weren't the eyes I was used to, the ones that looked on as she applied band-aids and watched me play in the park. The eyes that always knew just what to do.

"Hi Benny!" she said, setting down her packages and scooping the younger girl's spindly limbs right off the ground. Benny flashed a last look at me before returning her smile—not a warning, or even a question. She looked a little sad and shaken.

"So," my mother continued. "Jessie was asking about your birthday."

Bendida's eyes grew wide, then wild, passing between us in slight desperation.

"OH," she said. "Oh. I get it."

My mother continued nuzzling into her hair as if this was a normal day, an ordinary visit. She'd always adored Benny, as long as I'd been alive, and suddenly I wondered if she hadn't perhaps adored her much longer than that. I tapped my patent leather birthday shoes on the ground, feeling my white tights itch around my knees and ankles.

"Jessie, it's *your* birthday," said Benny carefully, her head dangling down to roughly the level of my face as she lay supine in my mother's arms. "Who cares about my birthday?"

She jumped to the ground and threw her arms around me, tugging me along to dirty our clothes in the backyard mud. I followed, little knowing what else to do, and looked one last time at my mother, who had begun organizing the birthday packages into a pile. She saw me looking, but didn't take the bait of my confusion or my growing frown. Instead, she continued what she was doing, and in one small gesture of acknowledgement, she shrugged.

. . .

It was some years later, with me already fourteen or so, when the family got together and decided that Benny had been with Uncle Len and Aunt Maureen for long enough to arouse suspicion. There was no tense vote, no hushed voices or secret ballot: Everyone just agreed over a civil cup of coffee that soon her presence, her consistency, her perpetual baby fat would likely begin to draw the neighbors' notice. With tears of real grief, her ostensible parents draped the house again in decoration, this time a wash of black. I remember crinkling the dark crepe tablecloth between my fingers, feeling how tangibly a house can be filled by absence.

Bendida stayed in her room for the duration of the wake with the door locked, packing the remainder of her things. She thought it was silly, not to mention a waste, fitting out a tiny coffin and paying the cost of burial space. But Len and Maureen wouldn't hear her protests and lovingly chose a shady cemetery plot within walking distance of their home. In the weeks preceding the move, they coaxed Bendida into amusing herself by filling the small box up with stones, to give the pallbearers something to struggle with. Len said that the volcanic pieces were perfect for Benny, because they were hollow like the bones of a bird.

After the funeral, Lenny and Maureen waited until nightfall and then drove Bendida to my parents' house, where we had painted the spare bedroom light yellow and purchased a new bedspread covered in flowers. The small details of the room shone out at us as Benny surveyed them, having been the subject of much quibbling and indecision. My tastes tended towards distressed oak, soft pastels, and patchwork quilts—things I remembered from years of playing Candy Land and building imaginary fortresses in Benny's room at Len and Maureen's. I knew exactly how everything should be and was proud to be able to provide for her, in that way, what she needed. Some pale portion of continuity. My mother, however, walked firmly up to unfamiliar styles, plain flannel sheets and pajamas laced with rocket ship platoons. In the end she won out, the purveyor of credit cards and ample station wagon storage space, but I assured her it was a hollow victory, overwhelmed by how wrong she was.

"It's not as though her room has always looked that way," she said to me as I whined and wended my way to the car. "Why do you think that Uncle Lenny and Aunt Maureen went to all the trouble of holding a full-scale funeral? With a priest?

Lenny, the atheist?"

I rolled my eyes and strapped myself in, hoisting my feet up onto the grimy dashboard. "Probably some ass-backward attempt to keep a piece of her in their lives. A headstone and an epitaph."

My mother smiled and shook her head, not looking at me. "To let her know that it was over. To give her a chance to start again."

. . .

Time, for Bendida, is an ordinary object, worn smooth by being worried over, and finally set aside. She reacts differently than other nine-year-olds—to disappointment, for example, or discontent. I've seen her start to crumble after getting too few hours of sleep and then being denied some much-wanted comfort, like buttered pecan ice cream or a play-date with her best friend of the hour. But as her rosebud bottom lip begins its gentle quaking, she pauses and seems to calculate the days since she last got her way and hears the insignificant drop in the bucket of time that even the most wrenching wait will cost her.

She sheds hours like water droplets. The days roll off her back unnoticed as we cling to the earth to hear its heartbeat.

. . .

I never got roped into ballet or painting or poetry, or any of the other fair vices that suckered my friends with beauty and left them dissatisfied with nine-to-fives and Volkswagens. Having Bendida in our house throughout my teenage years was enough of a snake eating its own tail for me, and I learned early that if you love something bigger than you, stranger, stronger, then the mundane tasks of earning money and keeping house come to seem like viable satisfactions so long as they help you in your greater aims. Without any calling to the fine arts, Benny was the fairy tale that I was raised on.

My irritation with her presence in my early teenage years—having to keep my friends out of the house, lying to boyfriends, sharing my space—quickly became eclipsed by the fervor of Bendida's belief in love and the strange ways she'd learned to understand it. I could always go out and make mistakes, kiss a boy at a party, touch his hand illicitly in the hallway at school, but my excitement was never greater than when I came home to tell Benny about it all.

Her thrill was tangible when I snuck up behind her and whispered in her ear, "I'm in love, Benny." Though her body remained still I could sense the hairs rising on the back of her neck, as if genetic muscle memory were struggling to stir.

Perhaps I was too open with her, too loose with my thoughts and vocabulary, but I was certain she'd learn on her own anything that I didn't tell her. Often, in fact, I was convinced that she'd heard it all before.

"Where did you learn that word, Benny?" I asked her once, having dropped a tomato-stained spatula in alarm at her vocabulary as we cooked dinner together.

She grinned at me wickedly, proud of making me blush. "I have time to read a lot of books, you know."

In her mouth, words like "kiss" and "caress" were darkly conspiratorial. She knew what they referred to, but being unable to desire them herself, she was left to covet the cravings of others. As we stirred spaghetti sauce in the stove-hot kitchen, she drew hearts with arrows through them in the fogged up windowpane.

"Do you know what I hate?" she asked me, erasing her work with the outside of her wrist.

"Hate's a pretty strong word, kid," I cautioned. As I grew older, I'd fallen into mothering patterns with Bendida, almost forgetting the days when she and I had measured our heights back to back. Stacked against my new thoughts, my words, my breasts, my hips, she looked much more like a baby.

"Yeah, but you don't understand." Her head was tilted slightly and her eyes had darkened, testing me. "It's important."

"Okay, well then tell me. What is it that you hate?"

"I hate people who stop loving each other."

I raised an eyebrow at her vehemence. Bendida was not a child of divorce; she traversed families like a beggar going door to door, but always one who is welcomed inside. She has a grasp, however patched together, of the complicated framework of adult emotions that hovered just slightly outside of her reach. She has never expressed love or hatred lightly: It is her least childlike of qualities.

"It's so... rare." She struggled for her words. "People should want each other. They're supposed to want each other. I can't want anything, and then people just throw it away. They want each other more than they've ever wanted anything, and then they just stop, like they die."

She used her forearm, tucked discreetly in a red wool sweater, to erase her drawings from the window. It was a move she'd learned from me, I thought. Or possibly I had learned it from her. When I was younger, our mannerisms were often confused in that way—no one was ever quite sure if it was Benny or I who came up first with a shimmying dance or flounce of discontent. But I always felt as if I must be the copycat, accidentally stealing something precious.

I mulled over Benny's words for the rest of the night, not quite sure what to make of them. It hadn't occurred to me before that my childish declarations of love would turn into ashes in Bendida's mouth when I inevitably betrayed them; that with no experience of romantic love or loss, the two concepts seemed much more disparate to Benny than they did to me.

Falling asleep that night I was overwhelmed with dreams of losing Bendida: of her going so far away that I might never be able to reach her, and of me, with my jokes, my boyfriends, my changeability, pushing her there as fast as she could go. I imagined her tiring of us extravagantly, walking away into the waves to become Triton's daughter instead of a wilting flower. The tide water in my mind began to choke and boil, tossing me around until I woke with a start and found Bendida's hair wrapped around my neck, stuck over my face with the condensation of her sleeping breath. My stirring woke her and she smiled up at me through a veil of sleep.

"Hi Jessie. I was," she yawned, "having a bad dream. Do you mind if I stay with you tonight?"

I swept her hair off of her face and my own, tucking it into an unsecured chignon at the base of her neck. Her knees were tucked up inside her nightgown, and curling around the small package of her body, I pressed my face against her shoulder.

"Of course, I don't mind. You can stay with me forever."

. . .

The day came when my parents began to think about retirement, and my mother brought up, over a cup of coffee, that they had been talking about moving Bendida. She had been in their house at least as long as she had stayed with Len and Maureen, and babysitters were becoming few and far between. My mother no longer even knew where to look for them, now that her ties to the high school were broken by the years intervening since my graduation.

"Where would she go?" I asked, startled at my mother's plain-spokenness. She had come to visit me in Olympia, where I was finishing up my M.Ed at Evergreen State College, and we were in a dirty café with posters lining the walls.

Stirring her coffee with a pliable spoon, she shrugged as

if she didn't know, but gave me several concrete examples. "Possibly the East Coast. You have a great aunt in Brooklyn who has the space and the inclination, but that could really only be temporary. Bendida's too young to stay anywhere where she'd essentially be the one taking care of someone."

She paused and surveyed the posters, fluorescent photocopies, advertising illustrious musical outfits like Six Day Itch and Lust Puppy. "And then there's always scattered people in Arizona, but I think several of them live in trailer parks and I don't know, not to sound uptight, but that might be too small. So, we're really thinking of my second cousin Andrew in Australia. He lives in Perth, and he's got the space, so that's one thing, but mostly I think she needs to get out of here. She's been in the area for too long, and she's gotten too comfortable seeing the same people all the time."

"Why is that a bad thing?"

There was another beat in the conversation, and this time I was old enough to sense the foreboding in it. My mother looked me straight in the eye and gave an honest answer to an honest question.

"Because we're going to die, Jessie. At some point we're all going to die, and then what would she do?"

. . .

A few uneventful weeks went by after my mother left, weeks filled with my preparations to graduate and move into a small house of my own in Seattle. Bendida was still safe in Eugene; I knew my parents were in no hurry to send her, of all places, to Perth, but I still felt a tugging at my skin, a slow creeping of ice in the badlands of my mind as I drew the inevitable conclusions: She could be kept, or she could be lost.

I pictured Lenny rubbing small stones together in his hand, grinding the ossified pieces of lava into a fine layer of dust that settled over the sateen of Benny's coffin. There are certain things that, once done, cannot be undone. I know that. My parents had made their choice, and so had Lenny and Maureen, and countless other generations before them. To my family, Bendida's quality of eternity made her expendable, whereas to me, it made her inevitable.

I stood up in my apartment and rubbed some heat into my cold hands. It was 11 p.m., and without thinking I picked up my car keys and drove the three hours south to Eugene. It was a pleasant drive, with the usual I-5 traffic on hiatus until the sunrise. When I snuck into Bendida's room in the black of the night, she did not seem surprised to see me.

. . .

We didn't plot out a destination: We just went as far and fast as we could to escape the silent songs of reminiscence and regret. They were unidentifiable, strangers, but they crept onto our shoulders just the same. They whispered to us, *you will know me.*

I drove into the morning gloaming with Bendida glancing up on occasion through sleep, a slight tension playing around her features. After a few hours of silence and road rhythm, I jumped at the sound of Benny's voice, jerking the wheel unintentionally to the left.

"Jesus, Benny, what?"

She shrank back into her seat and I cursed to myself, placing an arm around her shoulders.

"Sorry, sorry," I said in a hush. "I was just a little startled. What's up, kiddo?"

"Well," said Benny, "I think we're almost there."

We both knew the place when we saw it, with its forlorn "For Rent" sign swinging out front, glinting in new light. Since it was only seven in the morning we decided to get breakfast before calling the landlord, bursting into anxious giggles throughout our two courses of coffee, for me, and pancakes, for both. Our food was served on plastic plates, a circumstance just unusual enough to seem exotic.

"Do you think someone else will get it first?" Benny asked, tugging at my sleeve. Her legs swung anxiously under the table, as if she'd been the one to down two mugs too many of black diner sludge.

"Nope," I said, nudging her back, between two ticklish ribs. "You're my good luck charm, see?"

The landlord dubbed the place cozy, though a more accurate description would be *almost insufficiently small*, not to mention poorly insulated. All the same, it felt like home, a place where we could eat cereal in the mornings, with a yard Benny could roam through to rescue birds wounded by the neighborhood cats. She didn't know that the bacteria on feline teeth infected the birds irrevocably, and that even if we drove them to the animal shelter to recuperate, they weren't likely to fly away again. For my part, I didn't know to calculate heating costs into the rent, so we huddled for warmth beneath our jackets that first night when we didn't have beds.

The early weeks of our new existence were giddy and nervous, as we filled the cramped rooms with thrift store furniture and antique trinkets of dubious heritage. Benny made up a story for each item, detailing where each had come from, who had used it, how well it had been loved. Once able, we lived in a tender sort of house arrest, restricted by habit to our own creaking floors and unkempt garden grass. Only I'd escape sometimes, driving a well-worn road between our home and the local elementary school to substitute teach and be, in turn, granted that mean compensation which kept us in our toast and tea.

I hated to leave Benny alone. It was probably not a charming paranoia, but occasionally I thought I heard my mother's car outside, the distinctive putt-putt of an old Volvo motor coming to foil my plans, save me from myself. Benny, always more sanguine than me about our fate, went to elaborate lengths to comfort me, playing unannounced rounds of hide-and-seek to show me how much she knew that I'd never know.

"Benny?" I'd ask. And then I'd cry out, "Benny! Where are you?" Even though I knew the game, I never lasted longer than ten minutes before bursting into brazen tears. When she finally crept out of her hiding place, Bendida's eyes were on me like magnets. Never shameful, only questing.

. . .

I can tell she's looking inside me for the child I was, trying to strip away the twenty odd years I now have on her. And I wonder not for the first time how many iterations she's seen of this evolution, whether she wishes her own skin could grow sunspots, her face begin to wrinkle about the eyes. We are, I have determined, forever linked by a belief that's been burned into both of our brains: that love should last forever, and that it almost never does. Of course, her knowledge is earned, while mine, like so many of my most important insights, is borrowed. I wonder if Bendida would think, like I do, that the small punctured birds she tries to rescue are lucky, their last experience of life being one of overwhelming pity and affection.

"Jessie," she asks often, plaintive, soft, "do you love me?"

Her eyes go glassine, as if preparing nervous tears, though of course, I've never said no.

"Of course, I love you," I tell her, running my rough thumb over the plum of her cheek.

I suppose, though, she has had cause to wonder.

. . .

The room was dark when I walked in with a pillow in hand, smoothing the fringe out into a colorful mohawk. Outside was a faint dusting of first snow; the Washington weather patterns are different here than I remember them being closer to the coast, in thrall to a different side of the mountains, and no one in town seemed surprised by the early frost.

Bendida was hunkered over in her bedclothes; it's amazing to me how much a child needs rest. Sleep weighs down on her like a layer, like it's something new to be aware of, and I enjoy watching her well-ensconced in it—her heart beats hard, like a hummingbird's. I can see the veins in her neck throb in time with it, a gentle rhythm beneath her iridescent skin. She looks perfect: dark hair, round cheeks, eyelashes like velvet Elvis. That night I wanted, more than ever, to find the tools to protect her. From everything.

But in her warm quilt, knitted in the last dance of Maureen's arthritic hands, she was already sufficiently cocooned. Her hair was down to the center of her back, the length it grows to every winter, though we chop it off to her shoulders every spring. She heals, and instead of bearing scars she gains back every inch of her softness.

I crawled into her bed as I had done so many times before and wrapped myself around her body, put myself as close as I could get. Here, I thought, she's right here. But where would she be in the morning? In a month? When a stranger in our too-small town caught too many glimpses of her and called a foul? When I fell down the stairs, when I went crazy, when I died?

My breath pulled in, seeming to implode, not fill, my lungs. The air shoved soft tissue into the back of my ribs and I kept inhaling, kept inhaling, inhaling and pulling Bendida closer, with the pillow pulled across her face. Doesn't she deserve a permanent solution? I thought. To die in the pitch and roll of the night, embraced by love? To become more than a secret sorrow? It was so romantic a notion; she would like that. Finally, a love story with no love lost.

A sob escaped me as she kicked out her legs, her tiny body beginning to quake and undulate. First, with the muffled energy of a dozing child, then with surprising force and deadly accuracy. Through the pillow I could hear a scream, the muted ribbon of terror that I knew would come and would have to wear as a badge from now on. A cry emanated, vibrated, echoed, and skittered across the moony snowfield outside, and suddenly I couldn't judge its source—her throat, or mine? Was my mouth full of fury, or empty, dry as dust? I didn't know, and in a panic I pulled back and leaned against the wall as Bendida sat up, panting, in the bed.

"Jessie," she said, and in that moment the tune of sorrow that had once already crept upon me wrapped itself around my neck like it belonged there. *You will know me.*

"Benny, no, I wasn't, I wouldn't, I..." My words tumbled from my mouth like stones and piled, pebbles, at my feet. Bendida clutched the pillow I'd brought in to her chest like a talisman.

"You can't," she said.

"I know."

"No, you don't." She sighed, with years and years in her breath, leaking out of her mouth, spilling out into the room, and as I watched her rocking in the bed, arms and pillow around her night-gowned knees, the blood flowed swiftly out of my face until we were both very pale there, silent in the moonlight.

"You think so, I know, but it can't happen." Her small face twisted, with—effort? Annoyance? Maybe sorrow, but I'm not sure. What I know is that, sitting quietly in her pajamas, Bendida let me know in her roundabout, storied fashion, that every so often people had tried to help her die.

"People always think I don't know what I'm talking about

when I tell them not to, but I do." She thought for a moment. "Every time, it's a completely different person, but they always think they know best, they always think they know the exact right thing."

There are days when she'll bombard me with questions: How do bees know how to get back to their nests? Why can bears sleep through winter without eating when all of us get hungry after a couple of hours? How do you make plastic? She must have asked these questions a thousand times to a thousand different sets of ears, but I guess she's never received a satisfactory answer.

So I'm willing to take her word for it when she tells me that my idea, my sudden grain of terrible insight, is nothing new, has all happened before. She smiles when she sees how original and unforgivable I think I am.

———

ADRIENNE CELT is the author of the novels *Invitation to a Bonfire* and *The Daughters*, as well as a collection of comics, *Apocalypse How? An Existential Bestiary.* Her work has been published widely, and she lives in Tucson, AZ.

INTERVIEW WITH ADRIENNE CELT

January 2019

CARVE

You've been published in *Carve* twice, once in the Summer 2012 issue and once in the Winter 2015 issue, Matthew's last issue as editor. I revisited your interview with Matthew, which probably would have taken place at the very end of 2015. You mentioned that *Carve* was your first print publication. I was curious, at what point in your writing and submitting experience did your original publication in *Carve* come?

ADRIENNE

It was right when I graduated from my MFA program, I think. I had another story accepted earlier that year by *Southeast Review*, but it hadn't been published yet. I had been submitting a lot and getting some positive rejections—a bunch of different rejections, as all writers do. It was really exciting because I really believed in that story, but I had been having trouble placing it. I had submitted it a lot of times, actually.

When Matthew accepted it, he accepted it contingently and said he had a big edit he wanted to make, which was essentially a big cut of an opening section. I immediately saw how smart it was. I'd been holding on to the earlier pages because I liked some of the images in them, but he really saw to the heart of the story in that way that good editors can. I was really excited to accept that edit—it wasn't even something that I had to think about. From that moment on, the publication was such a wonderful experience because everyone at *Carve* was very enthusiastic about the story, and then the readership was also really enthusiastic. I don't know if I've ever published in a journal anywhere that was as motivated about getting the story to readers and continuing to connect it with readers—an effort which goes on to this day!

CARVE

I don't want to speak for Matthew, but I think we do share this dream of fostering space for conversation that doesn't go away. This anthology project was in part born out of a conversation that I had with an editor at a book press. I really admire him and I really admire the press, but we were having a conversation about how the benefit of book publishing is that books don't expire the way an issue of a magazine does when it's no longer the current issue. It becomes hard to sell those magazines. I understand that thought, but I was upset about the thought that our stories are no longer relevant once there's a more current issue. That is part of the reason we've built lesson plans and online writing classes around our archives.

ADRIENNE

I also understand that, but I think that the hustle that you guys show for the stories that have been published—bringing them back to readers, bringing them to students—is actually something that's necessary in book publishing too. It's true that books have more longevity in a certain way, but they can disappear too. The backlist of a book publishing company is also something that needs to be vigorously marketed or championed, brought to readers, if you want people to see it and if the book wasn't an immediate bestseller. I think there's a lot more interrelatedness between those two things than that comment suggests, even though, again, I also see where it's coming from. And as a writer, it can be funny to realize that your work that has this other life, totally separate from you. Odd, but wonderful—it's what you want, even though it's always a surreal experience to be confronted with it. Like, "Oh, people in Carve workshops are reading my story as they learn. That's so great."

CARVE

Yes—I love that "The Eternal Youth of Everyone Else" is part of our online classes. What else do you recall about your process writing this story?

ADRIENNE

I remember very specifically that it sprang out of a conversation I was having with my sister in the car while I was home for Christmas. I grew up in Seattle and most of my family still lives there. We were talking about letting go of a person from our past, and I had a keen sense of how difficult it was to relinquish not only them but also my own, old feelings about them, which made me really sad. That brought me to Bendida, who is stuck at not only a particular age but stuck with the perception that people inevitably have of her—that they change but she stays the same. It's human nature to want to hold onto something steady like that, but the thing that you're holding onto doesn't really exist after a certain amount of time. Even for Bendida, who stays the same physical age. She is still affected by the passage of time, so she's a child but she's not naïve. She has seen a lot and has been changed by it, so the attempt to keep her that way is impossible.

CARVE

One line from this story that haunts me is, "Time, for Bendida, is an ordinary object, worn smooth by being worried over, and finally set aside." It sounds to me like you're speaking to that—she's a child, but she's not naïve and she's had time to figure things out. But it's still sad for those around her, who are, in some ways, younger. Considering this story came from a real-life sadness about time, did the process of writing this story affect the way you think about time? Or did it just create a space to work through the sources of that sadness?

ADRIENNE

It's a good question. I don't know that it changed my thinking about time, but it did open up a little time bubble for me, which I could sit inside for a period and then have to move on from. In which I could process that sadness in a way where I was no longer thinking about the particular events that led up to it, but just about the feeling.

You know when you listen to a song and it makes you really sad, but you're not sad about anything? There's nothing wrong in your life but you just want to cry because of this beautiful melody, or these particular lyrics, the way that some people really love breakup songs even though they have a happy relationship, or no relationship. It felt like that, for me, to be inside this story. Which is also weirdly appropriate, or maybe not so weirdly appropriate, to the themes of the story. By the time I was done with it, I think I was done with that moment of sadness. But much like the characters in the story, I had to look at it obliquely before I could move through it honestly.

CARVE

In your conversation with Matthew in 2015, you talked about ghost stories and things beyond ordinary human experience. Of course, Bendida's condition, this immortality and inability to age, is beyond ordinary human experience. But it's representative of ordinary human emotion, human emotion that is common. In your novels there's also still a hint of the uncanny, this toeing the line between dreamscapes and reality.

Also, there are so many family secrets, and questions about intimacy and identity, immigration and war, and language. I wondered how you see your work engaging with those themes and ideas, or how they recur for you.

ADRIENNE

I definitely would say that's a good list for me. As I choose to write a story or a novel, I'm rarely picking from a grab bag of themes in that way, naming what I'm doing. That's more of a retrospective process, or a process that I reckon with as I develop the themes of the story or book. But the thing that always comes to mind, when I'm asked about themes that run through my writing, is identity, or maybe identity and power, and how the two are linked together.

Part of what interests me about the intersection between those two things is how you think your power will help you maintain your identity—and how many people then build their identities around how much power they can get. It's recursive. Get power to build an identity, build an identity that lets you get power. You put all this effort into being the person you believe you are, or should be, based on your history, your family's history, your place in the world, and what you accomplish, how you're recognized for your work. And yet those same things can fall apart so easily inside you, or stop being enough to make you happy. Power isn't enough to maintain identity. Some things just have to come, not from what you *could* do but from what you *do* on a daily basis: The power you have is tenuous, but the work you do accrues over time, and becomes legible as your life.

This is such a long strange answer to the question that you asked. I guess these are all things that I'm thinking through as I'm writing, and I guess also that I find our human concept of power a little uncanny. Identity too. We're very slippery beings, and our sense of what's meaningful changes over time.

CARVE

I'm so interested in the word "power" in this context. It's not that time is defined in a specific way across all of your work, but it's something that's always considered. Time's effect on relationships is really important in your storytelling. In both of your novels, there are questions about intimacy and iden-tity, but there are also these really imperfect men, and the sto-ries look at women's relationships with them over time. How is that connected to this thought about power?

ADRIENNE

I think that power is more fraught, or differently fraught, for women in our society—and that's true also for people of color, for queer people, for trans people, for anyone who is part of a group that's marginalized from the norm. For me, it has been focused on women specifically, partially because I am a woman and partially because one of the things that is often expected of women to gain either power or a sense of identity in society is to have children. In *The Daughters* that's very explicit—the book is exploring what happens to a woman who has identified herself through art, through singing, and who has now given birth to a child and taken a place in this great intergenerational saga of the world and of her family. In her case, the issue is dramatized through a curse, which says that each woman in her family will give birth to a girl who is progressively more beautiful and more musically talented than the last generation, at a cost. So she's also grappling with whether she believes in that curse, what it means for her, is it real.

For me, that was something that I have been thinking about and working out for a long time—not just related to power and whether or not I should have a child, but also related to the difference between your identity as a child and your identity as an adult. I was really scared that if I ever had a child it would somehow erase the meaning of my childhood, which I realize sounds really weird. But children have so much primacy in so many families—you get obsessed with them, with what they're doing, with what they're thinking. I was afraid it would force me to be in a place of stagnant adulthood. But I think that's actually very often not true. I've seen a lot of people who experience renewed wonder through their children, who are able to remember and relive parts of their childhood that way. So, who knows.

In *Invitation to a Bonfire* the question of motherhood isn't as present, because none of the women in the book are mothers—except Zoya's mom, I guess. All of the characters' mothers. But power and womanhood is still very much at play. It's also relevant that it's a historical novel, set in the thirties, so the avenues to power for women are very different than today. Since it's inspired by the Nabokov marriage, there's always been this question for me—why a woman like Véra Nabokov would make her career that of "being married to a great man," when she herself is very intelligent and very cultured, very educated. Yet he was what she was devoted to. She was so passionate about Nabokov's career that it didn't seem to me to be just a quality of its time. It seemed like that was what she wanted, she was getting something out of that relationship that was personal to her. That was something that I was exploring in the book—what she would get out of it, what someone else who was interloping in their marriage would get out of it. Of course, I don't expect the answers I drew were the same as she drew in real life. I think I made it rather more dramatic. But it was fun to explore, and that was a good jumping off point.

CARVE

Speaking of drama—in your conversation with Matthew, you were joking about how there's a dramatic bedroom murder scene in both of your stories that *Carve* has published.

ADRIENNE

God, that's true. I forgot about that.

CARVE

Not all of your work is high drama—your novels are not high drama throughout. Of course, *Invitation to a Bonfire* is very suspenseful, with a sense of mystery. I wondered if you would speak a little bit to how you balance drama without slipping into melodrama, if that's related to a process of laying out your plotlines or how capital-C Conflict versus tension works in your stories.

ADRIENNE

I look to the characters first. In any literary fiction—and I'm using literary really broadly here, because I think that anything that concerns itself with character, be it science fiction, or a thriller, or what have you, can do this work—you have to be concerned about the characters and their motivations, the things that they want, the things that they need, that's what drives the action. If, as a writer, you're paying attention to that, it becomes harder to slip into melodrama, because you (and hopefully the reader) begin identifying with the interiority of that person. Their needs feel both urgent and expansive.

If you look inside what makes any person do any particular thing at a given time, you can parse it out across their entire lives, everything that led them to that point. Nothing has one cause; everything's rooted in the person as a whole. I think that's especially true considering *Invitation to a Bonfire*— the things that happen in the end, and I don't want to spoil them, because I do hope they are suspenseful—but I think that you have to look at everything that has happened to Zoya in her entire life to see how she leads up to that moment.

In *The Daughters*, which is, as you say, less hugely climactic, I was really interested in looking at not only how all of a person's life affects the choices they make, the actions they take, and the needs that they have, but also their whole family history's lives. Lulu, the protagonist of *The Daughters*, is making choices and trying to come to terms with her life not only in terms of what has happened to her and what she has done, but in terms of her mother, who abandoned her as a child. And her grandmother, who raised her, and the competing stories that both women tell about their family history, and what its place is in the world's larger history—what was real for all of them and what may or may not have been real but certainly still guided their lives. That's something that I'm always looking to, even if I come to a story because of an image or a plot idea—it won't be satisfying to me unless I know why the characters are doing what they do on a very granular level.

CARVE

There's also somewhat of a difference in style between the two novels. *The Daughters* follows its protagonist pretty closely, and *Invitation to a Bonfire* has the quality of an archive. The narrative goes into Zoya's thoughts, but there are also fragments of newspaper clippings, letters from Lev to Vera. What was the process like inhabiting different voices, different genres, different tones, dipping in and out of different characters' heads and voices?

ADRIENNE

I'm glad that they feel so distinct to you. That's wonderful to hear. It sprang very naturally out of the idea that I had for the book, which came from the lives of Véra and Vladimir Nabokov, although I call them Lev and Vera Orlov in the novel. God, saying that now—I should reemphasize that they are not the same people as Véra and Vladimir Nabokov, but that was the inspiration. When I began writing, although Lev's first letter was the first thing that I wrote, Zoya's voice quickly became the most important thing to me as a driver for the narrative. I wanted to go back and forth between those two voices and hear what they each had to say about the situation as it was arising. Vera was behind the scenes causing so much to happen, but she is meant to be more of a cipher. I had to think a lot about how to bring her voice in so that she was not a silent partner for the entire book.

Most of the novel I wrote straightforwardly—that is, I wrote it straight through. I didn't have the idea for the archive project until my second or third revision, but the letters and the diary were both already there. Some of the things, like the newspaper clippings or pieces of books that get pulled in, were there, but in a more nebulous form, and I didn't know what to do with them. When I realized that it would make sense to cohere the documents in an intentional way, I had to think about how to integrate what were, at the time, random pieces of second-person or omniscient observation.

Similarly, the sections of brief letters or interviews with the police, things like that, initially came from first-person stream of consciousness pieces that I wrote for Vera because I wanted her to be able to insert herself into the story, even though those came later on in the book. But those, also, just didn't work. You can't have stream of consciousness narration from a character who hasn't written anything in an archive. It's not possible. I had to become more purposeful about what I was doing with each section that didn't already have its own paper identity. It wasn't that hard, since I had a lot of the material. It was mostly a process of thinking, where could this come from? The section from the lost history of the Donne School that I wrote—all I really had to do was think, who could have written this, where did it come from, where would Zoya have gotten her hands on this piece of paper? It became a puzzle project.

CARVE

Listening to you talk about this process is reminding me of something you said to Matthew in your interview a couple of years ago about the difference between your writing process and your process making comics. You said that for you, writing is an intellectual, ongoing thing. It's not necessarily planned out before you begin your project. With your comics, you do plan things out before you begin. I wondered how that's evolved since then—what is the relationship between those two processes?

ADRIENNE

I probably wouldn't phrase it quite that way anymore. I know what I meant when I said it, but I think the processes have slid closer to a middle space from both directions by now. With a book, I still don't plan everything out when I begin, but I do often have a sense of what the arc of the book will be, even though I'll be surprised within it and probably change things. I had a sense of what the ending of *Invitation to a Bonfire* would be, and then once I got there I realized it wasn't yet enough. Based on what the book had become, it was able to teach me more about what it should be. I think that I have more of that relationship with comics now too. I do have to plan them out in a certain sense as I'm drawing them, because I don't pre-fer to just intuitively draw across the page, but I rarely write out ideas for comics throughout the week. Usually, on Sunday when I draw comics, I have any themes or ideas that I've been wanting to get on the page and any images that would corre-spond with those, and then I'll start sketching out whatever idea has spoken to me in that moment and draw little small thumbnail images of what it will look like across the strip. So I do think that now I feel more of a sense of inspiration and flow than maybe I suggested in my previous interview.

CARVE

The format of your comics website is really interesting—you post the weekly comic alongside a brief blog entry, where you record what you're thinking about, things going on in your life. I'm wondering how that might be related to what you spoke about earlier—thinking about a bubble of time and then having to move on from it after writing through it, maybe in this case processing your emotional reactions to events through drawing comics and writing short reflections. How do you see your comics and statements intersecting with your life?

ADRIENNE

It's kind of weird because I draw the comics on Sunday and then I post them with the blog posts on Wednesday, so they aren't always deeply connected. In earlier years, what I wrote was often very brief—it was kind of a surprise to realize my website layout had a blog element to it, and I had to figure out how to fill that space. Now, I'm always trying to figure out how to bring together the Sunday afternoon feeling and the Wednesday morning one, since both do encapsulate particular emotions for me, just not always the same one.

My dad once said to me, "Your comics make me feel like you're so in tune with the world and you're so present in your life." I just laughed and said, "Well that's because I'm forced to be very present in that moment because I have to say something right then, and all I have is what I am thinking about in that exact moment in time, looking out the window of my studio at the garden." Sometimes I worry there's a repetitive nature to that "present" feeling, that makes me wish I planned the blog posts more, but I also think there's something useful in just letting the process be fluid.

I was talking earlier about how I think the true value of art for an artist often ends up being less their individual successes and more the accrual of the work over time. That's definitely true of the comics for me. I would even say that was part of my intention for it when I started doing it really regularly—there was a real pleasure for me in the fact that I could post one every single week and every single comic didn't necessarily have to be a success or a failure. I'm not even sure what metric I would use to gauge that. Either people really like them and connect with them or they don't, or sometimes I really like what I have drawn or I don't. I go through phases of feeling more like I have been successfully advancing in my drawing and sometimes I look at them and think they're all the same. That process is ongoing.

When I'm able to take a step back and say I've been doing this almost every week since 2011 I feel a sense of accomplishment, and also like I have intentionally built a part of my identity that wouldn't otherwise be there. There's nothing necessarily in being a novelist that suggests you have to have seven years of weekly comics as well. I have had to actually sit down and do the work every week, put the hours in to draw, learn to draw better and expand on what the shape of comic can be and where the meaning can lie in the art, in the layout, in the wording, and in the interaction between all of those things. It's become a practice.

CARVE

Your discovery of the blog feature of your website—it sounds like your thinking flowed into the container available to it, which I think is really interesting in the context of the forms of your novels and how your process is driven by your relationship with the character and what's going on in their head, in their voice. Reading through your book of comics, *Apocalypse How?*, there's a really particular tone cultivated in the experience of reading the comics one after another. With the comics in particular it might not have been an intentional accumulation of tone, but how do you think about voice with respect to your fiction projects, your comics, or both?

ADRIENNE

It's really interesting that you phrased it as pouring intention into a preexisting vessel, in regards to the shape of the website. I think, especially with books, it ends up feeling that way to me too—like the shape of *Invitation to a Bonfire* could only have been what it is. I wouldn't have wanted to write it as a straightforward first-person or third-person novel with no variation of form or without the insertion of the archival project elements of it. But I couldn't have known that when the project was just a twinkle in my eye. It really had to come out of what the book wanted to be. Have you ever heard the idea of a sculptor who is trying to sculpt an elephant out of a brick of marble and they say, "I just have to chip away all of the parts that aren't the elephant"? I think writing projects often feel that way to me as well—they have a necessary form that I just have to find, and voice ends up being a big part of that for me.

I also think that voice in fiction and in art, generally, is where the artist's personality tends to flex itself the most. You're only going to want to write well in the way that you write. You have to be true to your own intentions. That isn't to say that writers don't vary their voices in writing, or that they shouldn't, or that they shouldn't seek to, because I definitely think that writers benefit from experimentation and stretching themselves. But as an example, people have asked me whether it was scary to evoke a novelist as stylistically brilliant as Nabokov, and I have to say, for me, it wasn't. First, because, thank god, I just didn't stop to think about it, but also because my natural style is already a bit high tone. It wasn't as much of a stretch for me as it would've been for a writer whose voice is more stark, more spare.

In terms of the comic, although each individual comic can be an experiment in and of itself, I did consciously have a style in mind when I started writing them. In fact, the earliest comics all had a formula that I don't adhere to anymore but that probably was helpful when I got started. I can't even remember if it was intentional or if it was just something I noticed and then made intentional, but there would be two panels in which animals were speaking or conversing and then there would be a blank speechless panel with just an image, and then a cohesion or a punchline in the last panel. That appeared again, and again, and again. I think that form of thoughtfulness and the ability to make a big thought very concise is something that has influenced the comics throughout. Another rule that I had for myself early on is that the animals would never acknowledge that they were animals, but they also wouldn't call themselves people. I think I may have slipped once or twice at some point. But that was overall a rule, which I think is related to the slipperiness between reality and fantasy, or reality and the sublime, or the divine that you were talking about as something that slips into my fiction a lot—hauntedness, ghosts, weirdness.

CARVE

I think this begs the question of your work's relationship with reality. You studied abroad in Russia—did you draw on that experience for *Bonfire*?

ADRIENNE

Absolutely, without a doubt. For *The Daughters* too. For *The Daughters*, some of the ideas I wrote about to give Poland a sense of place were inspired by things I had felt, smelled, and tasted living in St. Petersburg and visiting Moscow. For *Invitation to a Bonfire*, having a sense of Russian culture, language, and sound very consciously went into the book. Some of it came from having read a lot of Nabokov. But having studied the Russian language was very, very important to me. I wanted to get the Russian right. There were two small errors—kill me—but I fixed them, so in the paperback they'll be fixed. A Russian woman actually wrote me a fan letter, which I really treasured, in which she said, "I really loved the book. I can tell that you studied Russian." Then she said, in a very Russian way, "By the way, here's what you got wrong." I found it really gratifying that she could tell from the way that I wrote Russian that I spoke it.

In studying abroad, not only was I immersed in the culture and in the place, but there's a very specific kind of light in St. Petersburg that affected me. I think anyone who's been to a really far-northern place has seen this kind of light, that seems to bend around corners and reflect off water in a very strange way. That itself has this weird tinge of the extraordinary. And also the way you can still see the echoes of the USSR in Russia, in a Russia that has the beginnings of being very enmeshed in the capitalist system. Then there's just the fact that Russia and America are both superpowers and they define themselves, a lot of the time, against one another. From listening to either one in a vacuum you'd get the idea that they're very different places, but actually, having grown up in America and having lived in Russia, I think there's a lot about them that's very similar. Especially in their sense of their own power and dignity. They're kind of like two people who are too alike to get along. That similarity was really important to me for Zoya—it's something that, in a certain way, plays out in her character.

CARVE

This reminds me again of the image from "Eternal Youth," time being worried over until smooth.

ADRIENNE

I think about that image a lot too.

CARVE

It sounds like there are multiple levels in your work. There's experience—the real experience of being in Russia. But even within that, in the light, there's something that's a little bit beyond the ordinary. Within the fiction, there's also a relationship between experience and the extraordinary, but there's a relationship between writing and working through a thought process through the process of writing. As you write through images, through thoughts, through themes, how is fiction related to catharsis?

ADRIENNE

I don't think that I usually choose an idea or a theme in order to seek catharsis. Usually, when I start a piece of writing that I'm really excited about, I'm much more excited to get to go into that place than I am to have relief from it in the end. In terms of *Invitation to a Bonfire* for example, I hadn't lived in Russia for a really long time. I hadn't studied Nabokov in a systematic way for a really long time either, although I did a bunch of rereading as I was writing that book. And yet I was struck by how suddenly and completely I became invested in his story.

I've told this genesis story in a couple of other interviews, but I was reading a *New Yorker* review of the collective letters of Vladimir and Véra Nabokov. In that article, it really casually mentions that Nabokov had an affair—probably multiple affairs, but one in particular. I had always viewed him as this great man who was very controlling but who had the redeeming quality of having had an incredible wife and having known what a huge value she was to him, and really treasured her and loved her, which he probably did. In that reality, I had not integrated the idea that he might also have had an affair and almost left her. I got so angry.

From that, all of the ideas of the book, related to that

or not, ended up springing out. All of the knowledge that I have about Russia, all of the memories that I have of being there, studying Russian and reading Russian literature, suddenly bubbled up to the surface in a way that I hadn't needed them to, at least not for a long time. I think that what has been interesting to me about that process—what we've talked about with the time bubble, that you can have an idea or a concern worn smooth that suddenly gets jagged and requires you to go back to it. It does, I think, end up resulting in a kind of catharsis. But to me, the catharsis is having lived through an experience rather than an external force to apply to a problem in my life and fix it. I think you go deeper before you can fix it, if you fix anything at all.

CARVE
You've described writing as an opportunity to go into a specific place. Do you have a similar relationship with reading?

ADRIENNE
Absolutely, yeah. When people describe reading as escapism in a denigrating fashion, I think, "What are you talking about? That's the best part." As a writer, I definitely come to writing from having had powerful reading experiences all throughout my life. I think that there is, of course, a slight difference, but for me, the difference is that in writing I get to be in the place for longer and more intensely. I think that I leave more of myself in it, whereas with reading, it leaves more of itself in me. Of course, I get to be a little bit less concerned with how it's structurally put together and whether the voices are even, although you can't completely turn off that faucet once you've become a writer.

CARVE
Invitation to a Bonfire and *The Daughters* feel somewhat tonally

different, so considering this relationship you have with reading, is this experience of inhabiting stories and books different depending on what your writing project is? Does the tonal quality of what you're reading have to match or be different from what you're working on in your own writing?

ADRIENNE

The writing process for those two books was so different, it's not a surprise to me that they feel tonally different to a reader. *The Daughters* took a lot longer to write and it was written more episodically. I ended up putting it together in different orders a lot of times to see how the past and present could do the most work putting pressure on one another to create a satisfying hold. *Invitation to a Bonfire* came to me more like a fever. I wrote the first draft of it very quickly, and I think I was a little bit more assured in what I was doing throughout that process—which I would love to attribute to getting better at writing novels through experience, but I'm working on something now that's taking forever, so I don't know.

In terms of what I read when I write, I think—and this was true for both books, and writing in general—when I'm writing well I'll get a craving to read something; a very, very strong craving. But the thing I want to read rarely has much to do with what I'm writing. The stable element is just the craving itself. When I was writing *Invitation*, there were a few more things that I read for educational or research purposes—I read some Nabokov and I reread *The Secret History* by Donna Tartt as I was thinking about structuring it. But mostly, there's always some amorphous artistic itch that I have to scratch, through reading. I'm not one of those people who stops reading when I write at all, but I don't try to surround myself with things that are incredibly similar to what I'm trying to do. I don't think I consciously choose things that are really different, either. I just get hungrier in a more immediate way—book hungry.

CARVE

What's something you've read recently that is stuck on you?

ADRIENNE

This may sound really random, but the last book that I read was *The Goblin Emperor* by Katherine Addison, which is a fantasy book that's also, essentially, a court drama, just with elves and goblins. But I loved it. It did such a beautiful job really focusing on the needs of the characters, and their actions and feelings in the moment, that I actually kept forgetting they were elves and goblins at all, until someone's ears would be mentioned. They all had really expressive ears.

On a different note, at the end of last year, I really adored *Riddance* by Shelley Jackson, which just came out through Catapult. It's a really peculiar book. If you like a book that will delve into the uncanny in a very idea-based way, that book is for you. It's organized as a collection of fragments, communications, letters in a similar way to how *Invitation to a Bonfire* is, but it's about a school for children with stutters who use their stutters and other really arcane and bizarre methods to act as voice-pieces to the dead, to travel the world of the dead. But saying that is such a limited description of the book. I have a hard time describing it even now—I'd really have to read it again to do any sort of justice to it. The form of the novel pushes all of its ideas through the body in a fascinating sense. I'm probably going to have to go back to it because it's written in a way that I have not seen before.

CARVE

You mentioned you're working on a new novel—what can you tell me about that project?

ADRIENNE

Nothing! I've been working on it for a while and I have a chunk done. I guess I can say that it's really structurally strange. It was intentionally so. It's very personal, but it's also very intentional in its structure. That has been a strange ladder to climb up. I really love it and I'm excited about it, but I don't feel like I can talk about it quite yet.

CARVE

A few years ago when you spoke with Matthew, you talked about working from home, working remotely for Google, and how you had a beautiful office that was sacred for writing and you would go into the kitchen for working. It sounds like your weekly schedule is somewhat the same, creating comics on Sundays and posting on Wednesdays. I wondered what else about your process has remained the same and whether things have changed spatially.

ADRIENNE

Very similar in that I have the same house and I have the same studio, but I can't remember if we had renovated the garage yet when I talked to Matthew. When we first moved into this house, there was a sunroom that I wrote in. Then we renovated the garage into a full studio for me, which is totally awesome. The problem with it was that I ended up using it for work too, which did kind of mess with my head. I very recently left my job at Google, so now I'm experimenting with writing full-time. I'm still so new to it that I feel like I have almost nothing to say about it yet, except that I'm excited for it. To experience life with the freedom of a residency and not feel like I have to work eight hours a day on a really rigid schedule, and have a little bit more space to think and move and read during the day and go take a long walk as I'm working on a project and still get to be super focused. Which is a huge, huge privilege, and wouldn't be possible if my husband didn't have a good day job and I hadn't been working at Google for years and built a nest egg, which I think it's good to be explicit about. I'm still struggling with getting out of the mentality of working with an eight-hour day in a very desk job-y way. It's still an experiment-in-progress. I'm hoping to also work on a graphic novel now that I have more time, because that will take forever.

CARVE

You had mentioned a graphic novel a couple of years ago—it's exciting to know that's still something you're thinking about.

ADRIENNE

I had a project that I was working on then that I have since finished some pages of, but I think I'm doing a different project now. The book that I was working on then, the graphic novel, came from a script that I had written in grad school for a screenwriting class. I now know how long it takes to plot out and draw even a small part of a graphic novel. Since I wasn't as excited about that story anymore it didn't feel worth it to me to really commit to it, so I have a different project that I'm a little more excited about. But I'm not throwing those original pages away, so who knows. Maybe four years from now I'll be like, "No I went back to the other one."

CARVE

What mantra is guiding your work right now?

ADRIENNE

Keep going. I think that's pretty much the most important thing for any artist to tell themselves.

The Odyssey

JIA TOLENTINO

September 2012

An 18-wheeler carrying ten thousand kilos of watermelons had wrecked spectacularly, spilling its cargo from a height of two kilometers, near the peak of the Tu-Ashu mountain pass that looms over the cold northern provinces of Kyrgyzstan. Around the winding curves of the road, strange asteroids were falling. Drivers braked, dodging scraps of tire, twisted metal, watermelons splashing open on the road in fecund bursts of pink and striped green. A long line of dusty vehicles stretched away from the wreckage. Drivers wearing black Adidas track-suits stepped out of their cars and peered over the cliff in search of the emergency crew. They lit cigarettes, paced, muttered, pissed behind boulders. It was late November, and dirty snow covered the ground. The thin, gold light turned gray as the sun fell behind the mountains, and the air whistling around them was icy.

At the end of the line sat Ulan Esenovitch in his new Honda Odyssey, bemusedly watching the watermelons conduct their slow, violent ballet. He leaned out of his open window and, yawning, tasted the sweet crispness of the air. He reached for the back window and rolled it down so the new dog could stick her nose out.

There was only one road that crossed the mountains separating Bishkek and Talas City, and for the last hour, Ulan had been stuck behind the burgundy sedan that was now parked close to the cliffside. The passenger door opened, and a girl emerged stiffly. She turned away from the car and stared into the mist, unmoving, as the wind blew her white school apron around her jeans. She had been walking on the side of the road with a friend when the sedan slowed down and swallowed her, four arms quickly extending from the backseat to pull her hands, grab her shoulders, and fold up her legs and kicking heels. Bride kidnappings were always brief, but in this case her new husband—the driver, as dictated by tradition—hadn't even come to a full stop. Now he and his friends were squatted on the ground and celebrating, passing a bottle of vodka back and forth, singing so loud that Ulan's dog whined with excitement.

Since the kidnapping, Ulan had been feeling waves of irritation, wondering why buying a car wasn't easier. It had taken him a week to unload his rusted Audi and acquire the keys to the Odyssey—a long, dragging week in the maze of the automobile bazaar, where the oily salesmen lied about mileage and refused his requests for a test drive. He was satisfied with the Odyssey, but who knew when it would break down? A wife, acquired in an instant, would do laundry forever.

High above them, from the opposite direction, a crew had ascended to clear the wreck off the road. Drivers were trickling back to their cars, some cradling watermelons. The blank-faced bride got back into the sedan. Ulan turned the key in his ignition and hummed an old folk song as he began the slow climb upwards. He drove across the spectacular peak of the Tu-Ashu, from which he could see into three different countries—a vantage point that made the range seem endless, a long continental spine. To the west, he glimpsed the silhouette of a bighorn sheep. He wondered where it had come from: perhaps Pakistan, or Uzbekistan, or maybe icy China. Thinking of imagined places, he drove down into the valley, the pastures in front of him saturated with color as sunset slid imperceptibly into night.

. . .

Four hours later, Ulan pulled into his driveway, where all his neighbors had gathered to greet him. Their hands went up as soon as they saw the Odyssey. "Happy tidings with your new arrival!" they shouted. He groaned, looking at his wife, who held a tray of shotglasses and wore a simpering smile. The car wasn't even new: A 1994 model, it was already three years older than Ulan had been at his wedding. Grimly, he noted the empty bottles of vodka—his own vodka—littering the concrete.

Ulan got out of the car. He kissed his wife, greeted his neighbors, patted his two daughters on their heads, accepted compliments, shook hands. The dog sprang out of the back seat, and he went after it, leaving his neighbors to descend upon the vehicle. He brought it to the old tin house in the corner of the driveway and chained it up. He crouched there, weary, as the dog butted her head against the walls of her new home.

His friend Nurlan walked over to him. "Did you get a good price, brother?"

Ulan stood up and took the cigarette Nurlan offered. "At least the dog was free." The two of them watched the fuss around the Odyssey: hood pushed up, tires prodded, kids climbing all over the seats.

His wife had brought up the dog the night before he left. "You will be taking on many more long trips with this car," she'd said suggestively.

"Probably." He was a taxi driver.

"Well!" she said. "We could use the money. And I think it's time that we got another guard dog. I don't feel safe alone with the girls. I already called Izada. Her dog had puppies in the spring. She lives near Bishkek. It won't take you long to stop by."

Disliking errands, Ulan looked at his wife askance, but she was set. "Get a boy."

But it had turned out that the biggest of Izada's dogs was a female, a plucky dog with a snout shaped like a block. Once everyone left, his wife would be pleased with her new guardian, but for now she was occupied. He wondered if she had gone door-to-door to announce the Odyssey's impending arrival or if she had texted everyone instead, wasting precious cell phone credits. Both possibilities infuriated him. He wondered if she'd bothered to make him dinner.

Someone turned the radio on, filling the driveway with Russian pop, a thumping bass and feminine cooing. His wife crowed and grabbed two of her girlfriends. Two other women handed off babies to their eldest daughters and started shaking their hips to the beat. "Another round!" his wife shouted, and the neighbors cheered. Ulan's head pounded. He reminded himself that he was a lucky man.

. . .

Later, after the last of the neighbors had parted, Ulan sat on the couch watching his wife prepare for bed. He thought about the other things he could have purchased with his dead uncle's small inheritance: a larger TV, perhaps, or a sheep or two. They had considered sending Albina to private school, but the tuition at the Turkish lyceum was exorbitant, and anyway, she was—as Ulan and his wife admitted privately—not the smartest child that ever was.

His wife turned to him, her face still radiant from the day's attention. "You know what Jazgul said today? 'A beautiful car, for a beautiful family.'"

Ulan lacked the energy to reply.

The two of them slept in the living room, Ulan on the couch and his wife on the floor atop long padded cushions called *tushuks*. In the bedroom, he could hear Albina and Alina giggling: Parents and children had switched sleeping arrangements a few years back, after the girls invented a monster in the china cabinet. Outside, the dog was wandering around its house, its chain scraping the driveway. "And, of course, I like the dog," his wife said. "Even if she is a girl. Doesn't she remind you of Kaku?"

Ulan smiled. Kaku!

"Didn't Kaku—"

"Yes," Ulan said. Kaku had been hit by a car when he was nine.

His wife clucked sadly. "That's right, I'm sorry. You know, maybe you'll make a fortune with the Odyssey, and we could move back to the city—the girls would grow up so smart in those schools." She sighed. "We could get an apartment. Take showers."

Ulan lay back on the couch wearily and pulled the blanket up to his chest. Taxi drivers had no hope of moving to the city, which already overflowed with idle cabs. In fact, no one could move to Bishkek these days except for rich teenagers whose parents could pay the bribes to get them to university. Along with thousands of others, Ulan and his wife had been pushed out to the villages after the Soviet empire fell. Ulan had been a municipal engineer; now he was a taxi driver, and a lazy one at that, one who forgot to clean out his car and hired young children to shout his destination at passersby while he spat sunflower seeds in the alley. And what did his wife need to be clean for anyway? "Sure," he said. "I'll take on more trips to Bishkek."

"Good," she said, and switched off the light. Ulan let himself drown, finally, in the thoughts that he'd been stifling all day.

He had to credit the Odyssey, whose roomy backseat had lent the encounter a new ease and recklessness. He'd been more forward than usual, rougher, imagining in a rare flash of ego that the other man was aroused by the new minivan, that he found Ulan intriguing and powerful. He pictured it now: the nameless body bent over him, a head of rough graying hair, the gorgeous thick slap of muscled flesh. The man had smelled of familiar cologne, and several times Ulan had wondered if they had spent this hour together before. He couldn't be sure. In the family darkness Ulan felt an erection growing and took a deep breath. The room was painfully silent. His wife's breathing had slowed to a regular snuffle, but she woke easily and he knew that every rustle would be magnified. Quickly and regretfully, he calmed himself by thinking of the electric bills, his wife's chipped nail polish, the dingy beige straps of her slip.

. . .

He had found the field accidentally, years before, after nearly falling asleep at the wheel on a solo journey to Bishkek. Looking for a place to pull over, he turned onto a small dirt road and followed it through the woods until the trees cleared out and his headlights illuminated an open field with a cluster of parked cars in the middle.

Like most taxi drivers from his region, Ulan usually spent the night with acquaintances in the capital or drove straight to Bishkek and back. Still, the roads were long and the weather in the mountains was unpredictable. It wasn't uncommon to see a lone taxi parked on a monotonous stretch of road. He'd never seen this many cars together, but he was pleased—it would be safer. He pulled the car to a stop, turned the lights off, and got out to stretch his legs.

The door of a car near him opened and a man stepped out. He looked at Ulan, the peculiar slant of his mouth traced faintly in the moonlight. A sudden burst of adrenaline flamed through Ulan's body. The man walked over and touched him with large, worn hands, then sunk deliberately to the ground, in a moment that Ulan remembered reverently, a second that lasted forever but could not be taken apart. The air thickened. Neither he nor the man had bathed recently, and the sounds and odors were disgusting, irresistible.

. . .

Five years had passed since that first night. Now Albina was ten and Alina was eight. Ulan's wife had remained girlish into her mid-thirties. She was a good mother to the girls, placating them easily when they rushed to her with the incomprehensible, urgent emotions that so confused Ulan. Absorbed in her small tasks, his wife had not noticed the initial shame that had kept him in the village for months, afraid of the temptation that would overtake him if he took another trip to Bishkek. She hadn't seemed to notice his mania when the shame faded, the renewed frequency of his long trips to the capital; it escaped her, the way that Ulan no longer felt at home in the village.

But he could not stop going to the field, no more than he could stop coming back to the village, so—he told himself grimly—this life would endure forever. He separated himself from himself, and bargained: Once in the village, he would forget the field, be a father, a husband, a good man. But his lifelong even temper was blurring. On certain days, he woke up feeling like he had never seen his house before. When his wife poured him tea at breakfast, he could barely hear her voice; her face seemed obscured by gauzy layers. Under these spells, he drove his car without looking at anything and spoke rudely to his customers, forgetting where they had asked to be dropped off. He felt obsessive energy; on these days he moved like a ghost, his body an ambulating shell for visions from the fogged evening pasture.

He no longer had the energy to berate himself, but some things still set him adrift in guilt: his daughters running to greet him, his wife solicitously heating his milk for tea, the bells that tolled above the village mosque, which was always empty. Like many of his countrymen, Ulan was only moderately religious, but he found himself more and more drawn to the idea of a moral code, the stricter the better—a set of rules that would restructure his mind. Once, in the middle of the night, he found himself pulling the Koran down from the high shelf: *Do ye approach men, and stop them on the highway?* At this verse he stopped reading. He went back into the living room and lay down on the floor next to his wife, holding her closely, breathing her smell of bread and onions. But he couldn't sleep. *Do ye stop them on the highway?* After an hour he rose, embarrassed, and went to the outhouse to rub himself fiercely, imagining a vast empty highway, a lone man, a tangle.

Even in these moments, he never allowed himself to think about what exactly possessed him. He wouldn't call it love. In this country they employed a softer term, more fitted to the kind of affection people felt for a life of wormy apples and potato grease and fat-cheeked children that kept popping out no matter how many contraceptive herbs your wife put in her tea. The people felt transcendence in their perception of the land, the clean air, the mountains. They didn't look for bliss at home. Peace, at best. Companionship.

Ulan had never beaten his wife. He hadn't kidnapped her, either. He'd asked for her hand at a city *discoteka*, some Saturday night in the spring of their senior year of high school. In the sweet early morning they had held hands, giggling tipsily as they walked home to the apartment building where both of their parents lived, knocking on first her door, then his. Their wedding had been a week later, a simple Soviet affair: She put on a nice polka-dot dress, he wore his father's suit, they signed their names at the state office and went home to drink champagne with their relatives. After they were given the master bedroom for the night, they collapsed without consummating their union. Both of them had fallen asleep quickly, dizzy and relieved.

They had never discussed the infrequency of their relations, but Ulan didn't mind doing it when he was drunk. And now he had the images from the field to help him—those ghosts full of lustful anger, possessing him, pushing him deeper into the musty bulk of his wife.

. . .

A few days later Ulan woke up with an urge to walk the dog. His mind wandered through old places as he took his tea, and afterwards he dug out some rope from the back of one of their cupboards. Outside, the snow was muddy and the light was pale. The dog was in her house with her tail sticking out, fringed with ice. They had named her Chaika, which meant "seagull."

His wife stuck her head out of the door. "What are you doing?"

Albina and Alina, bleary-eyed in their pajamas, shoved their feet into their winter boots and bounded out to him. "Yeah, Dad, what are you doing?" they squealed, peering into the dog's house then backing away shyly.

"When I was your age, in Bishkek, I walked our dogs," he told them as he coaxed Chaika out. He knotted the rope around her neck, testing it, making sure it wouldn't slip. "You can come if you want," he added, smiling at his daughters, who looked horrified.

His wife raised her eyebrows. "Why are you walking the dog?"

"She needs exercise," he said. The girls shrieked with

laughter and ran back into the house, their hands over their mouths.

"You're going to look like a crazy person," his wife said.

Ulan shrugged. He pulled on Chaika's rope and unfastened the gate, then closed it carefully. The dog ran ahead of him and chased her tail in frantic circles. All around him the village was waking up. Gates were opening, wives were rolling out big empty barrels to be filled at the well, young boys and girls were taking their cows out to the mountain pasture. A boy named Azamat called out to him. "Big brother, what are you doing with that dog?"

"I'm taking her to pasture," Ulan called back, gesturing towards the girl in front of him, whose cow was eating grass. He was joking, but as the words came out he felt serious. He decided that he would join the children, leading the dog like a cow on the long, slowly rising path to the mountains.

The kids entrusted with pasture duty were still young enough to be wary and polite around adults. They nodded respectfully at Ulan and left him alone. Together, they walked for nearly an hour over hills and worn-down paths, the snowy mountains shifting and looming closer at every turn. Ulan's breath puffed raggedly into the cold air while the kids, unperturbed by the exertion, carried on talking about crushes, siblings, football games. Chaika trotted along gamely.

When they came to the pasture, a gradual slope on a browned foothill sheltered from snow, the kids let the cows free and looked at Ulan. "Go on," he said, smiling. They walked off, and he sat down, letting go of Chaika's rope. She collapsed on the withered grass next to Ulan with her tongue hanging to one side. She really did look like Kaku.

Ulan had loved walking the dog when he was a child. At first, it had been a way to see Bishkek without supervision, to steal candy from outdoor vendors and peek at the couples kissing in the quiet, leafy recesses of the parks. But soon he found that he enjoyed escaping with Kaku into the gridded streets. He loved the standard-issue factory uniforms and the anonymity of rainy days, when the pedestrians disappeared under thousands of identical black umbrellas. He had grown up with a good circle of friends, all of them romping around in Soviet abundance. His father had worked at a munitions factory, taken home steady pay, and received rewards for good performance. Back then they'd all lived in high-rise apartments and owned washing machines. They never imagined an adulthood spent in the villages burning their trash for heat, their college educations long ago wasted—but why would they have imagined such a thing?

Parts of the city were still prosperous: the discreet diplomat's corners where rich men kept houses with heated floors and Western electronics and thin, blonde wives. But the rest of Bishkek had become gray and shabby. The pipes and streets and big apartment blocks were decaying; stores, banks, and even doctors had begun to lean on commercial advertising to stay profitable. Foreign billboards towered over every corner, dwarfing the spindly columns where propaganda art had once been displayed.

When he was a child, he could see the poster on Sovietskaya Street from his window. Its slogan was stamped in red block letters: "Don't blab! These days, the walls have ears." Below the words were two strong-jawed men in olive military gear. One of them clutched a telephone with huge hands; the other reached down to take it away, matching his comrade's skeptical gaze with one of reassurance. The men were standing close. With every look, it became more and more possible to Ulan that the standing man was looking at his comrade's arm, pressed snugly and firmly across his stomach, groin, thigh. There were secrets everywhere.

The billboard made Ulan feel considerably patriotic. With such feeling did he love his country! He ignored the other full-body twinges he felt when he looked at his lithe Russian track coach—about whom people always said things—or the older boys at school. But then one day his coach disappeared, and a rumor circulated that Andrei had been taken to the mountains and beaten to death. Ulan came home from school feeling queasy. He lay on his bed and stared at the poster, thinking about how his coach had once gently massaged a cramp out of his calf. "The walls have ears," the handsome soldiers said. They looked stern now, unforgiving.

Chaika barked, wrenching Ulan back to the pallid mountains, the deep shadows of the valleys, the overworked potato fields. It was a brown landscape in a frozen sky. He picked up Chaika's lead and walked down the hill.

. . .

The next weekend, Ulan took his first trip to Bishkek in the Odyssey. He always enjoyed holiday drives, despite the ice and the traffic, and he was pleased to find a Kazakh family that was willing to both pay their children's passage and put the children on their laps. The ride was lively, with his passengers sharing their soda and singing along to the radio, and in the city the big avenues were strung with lights. The street vendors, bundled up, hawked cheap trinkets and party favors. He dropped his passengers off at an apartment building, stopping at a nearby stand to buy two glittery rabbit masks for Albina and Alina to wear for New Year's. Snow began to fall, and Ulan turned on the Odyssey's windshield wipers as he turned back onto the road that would take him out of the city.

He reached the field early, although it was dark enough so that mid-afternoon seemed like night. He idled his engine, put on his gloves and zipped his leather jacket. At that hour, there were only a few cars there. The snow was falling so thickly that they would all have to dig themselves out come morning.

When no one emerged from the cars, Ulan's excitement faded, leaving him suddenly tired. He turned on the space heater that he had rigged to the battery and reclined his chair, yawning.

A knock woke him up, setting his heart off at a breakneck pace—always, this flash of fear. He unlocked the door. A man opened it. He was older than Ulan, with a pockmarked face and a cap dusted with snow. As he climbed into the passenger's seat, Ulan quickly swept the rabbit masks away, throwing them into the back.

"Ah—the Year of the Rabbit," the man said.

Ulan nodded, thrown off: Normally, the men didn't speak.

"Are those for your kids?" he asked.

Ulan nodded again, clearing his throat awkwardly. "I have two. Girls."

"I'm sure they're beautiful."

A pang hit Ulan in the chest. "They are. They made this," he said, pointing to the dashboard ornament, a blue Turkish evil eye charm made out of felt. Albina and Alina had crafted it carefully for his last birthday.

The man smiled, genuine and easy. "It's beautiful, too."

Albina and Alina—the Odyssey could not accommodate the four of them at once. Ulan went soft and shameful. He'd have to ask the man to leave. It was all ruined now. He opened his mouth and the man reached out and shut it. He moved his hands down to Ulan's shoulder and gripped it, feeling his muscles.

. . .

Ulan woke up curled behind the man in the backseat of the Odyssey. Surprised, trying not to move, he looked around the minivan, which was flooded with moonlight. He squeezed his eyes shut, placing his hands gently on top of the man's hips and resisting the urge to clutch at him. The sense of devotion in his body was paralyzing. No one ever stayed. They always pulled up their pants and retreated, gone in a gasp of fresh air, sometimes getting in their cars and immediately driving away.

He had been confused when the man—whose name was Anarbek—pulled a condom out of his pocket. "To protect you."

Ulan had never used a condom and wasn't sure why Anarbek was suggesting one now. "But you can't get—you're a man, so—"

"I have bad blood," Anarbek said gently.

They'd gotten lost again then. At one point Ulan reached down to turn off the space heater, and he felt the unfamiliarity of the condom and still didn't understand. Afterwards, the two men had talked, but he was so absorbed in the novelty of learning about Anarbek's family, about his farm and children—even knowing his name was a first—that he had forgotten to ask what he meant about the blood.

Now in the early morning he cleared his mind, speaking to himself directly: He let himself remember some fatal illness, SIDAS, or CIDS, or something, that plagued far-off countries and was passed around in the Russian saunas in Bishkek. This was all he knew. There were no doctors to whom you could admit these sinner's fears. This concern, along with all the others, would soon be buried.

Now Anarbek stirred slightly and started to shift, turning to face Ulan, who quickly removed his hands from Anarbek's hips.

"I should go," Anarbek said, his voice scratchy.

Ulan nodded, averting his eyes.

"I wouldn't—I just need to get on the road. Toktogul, you know."

"Oh," Ulan said. "Of course. It takes me two days to get there."

Sitting up in the clammy backseat, they clasped hands in the Muslim way, then hugged each other for a long time. Ulan felt the air fracturing, the vital pieces falling away. "God willing, we'll meet again," Anarbek said. Ulan's throat caught and he couldn't reply. Anarbek smiled at him and left, closing the door quietly.

Ulan lay back down for an hour. When the sun came up, he left, still feeling as if there was something unanswered, forgotten. He stopped on the road for a wheel of fresh bread. Barely registering the children underfoot at the bread stand, he opened his wallet and found it empty. Yesterday there had been a 100-som bill, he was sure of it. He asked the *babushka* to wait and went back to the car, refusing to carry the facts to their logical conclusion. He found a ten-cent coin tucked under one of the floor mats. He paid for the bread brusquely and tore into it, staring ahead into the pale sunrise as he started the six-hour journey home.

. . .

A few days later came the celebration of the foreign New Year, which was held in a neighboring village, in the big school tearoom that was often used for parties. Albina and Alina had both binged on candy upon arrival and fallen asleep before midnight in a corner on top of a pile of coats. Ulan looked at them: two small full-skirted figures, bent legs in white tights, their rabbit masks askew on their heads. His wife refused to wake the girls up, saying they'd be cranky, but Ulan felt sorry for them. They'd be so disappointed that they'd missed the party. They'd been trying on their outfits since summer.

He looked at his watch, which appeared blurry: four o'clock. He wanted to go to bed. But they were two villages over, they hadn't had a big party since the spring weddings, and everyone would still be at it for hours. The music, bass inflated, was blowing out the speakers and pounding through the walls. Everyone had moved outside once all the kids started falling asleep, and Ulan could hear them whooping and dancing, pounding back shot after shot despite the hour and because of the cold. He had remained inside, needing a break; the room looked empty and huge without its revelers, and he slumped on the shiny floor next to a heap of trash and a prostrate seventh-grader who, judging by his breath, had been sneaking champagne.

Nurlan came breathlessly into the gym. "Your wife is very drunk," he said, squatting on the ground next to Ulan and shaking off a piece of tinsel that had attached itself to his foot. "So is my wife. They're slapping other men on the behind."

Ulan laughed. "Our poor cow. No one will milk it tomorrow morning."

"Time to go, don't you think?"

"I'd rather go join our wives," Ulan said, picturing one of his burly neighbors, who, when drunk, often pressed his forehead to Ulan's and emphatically called him brother. Nurlan looked at him. "I'm kidding," Ulan said. "Let's go."

Soon they were piled into the Odyssey, on the long straight road. The black mountains rose on either side of them like a moonscape. The women, although full of fight when instructed to leave, had passed out instantly. Albina and Alina were collapsed on either side of Nurlan's small son in the third row. Nurlan cheered approvingly as Ulan stepped on the gas. "*Too fast, too furious*," he said in English, and they laughed.

Nurlan rolled down the window to light a cigarette. The air flooding the car felt bracing and sweet. Ulan felt good again, back in balance; he wondered why he didn't drink more often. He watched Nurlan fumble with his lighter and drop it next to the seat. Reaching down, his friend pulled up a bright blue condom packet. The blood drained out of Ulan's face and hands. Nurlan turned the packet over slowly. "What's this?"

"It's not mine," Ulan said quietly.

Nurlan slapped his leg, laughing. "Good one! You've been

visiting the whores in the city!" He leaned conspiratorially towards the driver's seat. "I never use these—hate the feel, you know? But I should. We all should! I can't afford another child and the woman just caught something. She's got bumps on her. Disgusting."

"What do you mean? What do you mean, caught something?" Ulan asked, his stomach suddenly queasy. How could he have forgotten about this? Glancing in the mirror at their drooling, dressed-up wives, he saw only himself, waking up in the deep blue pre-dawn, his body fitted to Anarbek.

"Who cares?" Nurlan said. "So tell me, are the whores good in Bishkek? I have to settle for the ugly old ones near us. Do they—" He stuck out his tongue in the corner of his mouth. "Of course they do. Wish our wives would. How much do you pay them?"

Ulan thought of his emptied wallet, the gentle way Anarbek had excused himself. He shook his head and sped up even faster. "I told you, it's not mine. Let me see that." He held out his hand, and when Nurlan gave him the condom, he threw it out the window. Nurlan started to say something and Ulan cut him off. "Not mine."

. . .

He dropped Nurlan and his family off in silence. His heart pounded; he couldn't believe how close he'd come to being caught. His hands were shaking slightly, with relief but also with anger, with a growing sense that something was going to rip out of him. He drove through the open gate—he'd forgotten to close it—and jolted the car into park. "We're home," he told his wife, shaking her abruptly. She moaned quietly. "We're home," he shouted. "Albina and Alina, we're home!" His wife didn't want to wake up. "We're home!" he shouted one more time, flipping on all the lights in the car and then jumping out, slamming the door. He looked over his shoulder at the Odyssey, its insides glowing: The girls looked like they were about to cry. He didn't care. He could see his wife scratching at her eyes, smearing blue eyeshadow all over the side of her face.

It was pathetic how she'd had that shade since they were in college, Ulan thought as he turned away towards the house, unlocking the door. Why pretend to be beautiful? At best, the women would end up with someone like him. He pictured his wife's black nylon makeup bag, dusty and stained from shattered eyeshadows, full of half-inch lipsticks and broken lids. The girls sometimes tried the makeup on, standing on chairs to purse their lips for the one tiny mirror in the entrance hall. It made Ulan sick. All that Albina and Alina cared about now was their cartoons and their private nonsense, but soon even they would start mimicking the whores on the fashion billboards, the ones with glossy mouths and black eyes like they'd been punched. And like all the foolish girls in this country, they'd end up looking like regular whores, and they'd be poor forever because there was no money in driving a taxi, and they'd steal money to buy high heels and they'd shake their hips when they walked through the market and Nurlan would refuse to wear a condom and they would catch something if they didn't already have it from their father. What had Anarbek meant about blood? Ulan suddenly hated himself for never having the courage to ask or even fully see the question.

But it wasn't his fault, he told himself. It was this place, this village, these men who loved to joke about whorehouses but would kill a man like him. He was nothing like Nurlan. He didn't understand when everything had gone so wrong. He was a good man. He didn't beat his wife. He provided for his daughters. He took care of the dog. He was doing everything he could to be a good man. He'd tried to stop visiting the field. He'd worn the condom. He'd been the top of his class in college and now he was a poor taxi driver. It wasn't his fault. He didn't beat his wife.

As he paced the house, his wife shambled in, corralling the two girls. She didn't even look at him as she swayed down the hallway towards their bedroom; she'd sleep with them tonight. Ulan felt deep contempt towards her, towards the whole village. It wasn't just the children—they'd all been clutching for months at the anticipation of the New Year's party. Who knew happiness by anything other than what it wasn't?

He'd forget about the wallet. It wasn't like he'd paid Anarbek.

Ulan took a deep breath and decided to go feed the dog. Outside, he saw the tin structure in the headlights of the minivan, which was still on and running. It was empty. Chaika had pulled out the stake that held her chain to the ground.

"Chaika!" he shouted. She must have pushed the gate open. He hadn't forgotten to close it. He jumped in the car and backed out of the driveway recklessly. He sped down the dirt road. The sun was rising now, casting the mountains in soft pink and gold. "Chaika!" he shouted again, rolling down all the windows. "Chaika dog!"

He drove through the village for a few minutes, shouting out the windows. Then in front of the dark school he stopped the car abruptly, slamming his hands on the wheel. She wasn't anywhere. She was an animal. She'd get eaten in the mountains or run over by the drunk drivers who were careening home with their windows open, hooting.

When Kaku had been run over, Ulan hadn't seen the car, only the dog on the ground, her form emerging from a cloud of dust. He ran to her, confused, and her body jerked and pounded. He went numb when he saw the blood near her mouth, and he dragged her out of the road into a small side street. He lay beside her, touched her fur, still warm and soft. Eventually he cried when she did. He didn't remember what he might have been thinking. He didn't want her to stop shaking. He fell asleep slumped over Kaku in a corner of the alley behind an electrical box. His mother found him hours later, still sleeping, shivering in the dark evening chill.

She'd shaken her head sadly. "Poor Kaku," she said. She reached down to touch her son, rubbing his small back. He woke up and instantly started sobbing. She forced him up, leaving the dog, and held his hand as they walked home.

It was only a block to the apartment, but Ulan shuffled slowly, unwillingly. Suddenly, in the middle of the sidewalk, in front of a brightly lit ration office, his mother knelt down and turned him to face her. Her look hardened. "Ulan," she said. "You're a grown man already, don't you know that?"

This made him cry harder.

She shushed him. "You don't want your brothers seeing you like this."

"We left her," he said shakily.

"What else could we do?" she said. "Take her with us? Carry her around until the house stinks and you can't cry anymore?" She wiped his face off firmly and stood up, pulling him along, talking to him quietly, soothing him against his will, telling him that sometimes you just had to leave things behind. Pain was something you brought on yourself. He was too old to cry like his silly girl cousins. He was a man, a full-grown man. There would be other dogs.

. . .

It was the New Year, the Year of the Rabbit. Ulan had seen the whole beautiful sunrise as he drove east across the mountains, and now the day was cloudless and blue. He'd reached the field at eleven. He'd cried out in pain when the man left his car. He was on his way back, still mourning.

When he passed the high point of the Tu-Ashu he turned

on his cell phone and called his wife, who picked up instantly and started to yell. He cut her off. "I'm sorry. I'm very sorry. I was out looking for Chaika all night. I thought I saw her run into the hills and I followed her, and then I fell asleep. I'm sorry to have worried you."

"Chaika?" she shouted. "What do you mean, Chaika?"

"She got out last night. Haven't you noticed?" he said.

"Sometimes I really don't know about you," his wife said. "Sometimes I think you're crazy. Chaika's here! I found her in the cellar eating apples."

Ulan hung up. He pulled over to the side of the road and got out of the car. All of Kyrgyzstan stretched in front of him. He stood up and squinted into the sun, then sunk down against the warm metal frame of the Odyssey, cradling his head in his hands, overwhelmed by the mercies, the asymmetrical contracts of love.

JIA TOLENTINO is a staff writer at the *New Yorker*, formerly the deputy editor at *Jezebel*, and a contributing editor at the *Hairpin*. Her first book, the essay collection *Trick Mirror*, will be published by Random House in 2019.

INTERVIEW WITH
JIA TOLENTINO

December 2018

CARVE

So, I revisited your original *Carve* interview with Matthew to get some context about this story.

JIA

Oh my god. It's been a million years.

CARVE

You talked a lot about wrestling with the idea of following your interests, which at that time were really defined by the culture of Kyrgyzstan, and also dealing with the thought that it might not be your story to tell—focusing on the lives of the people and not generalizations about the culture itself. This would've been the fall of 2012.

JIA

Right. So, right when I started my MFA program.

CARVE

Yeah, I think you might've talked to him even before you got to Michigan.

JIA

That sounds about right.

CARVE

This is to say, I wondered if that thought process about story-telling was related to your movement away from fiction and into more nonfiction. At the time of that interview you were working on a novel.

JIA

Yeah. I mean, it took me until about a year into my MFA program to feel comfortable even calling myself a writer. Even though I had been working as a copywriter, I was not comfortable saying that I was a writer. I worked on that novel for all of grad school, probably for a total of almost five years. Then, sort of late in the process, well after I was finished, I told my agent that I didn't want to put it on the market.

In retrospect, when I was in Kyrgyzstan I was extremely young. Young in my brain, and in my heart. I worked on the book during the period in which I became a professional writer, so, by the end, the way I approached writing was very different than how I approached it at the beginning.

There was some amateur uncertainty I couldn't scrub out of the book, which I am sure is related to that cultural question. It was a huge part of my hesitation to put the book on the market, because, you know, I'm not Kyrgyz. I care deeply about that country. And I have been back. But you have to be really, really good to get away with doing something like that, and I was just never sure that I could write fiction that was good enough to.

CARVE

I appreciated how in that interview you acknowledged that MFA programs tend to make writers look at what's trendy—in some ways, writers in MFA programs are learning how to perform trends and technique for publication. I feel like I see that as an editor of a magazine that publishes a lot of emerging writers. I think the thoughtfulness with which you approached publication as a new writer, having completed a novel and then not wanting to put it on the market, shows a lot of self-control.

JIA

The fact that I was already writing professionally helped with that decision. I was writing so much on the side that I rarely lacked for an outlet or for the sense that I was being read. And the gestation period for a novel—it's just so endless. I'm just now finishing my first book, and it'll be published next August. I think one of the big motivations that causes people to put a first book that maybe isn't ready on the market is that desire to be read. That motivation wasn't a factor for me; I didn't feel like I had been working invisibly.

I write a lot about my own life in nonfiction, but as a writer my interest in fiction was always about being in the head of a person whose life I would never even come close to. I wasn't interested in writing fiction about someone who resembled me—you know, what could be more boring, a woman in her early twenties with the same mundane concerns as me.

So I reached for the opposite of my experience in a way that I'm sure reflects, even just in general, this narrative hunger for hardship that exists in both fiction and nonfiction, where people, often when they're starting out, tend to write about any adjacency to marginalization or structural hardship. That seems like the most interesting thing to write about. And that's not untrue, right? I edited personal essays for three years and, you know, I saw this as a theme there in a similar way. It's not necessarily a bad thing. But all of that is wrapped up in the reason that I didn't try to sell the novel.

CARVE

Sure. And I think writers in general tend to have this impulse to write fiction that borrows something from their own experience, their own lives. I read your interview with *Mythos Magazine* and you spoke about how you don't typically feel a sense of identification with characters in books, movies, TV—you see yourself at the center of your own story and not necessarily in the stories of characters. I'm also thinking about your reflection on *Girls* in the *New Yorker* and how you could see the reasons why some would feel an impulse to identify with that show, but you personally could write objective cultural criticism about it because you didn't really feel that. I wondered how that thought process plays into your relationship with fiction—with reading or writing fiction.

JIA

When I was editing essays, I rarely identified with the internal narrative texture of whatever the person was writing about. But I liked editing those, I liked working on them, because it offered the same possibility that writing fiction offers, which is understanding somebody's choices and empathizing with them. For me, the latter has always been a constant, and it's deeply pleasurable, but it has never really crossed the border into an experience of identifying with something so strongly, so personally.

CARVE

So that experience of personal identification is not what makes it important.

JIA

No. It's something that's very close to it, but not the same. Hopping into somebody else's brain for the length of a book or a TV episode does not require a puzzle piece that connects it to my own.

That being said—and I'm writing about this in my

book—there's a huge racial component to this as well. One of the reasons that I have not actively identified with literature is because there are lots of signals about how the identification process is supposed to work—not even in terms of what kind of people appear in what stories, but even at a language level. Something about literary fiction that drives me nuts is the novel that's written by somebody that clearly considers themselves very, you know, liberal. A progressive. But the whole novel is written with the understanding that, by default, everyone's white. And if a character is not white or not straight, that's when they get a descriptor, but everyone else is only described by their personalities or habits.

That is embedded at such a deep level in how I process narrative. And it is something that's more specific, or entirely specific, to books rather than TV and movies. It's the specific way that this is signaled in language that I have always hated. And still hate.

CARVE

And considering how white-oriented the literary canon is, even still in contemporary literature, like you said, character description in particular is tricky and problematic.

JIA

I don't mind a story that's set in a white world. A lot of people live in very white worlds. I wish they weren't the entirety of the canon, almost—but I really don't mind it, reading a book about all white characters. But there's a certain way that the descriptions work that makes me get a pit in my stomach because you can tell that the narrative, that the writer, is so unconscious of what's at work.

I guess it's similar to the beef that people have had with Lena Dunham in *Girls*. It's her lack of consciousness. But for some reason, I didn't really feel it with that and I do with fiction often, especially contemporary fiction set in a place like New York. I also think this correlates with just good writing.

CARVE

Right, compassionate writing?

JIA

Yeah. Or just smart writing. A lot of the books that I loved this year were by white women and a lot of them were about white environments, but whiteness was an implicit subject rather than an assumed backdrop, or something. Like *Florida* or *My Year of Rest and Relaxation* or *Motherhood*.

CARVE

Sure. This thought reminds me of Percival Everett, who has written and spoken about this, how in his books he's not writing a white environment, but he's also not super acknowledging the fact that he's not writing a white environment. You know what I mean?

JIA

Right. This predicament is really being broken open by writers who are not white and straight. You know, switching the default. That's where the real work is done, by people whose worlds are not by default white and who are writing to their own defaults. It is sort of discursively widening our sense of what an undescribed character might be.

CARVE

Yeah, absolutely. You mentioned how people perform being liberal and then write these books that fall into these problematic patterns, and you've written about the side-taking, opinion-forming, and polarization of the internet and how the internet is out of pace with what a real-life discussion about something like this would be like. It doesn't allow for the nuance that a real conversation would. In that interview with *Mythos* you referred to it as "excessive boundary policing," which is not action. This is a long-winded way of saying that what I love about your work is how you're comfortable in the space of not knowing what the answer is, with the conclusion being the premise, and not binding yourself to a conclusion as you enter into a discussion.

But I wondered—I mean, that interview is from the fall of 2017. In 2018, it feels like there's even less space for real discussion on the internet. How are you thinking about that? I'm thinking in particular about how you are active on Twitter, because I have to be honest, Twitter, and in particular writer-Twitter, scares the crap out of me because it's not very conducive to conversation or learning. Twitter can be a great tool to find writers that you might not find through other avenues. But I find myself intimidated by the risk of having my own thoughts on Twitter.

JIA

I think that's completely rational. I would never argue that it's good that Twitter has become an activity that is now seen as normal and productive in society, that people should constantly be broadcasting to an unlimited audience what they think. I mean, Twitter reflects and drives the sea changes that happen in the culture industry and in our broader discourse. I'm glad that I can be basically paid to have opinions now, and that the internet has made way for people like me to be included. But I would still say that Twitter is definitely not good.

Social media values the representation of something over the thing itself. So it will always make the representation of correctness, or action, take place over the actual correct moral action itself. I think if you hate Twitter, definitely don't try to use Twitter more. It's a bad place. I use Twitter, and when I do tweet I'm very unguarded—clearly I don't really have a lot of hesitation in my personality—but I actually don't tweet that much. I block it from my computer and phone for at least five hours during the workday and I have a timer that shuts it off after forty-five minutes of daily use. Both literary Twitter and journalist Twitter get overrun by meaningless niche drama.

CARVE

Yes, definitely.

JIA

And there's something about it—writers love to perform that they are writers. There's this indignance on Twitter, like when someone will be like, "Tweet this with something that you wish people understood about your profession." And then writers just like go on for days. And it's like, who cares? Twitter is really good, especially for writers and journalists, for creating this professional simulacrum—it's almost like you're working. It resembles your work so closely that it can seem like you're working. But get off of it and fucking work.

CARVE

Speaking of doing the work, in your conversation with Matthew you talked about not originally wanting to get an MFA, but after doing freelance writing for a while you realized you wanted some time to write for yourself and an MFA was a way to get that. Now that you're a staff writer at the *New Yorker*, I wondered what kind of boundary there is between your work writing and personal writing.

JIA

I work full-time at the *New Yorker*, and I wrote my book from September of 2017 until October or November of this year.

There's much less of a boundary in terms of subject now that I'm not writing fiction. Before, it was absolutely divided. But book work and work-work have been similarly slanted: This book picks up a lot of ideas that I've been writing about for the *New Yorker*, just at greater length.

Before, the way that it appeared to me was there is a divide between the writing that you do in public and the writing that you do in private. I started working in media on the side while I was doing my MFA—or I was going to school and working on the novel on the side, whichever one you want to think of as on the side. And then I moved to New York and worked for *Jezebel*, and all of my writing was for work, basically. Then I started at the *New Yorker* and it continued like that for a year or two, and I started to miss having writing that only I looked at. I thought that it was getting bad for my brain to be only writing in public. But it's sad that that's as personal and private as my writing has gotten lately—a year of secret writing before the book is published. I don't keep a journal or anything—Twitter is that, basically. I use it as a record of what I was thinking about on a given day, but it's so partial.

CARVE

You were an editor for years, and in your interview with the *Longform* podcast you talked about how editing is soothing for you, how it's rewarding to help clarify a piece, which is related to but different from the process of writing. Now that you're writing full-time, what role does editing play in your life?

JIA

I do really miss editing. Before I started at the *New Yorker* I was editing and writing, and now I'm only thinking about my own ideas. At first it felt disgusting, and then I settled into it, unfortunately. I really loved, loved, loved editing. What I didn't like about it was managing. *Jezebel* was such a high-traffic, high-volume thing and I had to do so much managing, which I didn't like because it was time away from writing or editing.

I'm ultimately glad that I got off the editing track because I do like writing all day. And what a relief it is to only communicate with my editor! So nice. And nice not to deal with invoices and stuff anymore. I am a really tough self-editor, and I think I take edits well because I was an editor and I know how annoying it is when people don't trust your edits. But I don't work with anyone else's writing actively or on a regular basis and I do miss that. You learn a lot from doing that, learn in a way that you don't when you're just reading, and I miss learning things through editing other people's work.

CARVE

The person who interviewed you on *Longform* revealed that you'd been turning down job offers because you wanted to stay at *Jezebel*. How, especially early in your career, did you know when to say yes or no to opportunities?

JIA

I've always been really pragmatic about it. I graduated in 2009, right into the recession. I didn't know anyone who was a writer, and I also have not had much of a personal safety net in my life. I've benefited, I think, from being really pragmatic, with very little wiggle room and also not counting on anything other than whatever satisfaction I knew I could personally guarantee myself in the work. I never thought I would be in this industry. The industry constantly seems on the brink of collapsing.

So I thought, okay, I'll apply to MFA programs and I'll go if I get one that fully funds me and gives me a stipend so I don't have to go into any debt at all. And I got into one, so I thought, okay, clearly this is what I should do. Then I was freelancing during that MFA and I got this opportunity to start editing a website that I loved. Again I was like, okay, clearly I should take this because here is a job that I can have in writing. Which, you know, what a miracle. I didn't think this would happen.

It was also that I loved writing fiction, but I also knew I couldn't make a living just writing fiction. I would have to teach, at the bare minimum. I knew taking the editing job was what I should do, and working at *The Hairpin* was an experience of having complete creative control and stylistic freedom. I learned to value that so much that when I got it at *Jezebel* again, with a much bigger audience and the ambient flickers of editorial independence dying all around me—*Gawker* was being sued, you know, places were shutting down. *Grantland* was shutting down. It was really clear to me that at *Jezebel* I had something that wouldn't last for long: completely unfettered freedom to run whatever I wanted, to write whatever I wanted, to write in whatever style I wanted, to be as vulgar or as formal as I wanted from piece to piece.

That was something that was more important to me than working at a place that was more respectable, or that was better known, or that people had less of a problem with. People had constant problems with *Jezebel*, some for good reason, often for not. But the freedom that I had at Jezebel was unbelievable. I just loved the people I worked with, too. I never considered leaving it just because another place was fancier.

But then I accepted the *New Yorker* job offer the day that *Gawker* went bankrupt. They had called and said, "Do you want to write twice a week and maybe try on print stuff?" And I was like, "Oh my god, yes." At that point, at *Jezebel*, I was editing full-time but I wrote a lot too. I couldn't stop writing, because I liked to, but it was getting to be too much. Plus the demise of *Gawker*. So it was a pragmatic decision. What I wanted was more time, and some direction, some extremely stringent editing from someone else, and here was this place that is a dream to work for, offering just that.

CARVE

Across your work, from your story in *Carve* to your virgin interviews in *The Hairpin* to the editorial work with *Jezebel*, you've done a lot of work examining and discussing cultural narratives, and this idea of bearing witness seems to be a thing that recurs in your work. What obsessions are driving you right now?

JIA

I'm thinking about the end times. In terms of capitalism. I think one of the big throughlines in my work now is this point of hyper-acceleration that we've found ourselves in that makes moral living in America feel almost impossible. That's one of the things I'm thinking about.

My book is a bunch of 10,000 essays on things that I was obsessed with enough to write ten thousand words on. One of the essays in the book is about what we were talking about earlier—how literary heroines, the canonized literary heroines, are all white and straight. How they're brave girls and then depressed, desirable teenagers, then they're bitter women who die. That's a journey that's always really bothered me, that I've never connected to, so I wrote about it until I felt that I understood it more.

But mostly, my interests have never really shifted too much. I've written a lot about sex, and cultural versus personal narratives, about how they overlap and influence each other. Because I think that sex, and power and sex together—these things are hard to write about well, or with the same complication that feels true to what happens inside a person's soul. I think I always tend to be drawn to things that I think are not written about well.

CARVE

As a reader, I think that's why I'm so drawn to your work—the way you can be articulate about things that other writers botch. I can't help but connect this to your 2012 *Carve* interview—you talked about the Kyrgyz language and its lack of synonyms, how everyone had Russian as a second language that could sometimes supplement communication.

JIA

Yeah. One language that was so relatively simple, and another language that was so much more complicated than English. It was wild—these opposite poles of syntax.

CARVE

That's so interesting. And I mean, I think some of the trouble with writing about complicated issues—it's linked to the limits of the language available for using to talk about it.

JIA

Absolutely, absolutely. The way I think about it—I've written about the "Me too" era like a million times since the Weinstein story, and part of the thing that really bothers me is that every time I write the word "women" I want to clarify and qualify it. But for the sake of concision, and, essentially, statistical acknowledgment—there are many reasons why you would just want to write, "when these things happen to women" or "when women are in these positions," right? But every time I use that word, in stories about assault or reproduction or whatever, I'm so frustrated with myself because I want to add five lines about gender, or find a better way of saying "people whose biology is consistent with female characteristics," or something. I am frustrated by my own tendency to reinscribe a binary in my work. I'm trying to get a little better at it each time, piece by piece. But in a lot of ways, it is a language problem.

CARVE

Yeah, that for the sake of readability you have to be reductive sometimes.

JIA

Right. I can't write a dissertation about gender every time I say "women." But I know I can be better and I want to be better.

CARVE

Talking about the word "women" has made me think about narratives and women, and I saw on your website that in January you're going to be having a conversation with the author of *Hollywood's Eve*. I wanted to ask you about that—I went to LA for the first time this summer and really wanted to read an LA narrative, but I didn't know where to start.

JIA

Did you read Eve Babitz?

CARVE

Well, I saw her books for sure, but I got overwhelmed by the "LA sections" of the bookstores and didn't end up choosing anything. I knew I didn't want to read Raymond Chandler, and most of the female characters I was finding were rich divorcées or teenagers in coming-of-age narratives.

JIA

Oh my god, you've got to read Eve Babitz.

CARVE

After seeing that on your website, I definitely fell into this internet research spiral about Eve Babitz. I wondered if you would tell me a little bit about your fascination with her and where I should start.

JIA

Well, have you read the Joan Didion LA stuff?

CARVE

Not really. I've read very little Joan Didion.

JIA

I would recommend reading them back to back because it's like reading a photo negative and then the image itself. They're both incredible writers about LA, but their instincts are absolutely opposite. Eve Babitz's writing feels spontaneously generated, but it's clearly very carefully crafted. It's crafted so carefully that it seems tossed off, which is an ability that I admire and probably is a personal thing, too, for me.

But Eve Babitz, really, she's just fun, and I find so much value in that. One of the things that drives me nuts about writing and writers is that writers can be real ponderous drags. That's one thing that I didn't like about my fiction. It didn't have humor. I don't think I'm a funny writer, but I think my sense of humor comes through in most of my work.

CARVE

Yeah, and the humor is tonal.

JIA

Yeah, yeah, for sure. But I didn't have that in my fiction. Maybe it was because of the subject, too. But Eve Babitz—I have found few models of writers who think very seriously about their subject but also consistently have in mind that they want to have a good time. That was a personal lodestar for me. There is so much pleasure in Eve Babitz's work. When I read it for the first time, it was like I had forgotten that all this was even possible.

Joan Didion—her writing about LA had been previously

definitive for me. But it's so neurasthenic and brittle—it's brittle and burned out and very white, blindingly white. Its aesthetic is just so clean. And you know, you don't read Joan Didion and think, this is a woman that loves to have fun. So it was just nice to read Eve Babitz and remember that there is truth in a different sort of tone, too. I found it personally very moving.

CARVE

I was also thinking about this because the cover your book, *Trick Mirror*—it kind of resembles an Eve Babitz cover, and your subtitle is *Reflections on Self-Delusion*. I'm so interested in the relationships writers have with their own thinking, or the artifice implicit in writing and placing parameters on the thinking, or whether those parameters are self-imposed or externally imposed, like by language itself, as we've discussed. It sounds like you're being self-examining but you're also acknowledging that it's, well, a trick mirror.

JIA

That's kind of the animating question of the book. I always feel like I write to make sense of something and figure out what I think. As a journalist, as a writer, I want to believe that writing leads me toward truth and not away from it. But I've also always had the suspicion that in that very act of sensemaking I am actually obscuring the truth for myself—like I'm constructing a narrative around it that conceals it from me.

Of course, this is an unoriginal worry, speaking of Didion, but it also works at a very deep level of self-conception. The stories I tell myself about myself are there for a reason, but I have also always felt like I should hang on to the suspicion that all of them are exactly untrue, you know?

CARVE

I can't wait to read your book.

JIA

I hope it's good. I want to say too, I do miss writing fiction. I just can't—my sense of interiority only sounds like my own brain right now. But I miss it, and it felt like a magical thing when *Carve* emailed about anthologizing this story because I never really tried to publish fiction ever again after publishing this story. I didn't send my work to literary journals. This was a story that I wrote for my MFA application, and I thought I should submit it to a round of literary contests. So it was a special singular thing—I only ever tried to publish fiction once and it happened at *Carve*.

CARVE

It was really special.

JIA

Yeah. And it feels really great to remember it now.

CARVE

What mantra is guiding your recent work?

JIA

That's a good question. I don't know. I am really anti-totemic: I try not to hold things up for too long. But I have been thinking a lot about a Simone Weil quote. It seems disrespectful to say this because, you know, she was writing contemporaneously with the rise of the Third Reich, on a hunger strike—it's so disrespectful to say this, but she wrote, "You could not be born at a better period than the present, when we have lost everything." I really love that. It has been giving me a lot, even though it's very disrespectful for me to use it in my very comfortable life, when Simone Weil would die on a hunger strike during the fucking Holocaust. But all of the climate reports and all this other stuff—it's like, what the fuck, what are we even doing? So it's nice to think that there is value in the present. In my personal life—which I assume will infect my writing—I've been trying to think about what kind of hope and purpose we can find that's predicated on loss.